MISSION

ALSO BY PETER ROBERTSON

Permafrost

MISSION

a novel by Peter Robertson

Gibson House 2013

For information, address Gibson House Publishers, www.gibsonhousepublishers.com.

FIRST EDITION

The characters, places and events in this book are fictitious. Any similarity to real persons, living or dead, events or locales is coincidental and not intended by the author.

ISBN: 978-0-9855158-3-6 (paperback)
Also available as an Ebook.

Book design by Anne Robertson

Cover and author photos copyright © Deborah Robertson

Published by Gibson House, Flossmoor, Illinois

Library of Congress Control Number: 2013936276

For Deb and Anne and Scott.
And for Bryan and Jack and especially for Fay, who would have been very pleased.

He was tragically boyish, impossibly thin, a post-death color of pale blue fading to white. He had cropped dark hair and a mouth empty and slack and wide open. There was no belt and his jeans were loose in a way that I knew wasn't some sort of dated statement of homeboy street style. He was just rail thin in his sad hand-me-down clothes.

Two college boys had jumped from their mountain bikes and were watching us now. Kaitlyn the EMT had gotten out of the water. She was shaking as she pulled a brown wool blanket from the back of the truck and wrapped herself tightly in it. The cop with the sling and the other EMT were still talking on their cell phones. Then the older EMT abruptly hung up and began pulling more equipment from the back of the truck. I saw the twin paddles of defibrillators, stock props on television crime shows in which everyone stands back as the grim-faced doctor waits for the correct voltage, then presses down firmly, kick starting the heart, staring at the flat line until it jumps and the attending nurse swoons.

The still shaking Kaitlyn and the other EMT now began to wheel their cart full of well-intentioned science down the path toward the patient body.

The cop with the sling joined us. He was probably around fifty, close to my age, tall and thin with his hair much longer than I imagined was typical cop style. With the stretcher in place, the younger cop and the older EMT gently lifted the body up. The loose trousers slid down to mid thigh. There was no underwear. The young cop looked at me and smirked. I stared back at him without smiling.

The older cop walked quickly over to the stretcher and, using his good arm, yanked the dead man's trousers up to

3

his waist. As he did this I saw him glance at the tattoo for a second, and I imagined him mentally filing the image and the single word away. He looked hard at the younger cop and all traces of the previous smirk quickly withered.

"It was good of you to help." The cop with the sling spoke to me quietly.

"It was nothing," I said.

He shook his head before he replied. "It was something."

There was silence. Then I spoke again.

"What happens now?"

"They make sure he's really dead."

"Why?"

"It's what they do."

"It's a waste of time."

He didn't argue. "It's still what they do."

As he said this I noticed about a dozen brightly colored braided bracelets wrapped around his wrist inside the blue sling.

The two mountain bike boys slouched over to stand in place beside us.

We all stood in a line. There would now surely come the inevitable shared moment wrapped in somber quiet. I assumed that, like me, the other witnesses would silently ponder the myriad mysteries of life and death. Why would they not, at a moment of unique perspective like this? Then one of the two cyclists chose to speak, and the wordless eloquence of the moment was indelibly transformed.

"Dude. Did you see the size of his dick?"

I did. And they did. We all did.

TWO

A torrent of early spring rain had fallen sometime in the middle of the night, and in the morning the lingering snowfall from a previous day had all been washed away. When the storms had moved away, the abandoned air had been crisp and pure and impossibly clear.

In the Colorado springtime, the snow on the Flatirons overlooking Boulder can melt rapidly, adding an abundance of crystalline water to the natural reservoirs located high in the hills. On rare and dangerous occasions, the melting snow and the heavy warm spring rains arrive at the same time, filling the mountain canyons in a matter of minutes, before rushing downhill in a surge that originates high and west of the city.

Boulder Creek is something between a stream and a river and a series of drainage ditches and culverts that run, trickle, dry up, and very occasionally flood their way right through the center of Boulder. It runs under the main streets, past the parks, past the well-used tennis courts, alongside the elegant condos and the more humble student residences, and under a series of low flat bridges carrying bikes, pedestrians and cars over the ever-changing waters.

People walk and run and bike Boulder Creek Path year-round. There's a child-friendly fishing area where foot-long trout are available for catch and release, and parks filled with metallic, angular sculptures and solemn wood carvings for Frisbees, leather-skinned housewives hard at their yoga and dogs with bandanas to avoid.

In the summer the young meet along the creek and

bullshit and tube in the water that warms up a fraction in the hotter months, while the city's homeless sleep uneasily en masse along the creek banks and under the overpass bridges on the generally temperate summer nights.

As it heads east, the creek breaks down into a series of manmade branches, not much more than concrete strips of drainage aqueduct that terminate suddenly, deliberately, dissipating into a wide flood plain that the environmentally attuned city considers a green enough methodology to subvert the likelihood of a flood.

As is my habit, I had woken at close to seven thirty that morning, brushed my teeth, washed my face, and put on my baggy swim shorts, my old grey Merrell water shoes, and a Belvedere Brewing T-shirt (the words Oh, Belvedere! were in large print under a picture of a bulldog improbably holding a full and frothy pint glass in his big paw). When I had walked onto the large yellow wood porch on the front of my small yellow wood house on Twenty-Second, the temperature was in the low fifties and the ground was soft and muddy and still very wet.

My bike is a five-year-old Gary Fisher hybrid with disc brakes and thin Kevlar tires, and it was chained somewhat optimistically to the leg of a loose patio chair. I had gone back into the house and found my grey Giro helmet, a bike bottle chilling in the fridge, and a sweatshirt that I quickly put on before walking back out to stand and gaze for a moment up at the new rust glow on the closest peaks of the Flatirons, and then further back into the range, where the snows still lingered stubbornly on the highest of the mountain peaks.

Half a block away on Pearl, a truck full of shuddering Futons had slammed on its brakes. I checked my iPhone weather app; mid sixties in Boulder by ten this morning was audaciously being offered, and we were promised no more rain for a while.

It was 8:22 when a text arrived from Nigel Prior, my business partner and my friend. It was both brief and to the point. "They say it's your birthday. I have sent you beer and I will talk to you later today. Please find someone pleasant to drink it with. Nye."

My keys, my iPhone, and my wallet all went inside the seat pack after I locked the front door. I unlocked the bike and slipped the water bottle into the cage. Then I put on my helmet and rode away.

Pearl had been empty at that time of the morning, and I playfully swerved and dodged the puddles for the first ten minutes of the ride. One of the drainage culverts ran along the right side of the road, past the discount Futon warehouse. The water was a cold black torrent, inches from the level of the road, and clearly audible, a hissing, ambient rush I couldn't remember ever having heard before. In the middle of the summer that same culvert stood stony dry and cracking for long weeks at a time.

A post grad girl on a paper-thin dull metal Apple laptop with a Hello Kitty tattoo where her left thumb met the rest of her hand had been the only other customer at Cygnet on Twentieth and Pearl. Rather than having a conventional door, the coffee shop opened up onto the sidewalk by the lifting of one continuous sliding panel made of equal parts painted metal and clear glass. Four tables had stood empty outside. An elderly Alsatian was loosely tied to one of the table legs as it slurped messily from a deep red plastic bowl. The heat was blasting inside the café and the metal door was raised to waist level.

"Terrible Love" by The National was playing very loudly that morning over four small overhead corner-mounted speakers, but the Hello Kitty girl had her own tiny earphones wedged firmly in both ears for protection.

Cygnet always looked something like a cluttered consignment shop stocked mostly with tacky crap salvaged from an English country pub. Jesse was Cygnet's owner, and he had silently placed a large coffee in my hand when I had shown up.

Jesse wore his hair very long, and it kept escaping from a hastily constructed ponytail. He also wore cargo shorts and T-shirts year-round, today's choice being a green and white football strip that doubtfully proclaimed his allegiance to Hibernian FC. He had begged me piteously until I had finally relented and handed it over.

Jesse had married in the last year and had appropriated two pounds for each month of blissful married life. He seemed unconcerned with his expansion. The Hibs uniform, on the other hand, was putting up a more than token resistance.

I had stood with Jesse at the raised door. I was half cold on my bare legs and half warm from my waist up. The feeling was actually not unpleasant for the first moment or two, but I eventually had to pull my sweatshirt off over my head before the top half of me passed out. I offered him some of my money, which he cavalierly and uncharacteristically waved aside.

Jesse had spoken then. "Happy Birthday, Tom," he said gruffly.

He looked at the front of my T-shirt, arched both of his

brows in a quizzical manner, and half smiled.

"I like the dog," he said.

"I saw him in a cartoon," I had answered him with what I hoped was an enigmatic air.

He changed the subject quickly. "The creek flooded hard last night."

"Was that the sirens I heard during the night?"

Jesse nodded. "It got up close to four feet. They closed down Boulder Canyon for a while and the underpass at Sixth. They're both open again. Are you riding?"

"I thought I would."

"It'll be slippery."

I had smiled at his unusual display of mother hen-like concern. "Thank you for the coffee. Nye's sending some beer later today. Should I bring it over?"

"What do you think?" Jesse had looked a little pained. "Is it the porter?"

It was a good question. "He didn't say. I think so."

Jesse had smiled darkly. "He must know it's my favorite. What do you call it?"

"Jolly Jack Tar."

"You always chose the name?"

I had nodded proudly.

"What else do you do?"

It was time for a modest shrug. "Collect the rent. Make stupid suggestions that no one asks for. Not too much else," I concluded lamely. "Please tell Natalie to join us."

"That means less beer for us." His tone had become suddenly mean and rather calculating; it was an altogether nastier aspect of his character.

"But she'll worship you for making the supreme sacrifice,"

I gamely reasoned.

Jesse had smirked nastily at that. "I'm getting marriage advice from you."

I returned the smirk and handed him my coffee cup. Then I crouched low and under the raised door.

My bike was unlocked and propped up against one of the outside tables. The old Alsatian had finished spraying her water all over the sidewalk and sniffed at my leg.

"Good boy, Saber," I said to her as I pulled my sweatshirt on and rubbed at her old dog chin, grey-white speckled and outstretched.

"Her name's Rose," Jesse had called out in a tone of tired exasperation. Only his freshly plump legs were visible under the café door. They weren't especially attractive.

Wanting to see the post-flood damage for myself, I had cycled up Pearl and turned left onto Sixth. The creek path under the Sixth overpass had been slick, but the flood barriers had stood unlocked and were wedged wide open. The runoff pools were filled to capacity, and the creek water was lapping high at the edge of the path.

I rode the creek west, following the path as it eventually latched onto Canyon and climbed gradually up into the mountains. I'd given up on dodging the puddles. The path runs along the side of the road then cuts underneath, well beyond the edge of town. From there on, the ride becomes a mountain trek, turning much steeper and relinquishing some of its urban gentility. Past a certain point, there are fewer pleasure walkers with unleashed dogs or small children, and the bikers and runners start to look gaunt and serious.

Uninterrupted stretches of muddy water forced me to slow down to a near crawl.

At Boulder Falls, ten miles or so west of the city, I had sat on a flat and unmistakably wet grey rock and drank the now lukewarm contents of my Belvedere Brewing Bike Bottle, emblazoned with a picture of a chubby old lady in struggling spandex on a racing bike, with the words "Fat Tires Slow You Down" underneath and conveying, to my mind, an open invitation to a costly lawsuit. Where the water fell thirty feet to the ground loudly and idyllically was the spot I had designated as the turnaround point in my almost daily morning ride.

The falls had seemed louder as I lingered there. There was a collection of wet rocks where I remembered only noticing dry ones, and the rickety collection of wooden steps up to the falls were damp and green and more awkwardly negotiated. There had clearly been a water surge, but I had no way of gauging the size and extent.

The ride back to town is always faster, mostly a matter of freewheeling downhill. I touched my helmet reassuringly with one hand. The few times I had fallen on this ride usually happened then. Nothing had been too serious. I had looked utterly stupid of course, and skinned my knees, and scraped the helmet, and received a more than abundant mocking from the smug and sedentary Jesse the next morning, on the singular occasion when I had been foolish enough to own up to my pratfall.

But this morning I had survived.

Now I stood beside the two Boulder policemen as the diligent EMT team worked quickly and hopelessly, performing a predetermined series of restorative rituals, gamely tending to the cold soft remains laid out on the stretcher. The cop with the blue sling and the gaudy bracelets thanked me again for helping and took my name and cell phone number. He also introduced himself as Reggie Hawkins.

I had watched earlier as the younger officer went hastily through the sodden pockets of the dead man. He seemed to be in a hurry and he found nothing.

Now we three waited as an untimely death was gamely offered a token resistance.

"What do you think happened to him?" I asked both men.

The cop with the sling shrugged with his other arm. "It looks like he fell in and drowned further upstream. The water must have smashed him around some as it carried him all the way to here. Some of the homeless stay too close to the creek when it floods. It's happened before. He's not the first. They don't usually want to be moved to someplace safer."

"Was he a homeless man?" I asked.

"Yeah, he was."

"Was he sleeping on the creek last night?"

He nodded. "I think so. It wasn't cold last night and some like to sleep outside all year long. They only go to the shelters at night when it snows or if it freezes. They want to be left alone and they like to sleep where they want."

"Do you know who he was?"

He nodded again. "I think we do."

I was surprised at that. "But how do you know that?"

Did the cop smile? "We got a cell phone call about half an hour ago. He must have seen the body in the water and he called it in. It had to be from another homeless guy because he told us the dead guy's name. He must have recognized him."

The cop looked at his watch. He seemed to be recalculating. "We got the call . . . then it took us ten minutes to get here . . . we've been here for about twenty minutes . . . that's probably about right."

He looked at me. "You were the first solid citizen to actually stop."

"What about the caller?"

"We think he left."

The cop smiled at me and continued. "He called on a cell phone. The dispatcher asked him to stay and wait until we got here."

I couldn't help looking around. The two mountain bikers had left, but there were now a few other people standing around. Except for an older man in a baggy red sweatshirt, they all looked solidly prosperous.

"He obviously didn't care to hang around." Reggie the cop smiled ruefully at me. "But we can find him if we have to." He said this last part quietly to himself.

I understood that emergency calls to the police are automatically tracked and the cell phone number is stored. In the middle of a dry summer, I had once reported a small grassfire burning out of control on a Chautauqua hiking trail.

The notion of homeless people having cell phones had once surprised me. I don't know why, because basic phones and basic phone plans are cheap enough, and all people want to stay connected, or at least most people do.

I looked at the still figure on the stretcher. The two Emergency Medical Technicians were slowly disconnecting their equipment. I watched the older EMT in the down vest touch the younger one on the shoulder as she lingered over the pale body. Did she want to keep trying? Was he trying to tell her that they should stop?

I asked the cop who the dead man was. To my surprise Reggie Hawkins hesitated for a moment. In a day or so it would be both in the media and common knowledge. But at this moment, Hawkins looked as if he might have told me too much. At this early stage, was the identity a more valuable piece of information?

I had no idea. So I waited.

"His name was Nitro," was what the policeman finally told me.

At what juncture does an idle piece of contemplation segue into an exercise in enduring obsession?

Because I thought only about Nitro as I rode away from the creek, and as I swam later in the morning, and as I drank later in the early evening.

He was perhaps half my age, and for all I knew he may well have died on my birthday. Was Amy his best girl? Or was she the first girl he ever loved? Was she his mother? Or his sister? Or the first pet he ever loved? Was he a married man? Was he alone? Was he mostly happy? Were his few unremarkable sins forgiven him in his passing?

Did his short truncated life pass before him as the mythic drowning scenario would have us believe? Or was the battering his poor head had taken what had prematurely ended his days in a savage coda? In either case, in a lifeless aftermath he had come to rest, pale and cleansed, washed up on the creek bank, carried to an all concluding destination by the risen flood waters.

THREE

After riding my bike, I try to swim most mornings in the indoor pool at the Lookout Lodge on Twenty-Eighth, which was my first short-term home in Boulder, when I moved here four years ago.

It has become an agreeable way to consume much of the free time I now find myself possessing.

I had lived for a long time in Chicago. I was married and divorced in Chicago, owned an art supply business on the north side of Chicago, invested my money wisely, and lived well, by my own narrowly defined parameters, all in Chicago.

My wife Patricia and I were married for fifteen years. When we parted, we sold an expensive house that we had both come to dislike, and we split our considerable assets with little debate or rancor. We had no children to either spoil or spar over. We had lived without each other for a good while, dual bastions of a chilled isolation that, in fairness, I lay claim to having almost singlehandedly manufactured.

Patricia moved almost at once to Portland, Oregon. Her longtime live-in boyfriend is ten years younger and seems to wear some sort of hemp-infused tea cozy on his head at all times. They live in a small messy house with two drooling retrievers, they see every indie rock band that visits that eternally damp hipster paradise (no mean feat, I should imagine), and they appear to be obscenely happy, if her sporadically updated account on Facebook is to be believed. Her rail-thin fashion model/icy schoolmarm figure has expanded out some, but not terribly much, and she has evidently forsaken the hair coloring and expensively tailored clothes that heretofore always matched up perfectly.

It is with no lack of regret that I state that Patricia looks utterly divine, and about a thousand times happier than she ever was with me.

My first few post-marital years were spent in the modest rented loft Nye found for me as my marriage broke into pieces. Most of my investment portfolio I let go. A few I sold well, a lot I just unloaded quickly, as the bull market of the proceeding years declined, and my interest in being able to tell the difference between good stock and shitty largely fell by the wayside.

At one point I spent close to a year traveling. I rashly set about rediscovering the time-blurred recollections and attendant deceptions that constitute our catalog of childhood haunts. I returned first to Lisbon, the harbor city I had visited as a seasick kid on a rowdy teenage cruise my mother could ill afford. I stood one late afternoon on the banked terraces of a football field high above the city, the scene of a famous Scottish triumph. I remembered how much it meant to me then, and I realized how little it meant to me now.

I returned also to Scotland, where I grew up, to a nondescript piece of desolate farmland on a high hill overlooking Campbelltown on the west coast. I had once camped out there, in a wet field with a quiet girl in brown corduroy trousers after we had impulsively elected to hitchhike our way across the country. I sat with the selfsame girl freezing and happy on a bench by a bleak road that curved sand-blown around the bay. Shrill seagulls whined and claimed most of our vinegar soaked chips; the little remaining money we had we squandered the next day, for two return tickets on the ferry boat that ran daily across the rough waters from the Mull of Kintyre to the island of Arran.

When I went back, everything was as I remembered it, but I wasn't there with anyone I thought I loved, and the effect was subdued.

My travels began with me awash in a desperate nostalgia and ended with my ridiculous metamorphosis into the anxious, solitary soul of a tourist, wearing his lowered expectations around his neck like a camera.

At one point my memory even ambushed me.

The town name was at once familiar, and I pulled off of the dual carriageway on an impulse. A neighbor's uncle was a village minister, and we had requisitioned his church hall for a weekend retreat when I was a teen. It had all been both upright and revoltingly wholesome. The hall had stood wrapped in oak trees at the bottom of the hill with a dawdling burn chuckling away in the back. The Presbyterian church had stood white walled and aloof on the hill overlooking the village pub, the post office, the ivy-draped manse, and the rickety mossy wooden gate leading off to a sheep farm.

Did I have the name of the place misremembered from years back? While the road still bottomed out at the foot of the hill, there now stood a roundabout with two exits that led, respectively, to a three-star hotel and an award-winning golf course, both of which were proudly open to the public year round. Everything else I remembered was either gone or misplaced, and I truthfully wasn't terribly sure which.

Everything I endeavored to do on my travels relentlessly reaffirmed the wise axiom that cautions us against going home.

Meanwhile Nye Prior, my gay, and black, and insistently

efficient number-one employee, eyeballed the internet as it slammed broadside after broadside at the retail industry, and before ArtWorks, our art supply company, took even one hit, he cast up anchor and set a bold new course.

When Patricia's father Ben Wise died, she inherited three art supply stores and a thriving mail order business. Since we were married, I inherited the selfsame by proxy. The stores were quickly sold, and I bought an abandoned pencil factory on Ravenswood Avenue on the North Side of Chicago. I called the venture ArtWorks, and we kept on selling art supplies and framing services from there. We still sold our goods and services by mail order, but we now supplied the new yuppic galleries and bars and restaurants springing up close by and provided the soothing art washes for dentists' offices and the beige and pastel expanses of hospital walls. Our big warehouse of a place very nearly supported itself, but I also invested my money well, and Patricia and I lived more than comfortably.

But we weren't quite happy. I wanted to have children. I never said it out loud because I assumed that Patricia didn't.

Nye Prior had come to work for me by then, and I shamelessly overworked him for a good while before I belatedly made him my business partner and we negotiated the first in a series of brilliant deals where he did all the work and I still pocketed half the money.

Before my divorce and prior to Nye's promotion, the mail order business was in Patricia's name, but she expressed little interest in selling charcoal pencils and X-ACTO knives as we began to divide assets. Nye asked her to let us have the business and generously offered her some of my money, which she generously refused to take. Nye found an abandoned warehouse in a south suburban town where the rent was laughably low, and the tax incentives for new businesses were well beyond generous. The internet was alive and kicking, and now we would sell our art supplies and framing services exclusively from there, no more catalogs, and no more retail store. We were online, and, imaginatively, we renamed ourselves artworks.com. Nye, now a full partner, found thirty black residents obscenely eager to work for him. Finding black residents in an all black town wasn't an especially daunting task, while finding people who badly needed work was also not really much of a challenge.

The black mayor of the black town was grateful, and, cavalierly ignoring any pesky residential requirements, he put Nye on the all black village board. The town loved Nye with a rare and consuming passion, and he repaid the village with baseball team sponsorships, boxes of new books for the local elementary school (he flirted, somewhat unwisely and dishonestly I thought, with the school's principal, who bought herself a brand new wig to celebrate the much reciprocated attention), and several Saturdays spent picking up broken glass and used needles from parks and spreading more than his share of communal mulch.

Much to our mutual amusement, the same village that pulled Nye close to its collective bosom chooses to completely ignore me, his clearly shiftless, pasty white foreigner of a partner.

Both my birth nationality and a finely nurtured reticence have conspired to handicap my personality I now belatedly realize; emotional outbursts are thus both rare and painful. But I have come to the realization that I have always loved

Nye Prior, and I always will. Having said that, I firmly and cold-bloodedly believed that by making him my business partner, he would endeavor to work even harder, if that were humanly possible. I am happy to report my absolute faith in Nye's quasi-Calvinist work ethic has been proven correct.

So now I possessed no wife, no stock portfolio, no large house, and half a relatively profitable online art supply business while doing no actual work.

Things were certainly moving along. But I also owned a large empty building in a hipster haven on the North Side of Chicago, where property taxes were well in excess of what we paid in the south suburbs for a mortgage and taxes, and over three times the floor space.

But my industrious Nye would come to the rescue once again.

We have known each other for a good while now. He's younger by a decade, driven, and talks with a pained economy. Like me, he lives alone for longer periods than he would like but never complains. Unlike me, he works much too hard and doesn't need to invent ludicrous rationales for suctioning up his time. I do think I know him well and, if he has passions other than for work and technology I think I would have stumbled upon them by now.

I have noticed over the years that when someone hands Nye a drink he absentmindedly takes it and sips it for a while. It could be a white wine or a red wine, a chilled beer perhaps in the dead heat of the summer. If you asked him what he wanted he would doubtless say whatever and would wordlessly drink whatever was proffered, with no visible show of enthusiasm.

Craft beer changed all that for Nye. He found himself in a brewpub on the Illinois-Indiana border, where he was handed a pale ale. Nye sipped at it gingerly. Then he sipped again with mounting interest. And thus with little fanfare the beer beast was unleashed. Nye went to other bars. He tried porters and stouts and triple-hopped ales, and he liked them all.

A creature of habit and compulsion, Nye turned to the internet. He found hop suppliers and beer blogs, old breweries selling off their equipment cheap, and legions of newly zealous craft beer fans who, like Nye, and eventually like me also, wondered why they had been consuming weak swill without complaint all these years.

So we expensively converted the old ArtWorks building into Belvedere Brewing. I still owned the property. I even got to pick the new name. I also got to be the landlord and collect the rent from a company I half owned. Again I craftily brokered a partnership deal where Mr. Prior toiled, and I essentially loafed on the job.

From the start, Belvedere sold better food than the fake heartland mega-portioned overpriced fare most brewpubs provide. We made the place more industrial looking, less Cracker Barrel, than our competitors, and the pale well-inked hipsters on their single-gear bikes beat a path to our door, where we obligingly provided bike racks and several choice alternatives to a Pabst Blue Ribbon tallboy.

Nye took to brewing, to his big green wellies and his wet knees and his grunge flannel under his thick dungarees. He'd stalk the brewery floor at all hours, between the newly installed vats. If I ventured into his damp lair he'd thrust a handful of dry hops under my nose.

"Well?" He would demand of me imperiously.

"Smells like hops to me," I would suggest helpfully.

The dark beer lord stalked away haughtily.

Belvedere's first official offering was Galadré Ale, a pale ale. Then came Hop Everlasting, an IPA. Nye followed these up with Jolly Jack Tar Porter and Daphne and Hen, which was a brown ale. All were painstakingly christened by me.

All four are, if I may say so, truly delicious. All four are popular, all four are available on tap, in growlers, and in limited edition pint bottles, and all are featured on a selection of T-shirts, bicycle shirts, bike bottles, baby bibs, and sippy cups in toddler and adult sizes and on pretty much anything else we could think of as vessels of shameless branding.

I suspect that Belvedere is a lot of fun for Nye, who hides his giddy enthusiasm beneath an aloof and stern exterior. It doesn't make much money at this stage, but my rent checks are always on time. While artworks.com makes more money, it isn't much fun, although Nye seems flattered and guardedly happy to be a pillar of a long-blighted community in the south suburbs. Belvedere is punishingly hard work for Nye. He's close to forty, and there are very few old men brewing good beer; it's truly a young person's game, a labor of love, and, in Nye's defense, no one appears to be getting too rich at it.

I have watched with some amusement as Nye, doubtless taking a page from my manual of master slacking, has delegated away much of the day-to-day managing in artworks.com. His/our hired staff is highly efficient, and Nye has come to love draught beer a lot more than drafting pencils.

Today I have fewer assets than I once had. My used car

and my small house and my few clothes are all practical models, no longer luxury ones. I own one piece of valuable property, a half interest in two decent businesses, and, by my calculations, enough money to get through a quiet life filled with economy versions of most of the things I like, if the bottom doesn't fall out of the art supply and craft beer businesses.

Which it very well might.

So it was just over four years ago that Nye decided on a series of fact-finding missions to the biggest craft beer states in North America, all for the stated purpose of research into the methodology of his competitors or, more accurately, for the shameless pilfering of any beer secrets we could get our grubby little hands on. Nye, our leader, headed to Oregon, Washington State, and the northern part of California, and I, his lesser acolyte, his Tonto, his Robin the Boy Wonder, albeit a tad long in the tooth for that final moniker, I was dispatched to the state of Colorado.

I stayed in the Lookout Lodge for my first month there. I swam in the indoor pool at lunchtime in water that was much too warm for a real workout but was just perfect for marinating my beaten body after a whole legion of morning brewery tours. I stewed still more in the large and mostly empty hot tub at the end of the day and watched the sunlight melt into the Flatirons as I nursed an Old Chub in a pool-friendly plastic glass. I first encountered the myriad complexities of Boulder recycling at the Lookout, and faced far too many choices of good organic wholegrain bread at breakfast. At first I gingerly partook of the twice-weekly conversion of a ground floor hotel room into an ad hoc grocery store by a local organic dairy farm anxious to sell their pricey wares (my room did thoughtfully come with a small refrigerator). On most weekends a blues band played in the hotel bar, and my room was close enough to sit outside and listen to vintage Strats and Telecasters played through Twin Reverbs, Chub in hand, and watch the mountains as they faded into the dry twilight air.

From the Lookout, I drove my rented Jeep Liberty to brewery towns like Longmont and Lyons in the mornings. In the early evenings, I texted Nye with the names of the beers I tried and the ones I especially liked.

The hotel had free bikes for hire, ugly red chrome monstrosities with enough extraneous metal for the sponsoring realtor's name to be prominent from any direction. It was off-season and in the middle of the semester, so I easily got a bike most afternoons. I began to ride all over Boulder, and at the end of my second week there I texted Nye.

"I'm going to move out here," I told him without much preamble.

As always, he texted me straight back. "I see. How will Belvedere and artworks.com ever manage to survive without you?"

Primly I informed him that rent checks could be mailed fairly easily to Boulder and that I would be able to choose beer names by text just fine.

I liked staying at the hotel. My room was small and neat and one of the cheapest I could find in Boulder. I did my own laundry. The management seemed to be a communal collection of earnest, hardworking, hippyesque do-gooders, who had found themselves in possession of an old art deco family resort and were hell-bent on making an organically correct and environmentally friendly go of it. I certainly wished them well.

As I checked out at the end of my stay and paid a large but perfectly reasonable bill I asked a last series of questions. Could I use the pool most days as a nonresident, I wondered? And perhaps the hot tub also? I would be more than happy to pay. I told this to the young gentleman in a pale blue dress shirt, khakis and dreadlocks, adding that I planned to live in Boulder.

He smiled and asked me if I intended to have my lunch or dinner there after I swam, as I had most of the days I'd stayed there. He also wondered if I would be having a beer there too, again as I had done regularly. He seemed to be finding the conversation unexpected yet slightly amusing.

Were these trick questions, I wondered? If they were I couldn't spot the trap. I assured him that my daily swim time would certainly include both an Old Chub and one of their fine lunch entrées. It was clearly the correct response. He smiled at me then, assured me that the facilities would be available to me, and thanked me warmly for staying at the Lookout.

I informed him that the pleasure had been entirely mine.

That was more than four years ago.

Today I'm going for my quick swim, a tasty half-price beer courtesy of the sensible Colorado adherence to the all-day happy hour, and an early lunch at the Lookout.

I'm still wondering about the dead man in the creek. Wondering how you end up homeless and young and then dead in a place as pretty as Boulder? Wondering about the mysterious Amy. And wondering just what kind of a name is Nitro, anyway?

To my knowledge, Nye wasn't intent on unleashing any new signature beers in the near future, although his quest for the perfect stout was well nigh all consuming. So my services as the official namer of the Belvedere ales were not actually required at present.

That left me with even more time on my hands. I badly wanted a distraction, and I considered the oddly named Nitro, both his final days and the extended arc of his abbreviated life. The cops seemed secure in the knowledge that he drowned by accident, and I saw no compelling reason to dispute this. But I was interested in how his short life unraveled all the way to that heartrending place and time, even if his last few hours were seemingly without malevolence.

I'm a creature of habit, and this is how it works for me most mornings. Start with a piece of toast and a coffee at Cygnet before nine and bike up and down the creek for a couple of hours. Chain up the bike and the helmet outside the Lookout. Walk through the lobby to the bar and grab all the free daily and weekly newspapers I don't remember having read yet. Order a beer in a plastic glass. Order a salad. Ask the waitress to bring them to one of the tables at the side of the pool in about fifteen minutes. Smile boyishly at the waitress, the inevitable inverse of which is to wonder fleetingly if my smiling boyishly still works, or if it ever did, but no matter.

Use the rear bar door, which leads directly to the pool/ hot tub area. Grab two pool towels. Throw one towel, my

T-shirt, all the newspapers, and my shoes on and under a pool chair to establish poolside residency. Keep swim shorts on. Use the shower connected to the exercise room for a quick rinse off while keeping one eye on my iPhone, my keys, and my wallet on a bench nearby. If others are showering, keep swim shorts on. If alone, gingerly remove swim shorts. Make a cursory attempt to dry off with the towel. Leave towel in basket thoughtfully provided in shower room. Replace shorts if and when needed. Retrieve valuables from bench. Return to pool area and place said valuables inside one shoe. Drape towel over shoulders to provide much needed modicum of decency. Sit at side of pool and politely await arrival of beer and salad.

A flawless operation well practiced and perhaps a trifle dull but, if I say so myself, usually executed to perfection.

The salad, when it came, was dauntingly fresh, a bed of organically grown mixed greens with a parmesan peppercorn dressing that I was assured was homemade. I was hungry and put it away with a flourish. There was a warm chunk of multigrain bread on the side of the plate, freshly baked, that also offered little resistance. The beer was not too cold, malty and sweet. I scanned my pile of newspapers as I ate.

The college newspapers put out the best print news coverage in Boulder by a wide margin. Today's student-run Boulder daily carried the previous night's flash flood on the front page with no mention of any fatalities. That wasn't too surprising. The newsroom worked late, and they put the paper to bed even later, but that sad announcement would surely not come until tomorrow's early edition.

It did however serve up a few statistics that were of some interest. The flood had occurred at just before two in the morning, today, the sixth of March. It had lasted for about forty-five minutes and produced an inch and a half of rainfall. Naturally, most of the weather experts had seen it coming for a day or so. Working in tandem with the melting snow in the high canyons, the waters had raised the creek water by four feet at the flood crest and shut down three of the underpasses. Jesse had got the water level exactly right.

As I knew from my four years in Boulder, flash floods could occur at most times of the year. Last night's flood was the first in March but not the first this spring. That honor belonged to the flood of February tenth. March flash floods were apparently not too uncommon. February ones were rarer because there was less chance of spring rain, more chance of winter snow, and the colder temperatures produced less melting snows to aid the process. Spring snow thaw was unlikely in February, less unlikely in March, less unlikely again in April, and pretty much a thing of the past by May, when all the snow that was going to melt had melted in preparation for the first hint of summer. Flash floods happened at any time in the summer months, but they occurred without snow melting and therefore required much more unaided rain power.

At their worst, floodwaters could theoretically manufacture a ten-foot wall of raging water with at best a forty-minute warning. The likelihood of this happening was perhaps once every hundred years, but, in the mid-1970s, the creek did flood in this very manner, and a hundred and forty people died.

Today the canyons above the city house fifty gauges measuring rainfall and water level, while computer systems in the city and university trip a series of flood warning sirens. Floodgates close, and manmade runoff pools fill up on either side of the creek. City workers patrol the inundated paths and help evacuate the threatened areas.

All the above measures, the article continued, were highly laudable, and more than earth-friendly, yet they still failed to prevent the occasional drowning death every year.

Much of this was news to me.

There were a few self-serving quotes from television and internet weathermen, and a spokesman for the university's online flood watch system proudly proclaimed their computer-assisted warning response to have been more than satisfactory last night. I read through the self-administered kudos quickly.

The last few lines of the article were more interesting. The flood of February tenth had been much less severe than last night's, producing only one inch of rain over a longer duration. But as I learned at that moment, and as the newspaper's loyal readers would presumably learn tomorrow, they had shared a common characteristic.

They had both killed.

Andrew Travers, a fifty-one-year-old homeless man, had drowned in Boulder Creek on the tenth of February.

So now there were two flash floods and two homeless deaths in just under one month.

Have I mentioned the first time I had a premonition? Perhaps I haven't. Perhaps I should.

More than a decade ago, I sat in traffic in an expensive German convertible. I read a newspaper article that mentioned a childhood friend from Scotland who was missing in Northern Michigan. I somehow knew as I read that Keith Pringle was dead, as I also knew that I would have to explore, to dig some, and to confirm this sad reality for myself. I was younger then, in my late thirties, a little bit thinner, and a good deal richer. I drove a fast car in those days, I dressed with more care than I do now, and the price and status of my possessions defined me more completely than they do now, or so I like to think. I lived the callow life of a caricature yuppie. I ignored Patricia my wife, who clearly deserved better, and I underpaid and overworked poor Nye, my best-ever employee, and my true friend, who still works very hard, but at least does so in larger part for himself nowadays.

So I headed up north and I hunted for traces of Keith. I found violence around and inside me. I discovered that I did want to be in love, but that I wasn't in love with Patricia. Ever-loyal Nye wanted my marriage to work much more than I did. I was technically unfaithful once, but emotionally I was a constant offender.

I returned from Michigan to participate in the polite, orderly, but no less somber teardown of a marriage.

As I sat at the side of the pool, it occurred to me that Keith had not actually lived as a homeless man, not strictly speaking. But he had been in the process of drifting, there was water in the abrupt closing of his personal narrative, there turned out to be more than one death, and I had found myself looking into other people's fractured and imperfect lives with an unwholesome relish because, if I am being honest, it was much easier than taking the sad measure of my own dull days, my personal time loop of recurring ennui.

As I thought about then and now, I realized that, in

every conceivable way, there were parallels to be drawn, coincidences to be considered, even down to the mundane reading of newspaper accounts that first ratcheted up my interest.

I had time on my hands then. I still do. I was curious and weirdly driven, and these two corkscrewing motivations are every bit as valid today as they were then. Finally there is the question of a conclusion, and maybe even a consequence. I was aware that I had been searching for myself as much as I had been searching for Keith, and in the searching, had I at least uncovered something of value? Was I an improved man? Was I a warmer soul? Could I still use more improvement? A tentative yes to all these questions seemed the appropriate response.

And in my albeit brief consideration came the crystallization of my second-ever premonition, a full decade later, but every bit as strong, and every bit as convincing as the first had been: there was more to these two men's untimely deaths than simply a matter of river and rain.

After my lunch I swam and soaked and drank my beer by the side of the pool. I pulled out my iPhone. There was a text from the cop with the sling, Officer Reggie Hawkins, offering his thanks once again for my assistance that morning.

There was also another text from Nye, this one announcing a Belvedere issue of mammoth proportions that required both my urgent attention and unique perspective.

A Scottish singer was touring the States, and his management was looking for a Chicago-area date. Belvedere had a small stage in the back of the main room, and occasionally lesser-known indie acts were booked there, either solo singers, bands doing acoustic sets, or retro rockers with minimal amplification. We didn't make much on these shows, but, if we chose right, we damn near managed to make our brewery look passably hip. Given that Nye is almost forty, and I am almost fifty and have just used the term hip without any apparent irony, this was no mean feat that we were attempting. The singer's name was Alasdair Roberts. Really Nye? Did he think I knew every Scottish person?

But in his defense, I did tend to gravitate toward artists from my home country for no good reason, other than a wayward sense of patriotism. The funny thing was that Alasdair Roberts was indeed known to me, and I liked his music. But the real question was: would he pass muster with our studiously aloof clientele? I had no idea. Neither did Nye, clearly. We could do some research or we could take a chance. Our success rate wasn't too terrible. Our loyal punters might be forgiving. They generally were.

I took a chance. I think we should book him, I boldly texted back.

Nye's relationship to technology is a beguilingly contrary one. He loves new computers. He barely tolerates email. He is addicted to texting, at least to texting me at any rate. He plans to die old never having been on Facebook, yet he lives to tweet and scour blogs. If there is an abiding logic in all this, I haven't yet seen it, but then, I have little chance to ponder, as I'm required to answer his damned texts, which come in at an average of one per half hour, from the early morn to late into the night. So much for a sleeping partnership.

So I have, in theory anyway, twenty-six minutes to get back to my house on my bike from the Lookout before Nye texts me again.

Oh, if only he was that predictable. But the good news is that I'm back at the house with ten minutes to spare in my imaginary itinerary.

The runoff pool by the side of the creek at Frontage had showed no evidence of recent death as I rode slowly past it. The police and EMT unit were gone and the body had been removed.

I slowed down anyway. What was I expecting? Should there be some illusion of death, some afterimage or tangible essence still lingering there? Was I a little disappointed that there wasn't?

Instead there was a little west highland terrier in a red dog jacket taking a shit under a tree, and there was a man with his hand thrust inside an empty blue plastic newspaper bag standing nearby looking law abiding and miserable. That was all the après death essence available.

At my house the mailman was just leaving.

Patricia had sent a birthday card. That was very kind of her. The card featured a toothless hag drinking a beer with no punch line, and I stared at it uncomprehendingly. Inside was a printout of an email confirmation for a concert at the Fox Theater sometime in May. Two tickets at the will call under my name for Admiral Fallow. I needed to bring ID with me when I picked them up.

I smiled; another Scottish act. I sensed the insidious hand of Nye in this. They kept in touch. He had stayed with Patricia at least once that I knew of, in hipper-than-thou Portlandia, on his beer-finding mission to the west coast. Did he torment her with texts twice an hour? I strongly suspected that he did not.

Patricia's thoughtful gift assumed many things. That I would want to go, that I was free that particular night, and that I could rustle up a date.

I did.

I was pretty sure I was.

Ah. That last might prove to be the more challenging.

The FedEx truck showed up later in the afternoon with two growlers of Jolly Jack Tar in elaborate and icy packaging. I snuck a quick reassuring peek and reclosed the box, placing it inside the fridge with only a little required repositioning of essentials like whole milk and organic orange juice.

The afternoon was warm enough to sit on my porch in a sweatshirt and fire up my four-year-old relic of a laptop, hastily appropriated during a previous Nye Belvedere technology purge.

I searched, in quick succession, for flash floods and Boulder Creek and Nitro and Andrew Travers.

The first two sets of hits were mostly stuff that I knew or had read that morning, and I perused them in a hurry, skipping large segments. Nitro was pretty much worthless, although I got a few craft beer hits for various milk and coffee stouts that were fun to read and diverting.

My first thought was that I must have the wrong Andrew Travers. I read some more. But then again, perhaps I hadn't. The age would be about right. But it was a very public record of a life that had all but come to an abrupt end a few years back, even before he had drowned. Was that when he had become homeless? It was all there, up to a point, and it was all so wholly unexpected. I grabbed my iPhone and texted Reggie Hawkins the policeman back. Could we meet sometime soon? And could I ask him some questions? I fully expected him to turn me down on both counts.

After a while I closed up the laptop and just sat on my porch and watched as the sun began to drop behind the mountains and backlight the big sky.

At just after five I arrived at Cygnet with my two cold growlers still nestled in the shipping box. Jesse thoughtfully produced two glasses and we eagerly partook. There were only a few customers. Rosanne Cash and Elvis Costello were singing the old country song "Heartaches by the Number." Natalie took a welcome break from copyediting dull-as-dishwater trade journals on her MacBook, and she joined us. She kissed me on the cheek, sat down quickly, and held out a glass she had found for herself, which her husband filled. I watched Jesse's face for signs of selfishness and unmasked self-interest, but I could see none. Ah, the selfless charm of young newlyweds. The two men at the next table had tried hard not to look envious as we removed the heat sealed plastic from the top of the bottles. They had failed miserably. Jesse obligingly found two more glasses. Eventually my birthday was toasted. Boulder was toasted. Good beer was toasted. There was much clinking and sipping. One of our new friends suddenly left and quickly returned with a growler of his own, this one filled with a cloudy amber-hued home brew. Some kind of super-hopped pale ale was bashfully proffered, and it would have seemed utterly churlish not to acquiesce. The consensus view was favorable: an eminently quaffable beverage, we proclaimed ponderously, by no means shabby.

Boulder suffers from no shortage of craft beer enthusiasts, and our conversation dovetailed into much dreary talk of hops and finishes and sessionability. I was soon out of my depth. Natalie wisely returned to her paid work, and I took my leave at close to eight. The walk back to my house was paradoxically with a much lighter load, while I was considerably more loaded.

Along the way I stopped at Snarf's and mumbled articulately enough to procure a six-inch sub with ham and cheese and veggies and no dressing, to ingest as I wobbled home in the post-twilight.

On the porch it was still warm, and I sat and supplemented the remains of my sandwich with some sea salt chips and tried very hard to think about close to nothing.

It did occur to me that it was the end of my birthday, and I had completely forgotten to feel sorry for myself. Perhaps I was an improved man after all.

After a while, I was still sitting in the near dark, with an empty sandwich wrapper and a chip bag in my lap and no clear sense of how long I had been there.

I thought about water then. The drainage culvert on Pearl was perhaps a block away from my house, and, did I simply imagine it, or could I hear the rush of the high cold creek as it passed angrily on through?

Later my hand reached out and I touched the dead man's shoulder again.

We were almost alone, and we were close to the edge of the water. But it wasn't the creek this time. Instead it was a burn, a slow-moving sewer stream, with a sheen of dirt and oil that rainbowed in the occasional shafts of sunshine that peered through the tree branches. Old tires stood half submerged; a milk crate functioned as a stepping-stone.

The burn in question ran along the abandoned train tracks behind the council house where I lived as a child. It didn't exactly look like the same place. Dreams tend to very roughly approximate. But it was the place where I used to play. I knew it was, as I also knew that I was in the process of dreaming.

My dream locale was sketchy and ill defined, but it offered up enough genuine memories that served as emotional authentication. The iron tracks and the wooden trestles had been removed, but the trail of dark shale stones still lay where I remembered them. The massive storage building at the end of the line was brown paint flaking off weather-warped wood but was still half standing; it was used to store household coal decades before I played there. Now it smelled of stale piss from the legions of super lager alkys who sheltered there. Two other boys and I had once made a skinny girl of twelve strip down to her underpants there after school. She was soon cold and her nose ran and she began to cry. Eventually she told us to fuck off and leave her alone. We ran away, imagining we had won something in the sad exchange, laughing hollowly amongst ourselves to somehow prove it. We had started a grass fire there on the steep-sided embankment in that same summer holidays, and watched as it burned fast and out of control. The police and fire engines arrived eventually, and we slunk away to hide in our gang hut and giggle nervously. Our gang hut was a natural tunnel of bushes hidden behind a line of fir trees, and one day we found a note pinned to a nearby tree trunk. Some girls had found our secret place. It was great. Could they please share it with us? Could they fuck, we boldly wrote on the back of the note. We pinned the note back up and it was gone three days later. We were insanely proud of ourselves. One day a carrier bag full of women's underwear appeared in the hut. They were all disappointingly clean, much larger and more spinsterishly sensible than our imaginations would have liked. We left the bag where we found it and spent the next few days watching the hut for the owner of the bag to return. As we waited, we imagined a grimy soul in a strategically soiled raincoat—the guy on the cover of Jethro Tull's Aqualung, perhaps. We smoked our way through shoplifted packs of Embassy Regal and tried not to cough as we inhaled the smoke, but we saw nothing. And one night the bag was gone.

In my dream, there was now a girl standing beside me as I touched the body. She was Amy and she was the twelve-year-old girl, scrawny and snotty and sobbing in her all-cotton Marks and Sparks underpants. I couldn't see her face, but I knew with the unerring logic of dreams exactly who she was, or who they both were. She/they was/were still crying inside my head when the dead man opened his eyes and I was fully awake.

For the rest of the night I lay there unsleeping, knowing I had drunk too much and systematically reliving every wretchedly stupid adolescent moment spent close to that stinking piece of fetid water.

FOUR

The next morning was sunny and warm by the middle hours as I rode up and down Pearl and onto the creek path. At the falls, a pale teenager was playing Dylan's "Knockin' on Heaven's Door" on a beat-up Taylor acoustic to an indifferent girl in cutoff jeans and a Colorado State sweatshirt painting her toenails a shiny dark green. The song only had four easy chords, but you'd never know that from his solemn expression and the flurry of bum notes he unleashed as he tried to flirt and fingerpick at the same time.

Boulder has locals, and students, and tourists, and homeless people, all seemingly coexisting. Pearl and the Creek both boast some of each and, if I've never been able to identify the exact proportions of each, it's probably because I'm not fully affiliated with any one group. If I stay a while longer I can perhaps expect to become a fully paid up local, but that accolade may only come with more long years in residence than I actually have to offer.

Tourists shop the western end of Pearl all year long, but more so in the summer months. Locals seem to use it to get from some place to some other place, and students and the homeless hang out there, again with the temperature being the key factor dictating their numbers and their level of enthusiasm. That's perhaps not quite accurate. Some of the chronic homeless work Pearl year-round, begging, singing, dancing, sitting quietly with their heads down, slumped over a handwritten sign and a paper cup. More than the homeless work the street. The quality of street performer is as varied as their circumstances. Some are playing for food or weed. Others are highly respectable locals, kids in the high school orchestra or drama group, extroverts, or else the hapless offspring of pushy parents. There are loud buskers doing magic tricks that seemingly require twenty minutes of blustery bravado for every moment of genuine stagecraft. Tourists are generally tolerant while the locals once again scuttle past in a hurry.

One coffee shop has a used bookstore attached. One bookstore has a coffee shop attached. If there is a qualifiable distinction in the business philosophies of these two establishments, I certainly can't see it.

Pearl boasts one glorious dive of a basement-level bar with cheap pitchers most nights and watery dollar shots and a finely balanced cross section of Boulder demi-monde in the summer months when the campus is a ghost town, or in the early evening hours, before too many CU kids show up and get unforgivably loud.

Next door to the bar is a gentleman's club, where college girls can pretend to be slutty, and college boys can pretend to be lounge lizards. I've been there twice. The first time a woman with big teeth and a tight red skirt drunkenly took me outside in the alleyway and sucked me off with admirable skill and very few words. The second time I sang "Rocket Man" by Elton John in the seventies karaoke contest and hit the half price well shots hard. It was enjoyable, but the first night was the more sordidly memorable of the two.

One of the cheaper restaurants on Pearl brews its own beers in ever-changing varieties that I use to wash down bowls of vegetarian chili. They have yet to serve me a beverage that I didn't devoutly and covetously wish Belvedere had come up with first.

On the creek, the locals move fast even in summer, power walking, cycling in barely tensed spandex on racing bikes, walking their aggressively fit dogs, running at a bold clip while encased in headphones. The only exceptions are the few patient souls I witness fly-fishing, an exercise in navel-gazing futility practiced by precious few of the usually kinetic Boulderites.

The paths along the creek are carefully designated for either foot or wheeled traffic, and the locals are the most zealous of practitioners. Tourists stroll more leisurely and haphazardly, take cell phone pictures, sip at large lattes, feed the well-trained ducks, and amble. Students pedal at a slower pace than the locals, on crappier bikes. Their backpacks and jackets by North Face, they favor University of Colorado colors mostly, a sea of black and yellow. When it's warm they linger, smoke some weed and type on laptops, check their Facebook status; it's still a wayward kind of motion, not quite harried, but far from being at rest.

The realm of stillness belongs to the homeless in all seasons. Most find shade or shelter and cluster together for safety and companionship. Some browbeat and beg aggressively, while others simply doze through an unspoken act of suggestive entreating, their scruffy presence alone presumably sufficient to elicit sudden acts of random charity. Some are in small groups and exchange combat stories and survival tips. On one occasion I heard a homeless guy shouting about the agents of government lurking inside his head to no one actively listening. On another a homeless woman had her hand inside a man's trousers and was idly wanking him off in broad daylight with a handful of junior high school kids watching gleefully. One little shit even had his Android phone out, videoing furiously. The guy getting the handjob seemed to be sound asleep, but he never once stopped smiling.

For early in March, the creek path was hectic in the temperate sunlight. There are bench seats carved out of stone set close to the water. They offered the comfort of shade. This was where I chose to sit, with my iPhone and a copy of the daily newspaper and my bike propped against a wall beside me. Two young men played speed chess at a low stone table. Were they grad students perhaps? The object of the game seemed to be to move their pieces as fast as possible then slam down the timer to halt the clock. The skill level of each move was clearly of secondary concern.

One man threw a tennis ball into the water near a small manmade waterfall. Was he maybe homeless? A large mutt of a dog swam out time and time again to retrieve the ball. I watched with mounting disquiet. Was the ball moving closer to the waterfall each time? Was the dog getting tired? Was the water too cold?

I appeared to be the only person watching. Eventually the man tired first, called for his wet and panting partner, and they left.

The daily paper told me next to nothing more about the flash flood. The dead man was known as Nitro, and he was homeless. The Boulder police were in the process of investigating what appeared to be an accidental drowning.

Meanwhile the complex issues of who should sell and where should they sell and just how much medicinal weed could and should the city of Boulder sell laid claim to the rest of the front page, and I suspected that Nitro would be forgotten by tomorrow.

A text arrived from Reggie Hawkins, the policeman. He would be happy to meet with me. That was good, slightly surprising, but good. Did I want to have coffee tomorrow morning? I certainly did. Would the Trident work for me? It most certainly would. Would ten be fine? Ten would indeed be fine.

I texted him right back.

I assumed that Hawkins would be part of the Nitro case and would therefore have little time to talk with me. Then I reconsidered. Did the accidental death of a homeless man constitute an active police investigation? And if there was an investigation, there was no reason Hawkins would have to be an integral part of it. It also occurred to me that I had no idea of his rank.

Googling Reggie Hawkins suddenly seemed like a fine idea. So I did. Good God. Once again I thought there had to be some kind of mistake. Was there another Reggie Hawkins? Was there another Reggie Hawkins in Boulder? Who was a cop when he wasn't doing something else I was completely unprepared for? The odds were terrifyingly slight.

First Andrew Travers and now Reggie Hawkins. Two men with other lives, two men both close to my age. I suddenly felt singularly superficial. Where was my other life?

"Good Sir, pray can I offer you a reading?" I looked up in surprise to find an elfin handmaiden smiling down at me. Her peasant skirt and blouse were made of wafer-thin cotton and almost translucent with wear and age. She wore several rings and bracelets on her sprite-thin limbs. Her feet were tiny inside cheap leather sandals, and what looked like a deep tan was mostly dirt. She held her tarot cards outstretched. "I can tell you a little of your fate if you wouldst desire it." Her smile was equal parts eager and mysterious.

She smelled faintly of patchouli, and her hair was frizzy and fair from exposure to the sun. Her age was impossible to guess. Had I ever been called Good Sir before?

"I'm not much of a believer in fate, I'm afraid," I confessed to her.

She smiled at me then. She was apparently utterly delighted by something I had unwittingly said or done. "You do not hail from around these parts then?"

Now I understood. "No," I said. "I'm from Scotland. It's been a while."

She nodded to herself. "And yet you still have the wonderful sound of the brogue about you. It's a truly magical tongue. You should strive by all means to keep it." She was certainly being theatrical, although I supposed that sounding British would be an advantage in situations where medieval credentials were advantageous.

"I'll certainly do my best. Do you charge for your readings?"

Was she offended by my crass question? She stiffened. "I ask only what people reckon my words to be worth," she answered me with some pride.

Slightly ashamed of myself, I changed the subject quickly. "Do you live here?" I asked her. "On the creek, I mean?"

Her reply was guarded. "This is where I make my home for the present," she said. She paused and looked at me carefully. "But why do you ask that of me?" Her voice had abandoned much of its initial warmth.

"I was just curious." I tried to sound apologetic.

She began to turn away from me, perhaps looking for someone less nosy and more mystical.

"Let me pay you for a reading," I said.

"But you haven't had a reading. And you don't really desire one," she said shrewdly. "Do you?"

"No." I sheepishly admitted.

"Then why should you pay me?" she asked simply.

I had no answer.

She took a deep breath. "So what is it that you do want of me?"

"Did you know the man who died last night in the flood?" I blurted this out impulsively.

There was a long pause. Then she smiled slightly. "I know of many things," she said darkly.

This sounded a little too melodramatic. But she did seem to be getting back into character.

There was another pause. "His name was Nitro," she said finally.

"You did know him?"

"No. That would be a falsehood." Then she hesitated, and shook her head slowly and sorrowfully. "I knew a little of him. I knew who he was."

"What did you know about him?" I asked her.

"He was here at the water often. He was certainly a handsome young one. He liked to laugh a lot and the fair young maidens all took a shine to him. He surely liked to drink his ale and smoke his weed. I saw him doing that a lot." Was she amused or disapproving? I wasn't quite sure.

I asked her. "Who were the fair young maidens?"

"Why, the lasses from the college. They used to make fine

sport with him. They gave him the weed he desired."

This all sounded perfectly believable.

I had occasionally witnessed a little comingling along the path, where college girls and young homeless men got together to smoke and hang. For the girls, this was doubtless a chance to slum dangerously, for the men a chance to flirt with someone reasonably clean and, perhaps, in their minds, to sustain the slim fiction that they were new age bohemian voyagers, and not simply fucked up and nearly destitute.

I stood up. "Please let me pay you something."

She took a step back in protest. "But that wouldn't be at all fitting." She smiled at me and shook her head. "This isn't a reading." She was adamant.

"You've helped me and you've answered my questions. I took up your time. You could have given another reading and been paid for it." I could be adamant, too.

There was something else I wanted to ask her. It was a sensitive issue but I bulldozed on. "How will you live?"

She looked at me as if that was the strangest question she had ever been asked.

"I'll be joining a fair later in the spring and traveling west with them soon," she said matter-of-factly.

"How long have you been living here?" I wanted to know.

"But a few short months," was her curt answer.

"Please let me give you something." I must have sounded almost desperate.

She shook her head once more. Then she paused. "Did you want to know something else about Nitro?" Was her tone now sly?

"Very much," I answered her.

"I did see him a few nights ago. It was on the night of the

bitter cold when the Lazarus bus came for us and took us to the shelter. It was on a Sunday. I saw him at the shelter that night."

"What is the Lazarus bus?" I asked her, not even close to understanding.

"The Lazarus bus always comes for us on the nights that are the coldest." She was explaining patiently, but I was still confused.

"Where does the bus take you?"

"It takes us to the shelter."

There was a loop of information/logic I wasn't fully accessing. I did remember Reggie Hawkins talking about the shelters. Some of the homeless chose to sleep out most nights and some went to the shelters on the colder nights. Was Lazarus one of the homeless shelters where they slept? Sending out a bus to pick up people made perfect sense.

"Is there something else?" I asked her carefully then.

She nodded her head slowly. "I watched him. When he was at the shelter. He was crying in secret."

I wasn't sure what she meant by that. "He was crying in secret?" I repeated her words stupidly.

"He was so sad. I could see it in the deepest part of him. He was unhappy on the inside where he thought that no one could watch him. He liked to laugh and be a jester on the outside, for the good people to see, but underneath, in his very soul, Nitro was crying and I saw it in him. He couldn't hide his sadness from me. Or from the others who can see inside."

"Did others see him?"

She looked at me pityingly. "Of course they did. There are others who can see as well as I can. Some look to offer help. Some look to find a weakness."

"You have a gift for the seeing?" I told her smiling.

She raised her eyebrows slightly. "You are perchance jesting with me, Sir?"

"Perchance a little, My Lady," I confessed sheepishly.

"He had a name tattooed on his ankle," I said.

"What was the name?"

"Amy."

"She would be a lost love of his. Perhaps he mourns her passing."

"Is she dead?" I couldn't help asking this.

She hesitated. "In a manner of speaking."

As she said this I found my wallet in the seat pack and pulled out a twenty. I handed it to her.

"It might be a while until the fair comes to town," I said to her.

She looked at the money. She seemed to be considering. "Tell me then, were my words of that much value to you?" she asked me finally.

"I think so," I said truthfully.

"What is it that you seek?" she asked.

"I think Nitro died badly last night and I want to know what happened to him. Another man died in the creek last month, and his life was a strange one."

"Did his strange life lead to his death?"

"I doubt it," I admitted.

"But it interests you all the same."

I nodded.

"Then you should look." She smiled at me then.

I had given her the hastily abbreviated answer. The extrapolated version was slightly more complex. Thinking about Nitro lead inexorably to reconsidering the part of my life with Keith Pringle, and thinking about Keith meant excavating back into my own past. In the same way, the tiny amount I now knew about Andrew Travers, the other recent drowning death, resonated a little uneasily with me.

When she smiled, I couldn't help thinking that she somehow divined all the unspoken portions of my answers.

"I remember the other death," she said.

I wondered. "Did you know him?"

She shook her head. "No."

Then she asked me a very good question. "Do you look for answers for the men who died, or do you look for answers for yourself?"

"Can it perhaps be a little of both?" I asked her back.

"It surely can," she told me. "But the dead don't need answers."

At that she suddenly made up her mind. She took the bill quickly and daintily and then she walked away.

"Fare thee well in your journey of discovery," she called out to me.

"Good luck to you, Fair Maiden," I whispered back to her, knowing that she wouldn't be able to hear me.

A minute later, a hand brushed my shoulder as I pushed my bike along the path. I turned around. The tarot lady faced me with her hand outstretched. In between her fingers was a single card face down.

She spoke. "This was to be your first card." She hesitated. "I thought you would want to know." She turned it over slowly.

"What does it signify?" I wondered out loud.

She hesitated. "Many unexpected things . . . a lost child

perhaps . . . an old friend . . . a family member . . . a new love found."

"Is it a good card or a bad card?" I wanted to know.

She considered my question carefully. "It's neither good nor bad. The cards suggest to us only aspects of our stories. We can always accept the parts we like, or try to alter the parts that don't suit us."

And with that she left.

I rode back to my little yellow house later, when the sky had clouded over. The day was still warm but a soft drizzle had begun to fall.

My yard is small and densely covered with mostly wildflowers that I can't even begin to identify. Beneath the flowers lurks a thin layer of sand, barely an inch or so that covers the hard rock underneath. There is no garage. There's no space for one, just a bare patch of sand at the front, where no flowers grow. My five-year-old blue Subaru Outback sits there most of the time, brushed by a light patina of rust-red dust.

In an unusual frenzy of boyish impulsiveness, I bought my car and my house and my bike in my last week of visiting Boulder for the first time, four years ago. Financially I did okay in the process, although I might just have been lucky. Doubtless I could have fared better with a little more restraint.

By that fourth week, I was finished touring the breweries and attached brewpubs out of town and was biking my way between the Boulder craft breweries. I tried driving one day, but Boulder is a bike town, most trips are a lot faster that way, and I was happy to convert to the local preferred mode of transport. Besides, biking was turning out to be a lot of fun, and I needed the exercise.

I gave some thought to finding myself a realtor. I could have chosen the very blonde woman who had strategically placed her name all over my borrowed bike. But I found lots of houses for sale by myself as I pedaled around town. Moreover, I wasn't a big fan of the emblazoned bike.

Boulder was far from cheap, but I had some disposable cash to spend, and I only wanted a small place. I still didn't know much of the town. The west end of Pearl was super costly, North Boulder was nice and funky over by Broadway and less funky at the Folsom end, South Boulder was too far from downtown, and The Hill was close to the university and much too full of students. Further east on Pearl fell nicely between all these areas, and the yellow house on Twenty-Second with a big porch, all the flowers, and the For Sale By Owner sign outside was the one I kept riding past slowly at least once a day.

On the third pass, I caught the two owners outside, thinning their flower collection in the early evening, using a complex botanic equation I couldn't decipher. They gave every indication of knowing exactly what they were doing. So I said hello, and I told them how much I liked the outside of their house. They quickly invited me in.

The FSBO sign was a tad fraudulent. Neal was a realtor by trade, and his partner Gus managed a restaurant in NoBo on the corner of North and Broadway. They loved their little house but they, or more accurately Gus, wanted a condo closer to work, with more living space, more mod cons, more chrome, less of the fairytale gingerbread ambiance, more of the functional urban vibe, and Neal, who was quite a bit older, was clearly anxious to keep his younger partner happy.

They had certainly fixed the little house up nicely. The kitchen was small but full of high-end stuff that I'd never use. The living room was big and sunny. There was a powder room on the main floor and a good-sized full bathroom upstairs, where there was one huge bedroom and one huge closet that masqueraded as a second bedroom. The total square footage was barely 1500 square feet. But best of all, I liked the front porch, which wasn't that much smaller than the rest of the ground floor. Virtually all the furniture would be staying if I wanted it, Gus informed me. It was all wrong for the condo. Did Neal stifle an intake of breath at that moment? Perhaps he did. I already coveted all their stuff, but, sensing the ensuing preliminaries of the haggle, I prudently refrained from saying so.

We would be circumventing all broker fees. I would be paying cash, another fact that I was yet to divulge. We were both looking to move in about one month, when they could move into their new place, and when my loft lease would be up.

Their asking price was high. I had looked at comparables on the internet. We haggled some. I chose my moment and broke the news about the cash purchase. A bottle of decent Malbec was opened at that juncture, and the price dropped significantly.

And at that point, after spending the best, or worst, part of my adult life negotiating for one thing or another, I simply caved like a punter on the spot. Genuine desire kicked in, or newfound business apathy, and I found myself abruptly agreeing to the new figure. They seemed momentarily shocked. The subject of earnest money was mentioned. The going rate was discussed and five percent up front was deemed fair. I wrote a check for twenty percent, and we cracked open another bottle. We were now truly done.

By the end of the night, and that second bottle of fine Argentinean wine, Neal and Gus and I were friends. They were full of advice, talking up the virtues of the local Craigslist for my car- and bike-buying plans. As I left, Neal drew me aside and asked if he could come by on occasion and help me out with the garden. I assured him that he would be most welcome. I also told him to bring Gus, and I received a reproachful look in response.

The next day a blizzard of house contracts flew back and forth. I bought the Subaru from a gentleman in Loveland on Craigslist a day later. Neal and Gus told me I could leave the car outside the house anytime during the next month. The Outback was a 2.5i. It was a year old and got a clean bill of health from CARFAX. I was well pleased. The gentleman selling it must have sensed a certain sale, because he arrived with the car and the title, and his good buddy drove over too, in his own car—the same good buddy who then headed off to the Sink for a burger and a Milk Stout while we negotiated and who afterward drove his newly carless friend back home from the Lookout.

The bike buy took a fun day of research on the internet. But in the end I walked to one of several cycle shops on Pearl, found the same bike steeply discounted as the previous year's model in a color I much preferred, and, seduced by the promise of a seeming eternity of free spring and fall tune-ups, I slapped down a solid chuck of the two large I had extracted from the nearby Chase. The sight of crisp green produced an upgraded cage, a decent Trek lock, better tires, and a Bontrager seat pack.

I rode back to the hotel whistling the Green Day song that had been playing in the store as they fine-tuned my purchase. I detoured past my new house on the way. The For Sale sign was down, and I almost giggled out loud.

I was a true Boulderite now, with a decent bike, a used Subaru, and an overpriced piece of real estate.

I still had a couple of days left. I needed to return my rental car, check out of my rented hotel room, give up my rental apartment in Chicago, and get back here with all the shit I still wanted to keep by the end of a month. I also realized that my flurry of spending wasn't as well planned out as I'd thought or, to be more accurate, wasn't really planned out at all.

I wanted to drive the Outback to Chicago and back here a month later to move in. So I needed to drive the rental car back to the airport, where I could cash in one half of my return ticket to Chicago on Southwest for a credit I had one full year to use, then take the shuttle bus back to Boulder and the Lookout. I then had to leave my new bike chained up on the porch outside my new house for a month. Neal and Gus had graciously offered to babysit the bike. But I still wasn't happy about it.

On the plus side, I didn't have much stuff to pack in the apartment, and I was pretty certain that the Salvation Army might be induced to take most of it off my hands. My apartment lease ended serendipitously, and my car in Chicago was an econobox business lease for artworks.com that Nye would cancel.

I was absurdly keen to make the long drive back to

Chicago. Lincoln, Nebraska, looked pretty close to the half way mark, and I got myself a Best Western room with a queen bed at a manager's special price. I was quite unprepared for the unrelieved tedium of Colorado, once I cleared Denver, and three solid quarters of rural Nebraska, which I had to conquer before reaching my first night's destination. Still, I drove fast in my Outback with the iPod classic on shuffle, the hot tub worked fine at the hotel, and it was buy a big beer at a little beer price that night at the brewery/steakhouse in town. As if that wasn't enough, the Cornhuskers prevailed in overtime on every one of the big screen televisions, and free dessert was offered to everyone, rabid fans and tired, largely indifferent travelers alike.

All that was four years ago.

Inside the fridge was some organic split pea soup from Whole Foods that I'd barely dented. There was also half a baguette on the kitchen counter, too old to pass for fresh bread, but perfect for toasting in my snappy black Dualit toaster.

The porch was mostly dry even though the rain had picked up, and the Flatirons had vanished behind the low dark clouds. Neal had installed rain barrels on two sides of the house, and I sat with my toasted bread and my hot soup and listened to them gurgle away in stereo as the downspouts filled them up. Gradually the noise lulled me into a stupor, and my eyes half closed for a promised moment.

I woke up with a start much more than a moment later. There was a soft crunching sound, a sudden body movement glimpsed through the density of the wet flowers, and an out-of-place-color—a deep red or dark brown jacket or coat, perhaps.

But then it was gone and there was nothing untoward.

I ate the rest of my dinner slowly, and later I went to bed early, as the rain kept falling long into the night.

At some sleep juncture a gun is pushed against my head in almost every nightmare I can recall in the last ten years of my life. I kneel in the wet sand and wait for an eternity, for the death shot, for my death shot. Everything is slow enough for me to recognize that I could theoretically escape. I could simply get to my feet, walk away, and I would surely live. Yet I never choose this option, because I know I won't be able to walk if I do try to stand up. I am also aware that crawling away is also theoretically possible, and would actually save me, but I choose not to do that either, this time for some unfathomable reason. There is thus a protracted internal debate/mental loop triggered every dream time . . . I know that crawling away is my only option but I choose not to take it . . . I can't get up and run . . . I will therefore soon die . . . I know that crawling away is my only option . . . and so it repeats.

Adding to the numbing repetition of the moment is the depressing awareness that I am in a dream that I have experienced many times before.

My nightmare isn't especially frightening, because I recognize it as a dreary recurrence, just as I also know that I will live to replicate it over and over again. Toward the end of the reverie, which invariably seems to last forever, I always try to raise my eyes just enough to see who is holding the gun to my head. Again, I am perpetually conscious of who should be holding the gun, the only man who has ever held a gun to my head. But somehow I know that it is not the same person this time. I know this, even as I am unable to lift my head, as I am also incapable of getting to my feet and saving my life.

As I kneel and consider my suspended fate, the sun always starts to set across the lake in a series of segmented time-lapse long exposures, and at that moment I wake with the recurring sense that I have failed a series of simple tests yet again.

This time when I woke, it was also early in the morning, the weather was colder, and the rain had finally stopped.

FIVE

At ten in the morning, Boulder Police Officer Reggie Hawkins and I were the only people in the café section of the Trident who were not crouched over some version of a computer screen. We were also, perhaps not coincidentally, in the highest and least-well-represented age bracket of the assembled clientele.

The Trident is on the west end of Pearl, with a used bookstore attached, and four smoked glass and wrought iron tables outside, unofficially reserved for customers with big sleeping dogs to crawl under on warm days—the dogs that is, not the customers. Today was much too cold for that. The outside seats were empty for long stretches, then peopled for short spells by brooding young cigarette smokers huddled, scowling, and intense in the unofficial version of Boulder gothic: black North Face jackets.

Pearl was quiet. Directly across the street from the Trident sits a singularly rare spectacle on this end of Pearl: an abandoned storefront, which, if memory serves, was until very recently the site of a high-end motor dealer. I'm frankly surprised that a store like that would go under in a prosperous place like this, but then, generally speaking, Boulder money tends not to go toward sleek autos but is usually allocated instead on several pricey bikes per citizen, plus a smattering of sundry other types of outdoor lifestyle accoutrements.

Reggie Hawkins had arrived at the Trident a few minutes before me.

We sat near the back of the café, in a section mostly

used by young mothers with little ones, in hi-tech strollers, clutching their organic fruit juice in sippy cups. The back of the place provides easy access to the sandy play lot, half inside, half outside, solidly fenced in, and partially covered for year-round romping by the pampered little darlings. Some attempt at artistic expression has manifested itself in the layout of the play area. There is soft sand and running water and a large glass globe placed like a splendorous crystal ruler in the center of the area.

Hawkins still looked nothing like a cop to me. But then my stock model is the beefy Chicago one—ruddy faced, uniformed, ginger-haired shanty Irish variety—or else the casual, over-polished work shoe, polyester-trousered plainclothes model that never manages to fool anyone. Officer Hawkins no longer had his arm in a sling, I now noticed. He'd draped his leather jacket over the back of his chair, and he wore a worn denim shirt and a wrinkled pair of khakis. The same chunky collection of bright braided bracelets adorned one wrist, and a matching necklace was tied loose around his neck. Were there a few more bracelets today perchance? I spied neither a watch nor a wedding ring.

His look was superior old hippy, gotten good and wealthy but not yet a total capitalist copout, or else a college professor, the terminally hip guy that all the kids in his freshmen class really dig.

"Thank you so much for meeting with me," I said as I sat down. I noticed he still had half a tall latte left.

"Sure," he said. He watched me as I carefully placed my regular coffee on the table without spilling any. "I was kinda surprised you asked to meet with me."

"Why's that?"

Reggie looked hard at me. Then he smiled. His eyes were blue and pale and he didn't let them blink too often.

"Okay, so maybe I wasn't so surprised you wanted to meet. You asked some interesting questions at the creek. I figured you'd soon think of a few more."

"I have," I said.

He sat back in his chair. "So fire away," he said amiably.

"Why are you being so helpful?" I blurted this out. It wasn't what I had planned for a first question.

He laughed. "Are you complaining?"

I shook my head vigorously. "No, not at all. But I'm curious. Why did you agree to meet with me?"

"I did me some digging. And I know some things about you now."

"And?" I waited for him to continue.

"And they maybe help explain your curiosity. You're pretty new to Boulder. You used to live in Chicago. Ten years ago you decided one day to be a private detective. I was able to read the reports. It didn't go too badly for you that time although it could have easily ended with you dead. You found a missing man for the local cops up in Michigan, and you did it without their help and without pissing them off too much. There was some more death, but you weren't especially to blame for that. All in all, you did well. You slapped a few people around, and you went up against a local prick and pretty much brought him down all by yourself. The local cops there thought you did okay. They also thought that you bullshitted them some at the end but that you did it for a good cause. So now you're a pretty wealthy guy still, and kinda semiretired, with some time on your hands." He paused for a moment. "Maybe with too much time on your hands?"

"You think I'm wealthy?"

"Not as much as you once were. But you still bought yourself a house in Boulder for cash."

"The whole of my house could fit inside a small bathroom."

"Boulder is an expensive place."

"So where do you live?" I asked this a little defensively.

"Westminster," he smiled blandly. "All I can afford on my cop salary."

"What about your art?"

That got his attention. "I beg your pardon?"

"The paintings, the gallery shows, the articles about you in the Sunday papers."

He grinned sheepishly at that. "You looked me up."

"Just like you looked me up," I countered. "I also looked up Andrew Travers."

He nodded slowly then. "Yeah, I thought you might. That was a hell of a story. Billionaire becomes homeless guy becomes flash flood victim," he said.

I nodded. "You still think I'm wealthy?"

He shook his head several times. "Not compared to him."

I asked, "You still haven't told me why we're here."

He took a deep breath. "Okay, several things. Like I said, I thought the stuff I found out about you these years ago was pretty interesting. You had a hunch, and you went after it, and you were smart, and it turned out you were pretty much right too. Now I can see that you're kinda curious about Nitro, the dead guy in the creek. And maybe you're a little curious about Andrew Travers now too."

I cut him off. "I can't escape the feeling that there's something weird about their deaths."

Then he cut me off. "Let me tell you, there's always something weird about death. But let me ask you something: how do you know they're weird?"

I said nothing.

Hawkins nodded to himself. "Let me guess. You have another hunch? Well maybe you'll turn out to be right. But, between you and me, I seriously doubt it. Want to know what my hunch is?"

I nodded.

"I think you're just a little bit bored. I think you're reaching too hard for something to fill up your time."

The possibility had crossed my mind. "Perhaps," I admitted.

"So I agreed to meet you and to answer your questions. Maybe I'll be able to talk you out of this. But in the seriously remote possibility that you're right, you can help us solve two murders that only you believe are actually murders, and you'll get to make us look like idiots in the process."

"What do you think?" I asked him.

There was a pause. When he finally spoke it was measured and slow. "There are no mysteries here, and we're not gonna look like idiots. Finding two guys in the creek dead within a month of each other is sad but not that strange. The creek does occasionally flood, and homeless people do occasionally die when it does."

I nodded. What he was saying did make sense.

He sighed for a long time before he spoke again. "I think they both drowned by accident."

I asked, "All by themselves?"

There was another long sigh. "I think so."

"You're quite sure."

He sighed for a third time. "I am. And even if I wasn't, I just can't see how you'd explain it any other way."

"Have you tried?"

There was an intake of breath. "I did give it some thought."

We sat for a moment saying nothing. Hawkins spent the time rearranging the contents of our table. When he was finally satisfied, he leaned forward and he spoke very slowly. "Listen to me very carefully. We're going to talk a bunch more now. You'll learn some stuff that you probably have no business knowing, and you need to keep that stuff to yourself. Do you understand me?"

I nodded.

"Now you need to understand something else. You're not about to let this go anytime soon. That's my hunch. So, if you do, by any weird and wonderful chance, find out something of real value, you're going to call me before you do anything seriously fucking stupid. Do you understand that?"

I nodded again.

Reggie Hawkins leaned back in his chair. I watched him for a moment. Then I spoke.

"There's something more to this."

"How do you figure that?" He looked all innocent.

"Because you're not actually telling me to stop?"

Reggie sighed. "Okay. I don't happen to think that following hunches is in any way stupid. And also, since you did ask, there is one little thing about Travers dying that does bother me."

I waited.

"How come he was at the creek that night when it flooded?"

"What do you mean?" I asked.

"Some of the homeless stay at the creek almost every night. Nitro was like that. But Andrew Travers wasn't. He went to the homeless shelters every single night. The flood that killed him was late in the evening, so he should have been safe in some shelter when it happened. But he wasn't. He was out at night in the rain."

"Do you have a theory?"

He shook his head. "I wish I did."

Then he leaned forward. "Okay. Before you get to pick my brain I get to ask you something."

"Of course," I replied.

"I'm a cop and, as you found out, I'm also a painter. Both pay badly, although painting gets you fancy articles in fancy magazines that frankly, they only write because I'm also a cop. I don't follow finance much, although I've got twin girls going to college in five years, so maybe I should start. But you were a big investment kind of guy once. You still part own two companies, and you don't appear to do much work. You used to wheel and deal some. What do you make of Andrew Travers?"

I thought for a moment before I answered. "I'd heard his name before. He worked for Eagle Equity in Omaha, Nebraska. They're a well-known private equity firm. He was a senior partner. He worked there for twenty-five years. He joined them right after college. He made them a fortune, and he made one for himself."

"Explain all that equity shit to me . . . the layman's version."

"Private equity?"

"Yeah."

I took a deep breath. "This is the condensed version for

cop/painters. Eagle Equity looks for business opportunities. They use investor money to buy a controlling interest in struggling companies and they try to turn them around. They charge all kinds of fees for doing this. Advisory fees. Even fees for buying the company in the first place. These are usually very steep fees.

"How steep?"

"Often around a million a year to advise and perhaps two million to buy the company in the beginning."

"Then what happens?"

"Then Eagle goes to work. They reorganize companies, use acquisition strategies, hire, fire, sell off assets, outsource, streamline, buy smaller competitors, merge, leverage a buyout, whatever it takes. If it works they turn a business around, declare a dividend for their happy investors, pay off the creditors, keep everyone in the company employed, and keep all the fees and the leftover profits for themselves. Their money then gets hidden in tax shelters and offshore accounts for the senior partners like Andrew Travers."

"Sounds like a sweet deal where everybody wins."

I nodded slowly. "In this particular scenario, a lot of people do get to profit. It's often a lot more complicated than that. There are several layers of protection for Eagle, for a start. The purchased company themselves are the first to lose out. They pay the fees to Eagle and repay the Eagle investors, in that order, before anything else happens. That money alone can drive a struggling business into more trouble; having to pay Eagle and their investors makes a company more liable to liquidation than anything else. There's a lot of ways to lose for everyone except Eagle Equity. Here's an obvious example. If you worked for a company that fired you to make the company more profitable then you certainly lost. If your job was outsourced to somewhere where labor is cheaper you also lost. When Eagle take companies and force them to expand, buy subsidiaries, merge, and consolidate, the debt automatically mushrooms, and then maybe the whole economy falters or that particular industrial sector does. Then the company goes tits up. But first the Eagle fees come off the top, then the investor dividends come next, if there's any left. In some instances most people get to win, but in all the possible ramifications, Eagle Equity never loses."

"Is Eagle that bad?"

I smiled. "I'm a semi-reformed capitalist, so I'm prejudiced. Eagle collects fees for managing investors' money, they charge transaction fees for acquiring other companies, and they charge advising fees to the companies they buy. There are finder's fees and loser's fees. Travers started making around five million a year in bonuses derived from the fees alone in the mid-1990s, when he was only thirty-five or so, plus he got a share of the carried interest, plus Eagle's cut of investment profits, as well as any returns he got from investing his own money, which Eagle actively encourages their employees to do."

"So do we know exactly how much he made?"

I shook my head. "We don't."

"Any chance of us finding out?"

"I seriously doubt it," I said.

Reggie thought of something. "So if a company goes under and Travers put his own cash in, does he lose it?"

I nodded. "He does. But remember he has a lot of fee revenue coming in to offset his own liability."

"Does Eagle ever lose money?"

I shook my head at the absurdity. "The worst that can happen is they just make less. Eagle takes out their huge fees win or lose. Plus you have to remember they are very good at turning companies around. That's how they get their investors onboard in the first place."

"Do they always collect?"

I looked incredulous. "Do you even have to ask that? They'll sell the last few assets of a business going under to get their fees back, and in some of the strangest cases getting their fee out of a struggling business is enough to drive that company under all by itself."

"Is all this legal?" he asked me then.

I nodded. "Pretty much."

He shook his head. "It's a shitty business," he said.

"You'll get no argument there," I agreed.

"So that last scenario you talked about. The selling all the company assets and stuff off at the end; was that what happened with Armstrong Tool?"

I nodded. "It seems so. They were a small farm machinery manufacturer near Ottumwa, Iowa, and they were the last company Andrew Travers worked with for Eagle Equity. In his defense, Travers was reputedly a decent man most of the time. The companies he worked with usually did well. His success rate was what made him good at his job. He didn't like taking on high-risk jobs, and, that time, he even went on record advising Eagle not to buy into Armstrong."

"How did they take that advice?"

I snorted at that. "They took it exactly as you can imagine they would. Armstrong went badly right from the start. Eagle couldn't get any traction, and a family business in its third generation went under quickly within two years, taking almost thirty good jobs and the pension plan with it. Armstrong had been struggling before Eagle took over. They had a long history of losing market share and they had mounting debts. Eagle acquired them . . ."

Reggie cut in. "For an acquisition fee?"

I nodded. "You're learning fast. Then Travers advised them to buy out a smaller competitor, which meant?"

"Don't tell me. Advising and transaction fees?"

"Good boy. All this raised their debt, and business was still stalled. So Travers liquidated Armstrong, charged a liquidation fee, sold the plant, laid off the workforce, and auctioned the equipment. He might have raised enough to pay everyone off, give decent severance packages to the employees, except . . ."

"Except for the fees," Reggie offered helpfully.

"Exactly," I said. "The ten million still owed in fees to Eagle Equity. That figure left Armstrong truly gutted. And Eagle Equity always gets paid first."

Reggie spoke quietly. "You read about Ted Armstrong?"

I nodded slowly. "I read that Edward Armstrong the third drove his company Cadillac and his wife and his daughter into the Des Moines River one dark night."

"Three drowning deaths," Reggie spoke the words softly to himself. I said nothing.

Then Reggie spoke again. "So what happened to Andrew Travers?"

"You read the same articles as I did. He went before the Eagle board and begged them to get out of the private equity business. They naturally declined. Then he resigned. He even gave some of his money to the Armstrong employees. Then he divorced his wife, but not before carefully creating a charity with her and his teenage daughter in equal charge of pretty much every penny he ever made and invested. They've been giving his money away for a few years now. The ex-wife is forty-five and the daughter is twenty-two. They've become quite famous."

"Have you seen them?" Reggie asked me eagerly.

I smiled. "I certainly have. They are both very smart and very attractive, and they've given about thirty million dollars away so far. Matching grants for education and technology and disease control in underdeveloped countries mostly. Travers had over a billion dollars in Cayman Island offshore accounts alone, on which he paid virtually no tax. He hid more of his cash in shelters all over the world. Some were in Ireland. His money is still out there, generating more tax-free money. It'll take these two ladies their whole lives to give away all his assets."

"Did you have any business dealings like that? With places like Eagle Equity."

"Me?" I was surprised at the question

He laughed. "Sure, why not?"

I laughed a little nervously. "A little out of my league," I shrugged.

Reggie waited for me to continue.

"I suppose there were a wide range of investments in my portfolio at one time. It's perhaps possible that at one time I could have . . ." I stopped there and thought hard for a moment. The truth was I really didn't know for sure.

That was what had occurred to me when I first read about Andrew Travers; not just the strange trail of his money, and the possibility that my little investments had rubbed up at one time against his, but the descriptions of the rapid accumulation and the palpable excitement I felt as I followed the sharp trajectory of his career and his attaining of an almost unimaginable wealth in a comparatively short time.

There was a time when I would have gladly killed for his life . . .

Reggie dragged me back to the present. "And then Travers . . ."

I finished the thought for him. "Then Andrew Travers just walked away from his old life."

Then it was Reggie's turn to cut in. "And into his new life where he lives homeless on the streets in Boulder then drowns in the creek last month."

I nodded. "That's about the size of it."

Reggie sipped the dregs of his latte thoughtfully while I watched a mother yank a baby out of a stroller and sniff hard at its diapered bottom.

"Thanks for the business lesson," he said smiling.

I smiled back. "Did it help?" I asked.

"Sure," then he paused. "Well?"

"Well what?"

"So what do you want to know?" he smiled again.

"I have a few questions," I said.

"So start off with the easy ones," he laughed.

"Very well. Why wear all the bracelets?"

Reggie laughed and shrugged at the same time. "My daughters make them. They think it keeps me safe. I get about one a day. The deal is you've gotta wear them until they fall off naturally. No cheating. No pulling at the knot when they're not watching. That would mess with the good vibes. Eventually the damn things fall off by themselves. What do

I have now anyway?" He counted the lines of thread on his wrist. "Thirteen. Shit. That can't be lucky. But that's about the average. It makes them happy to make them. I haven't died yet. So maybe they work. Who knows?"

"Are you married?"

He nodded. "Fifteen years." About the same length of time I had been married to Patricia, I couldn't help thinking.

"Where's the sling?"

"I sprained my wrist playing tennis with the wife last week and just got the damn thing off this morning." He glanced involuntarily at his newly freed arm.

"And you are a painter?"

He shrugged. "Fine Arts major back in college. I just never managed to quit."

"What do you paint?" I asked him. I already knew the answer from the images and articles on the internet. But I wondered how he would respond.

He smiled. "I paint crime victims in imaginary settings." It sounded like a rehearsed answer to an often-asked question. I wanted to know a lot more about his painting, but I decided it could wait.

"How did Andrew Travers die?"

Reggie took his time before he answered. "He died a lot like Nitro. We found him in the early morning after the flash flood in early February. Travers washed up ashore."

"Did he drown?"

"Yeah. He was beat up way more than Nitro."

"His head?"

"Mostly. But he was truthfully pretty much bruised as shit all over his body."

"Where did you find him?"

"He was a good ways downstream from Nitro. We can't really assume that he and Nitro went in anywhere close to the same location. We can maybe guess that Travers' body travelled the greater distance, which would maybe account for there being more damage to the body. But he was older, too. And not so healthy. He was a little overweight. So maybe he just got bashed about more. The two floods weren't the same strength, but this isn't a science."

It all sounded perfectly reasonable.

"I'm curious. Does someone drown every time the creek floods?"

He laughed a little uneasily. "No way."

"Most times, then?" I asked.

"Nope."

"Just sometimes, then," I said.

"Right."

"Were there any flash floods between the deaths of Travers and Nitro?" I asked.

Reggie nodded. "There was a flood on February the twenty-second."

I was pretty sure that fact hadn't been mentioned in the newspapers, and I hadn't thought to do any more checking. I now realized I should have.

"Did anyone die then?" I asked.

He shook his head. "Not that we know of."

I took a deep breath. "So tell me something about Nitro," I said.

He drank down the rest of his latte.

"You're gonna want your money back."

"How do you mean?" I asked him.

"There isn't that much to tell. He drowned in fresh water. He also hit his head hard."

"Was it hard enough to kill him?"

Reggie smiled. "You do ask good questions. But no, he wasn't hit hard enough to kill him."

"Was there evidence of drugs and alcohol?"

"Damn. You are good at this. That's a positive to both. His blood-alcohol level was high. There was evidence of drugs both in the body and also a little wet weed residue we found in his pants pocket when we looked more closely back at the station."

"It could have been planted."

Reggie looked almost disappointed. "Come on. Why would anyone plant a pissant little amount like that?"

He was probably right.

"What about Andrew Travers?"

He shook his head. "His toxicology report came back clean for everything."

"Who was he?" I asked.

He smiled. "You mean Nitro? You took your sweet time getting to that one. You know what? This is the stuff I really shouldn't be telling you." He hesitated. "You remember what I said?"

I nodded and tried to look contrite. Then I sat and waited.

Reggie made up his mind suddenly.

"His name was Arthur Crowder. He was twenty-four."

"Had he ever been arrested?"

"Yeah. Once for possession of marijuana with probable intent to sell, and once for public drunkenness and underage drinking."

"Where?"

"Both arrests were made in Los Angeles. Both times he got probation."

"Does he have any family?"

"We contacted the grieving parents in an LA suburb; they hadn't seen their beloved Art in five years. They arranged for the body to be sent back there."

"What happened to Travers' body?" I asked.

"The ex-wife had it shipped back to North Platte, Nebraska. He was born and raised there."

"How did she react to his death?"

"She cried for a good long time."

I changed the subject. "The parents called him Art?"

Reggie nodded once.

"How long had he been in Boulder?" I wanted to know.

"We're not really sure about that one. Maybe a year or so."

"How do you know?"

"He signed up for a medical marijuana card."

"Is that hard to get?" I asked.

"Medical marijuana?"

I nodded and Reggie burst out laughing

"Did he get in any trouble here?"

"There's nothing on record. Maybe we're just nicer than the California cops."

"Is there anything else?"

"Not much. His parents say they pretty much lost control of Art by the end of junior high. He'd had good grades up until then and played pretty good traveling baseball for a time. Then he discovered beer and weed. He never made it through high school, and he left home at eighteen. There's no employment record for him after he turned nineteen, and that ties in pretty well with his last known address. He's been living under the radar for close to five years, here maybe a year or so and, we're guessing before that, maybe in and around Los Angeles for a time. We're still checking out the California stuff, but there isn't much."

"What was he like?" I asked.

"He seems to have been happy as shit most of the time. Liked to laugh and get stoned and drunk on his ass on beer pretty much all the time when he could get them. The people on the creek all seemed to love him like crazy. He had no enemies that anyone knows about. No one had anything shitty to say about Nitro as near as we can tell."

"What about Amy?"

Reggie shrugged. "That tattoo on his ankle? I asked his parents about that and they had no idea. Said he didn't have it in high school. They said there were plenty of girls, but they didn't recall anyone named Amy. At the station we took a look at it. It was done professionally and was maybe less than five years old, but it wasn't especially recent. So that makes it what, maybe three or four years old? We're pretty sure it predates his living here. We could check all the Boulder parlors. It wouldn't tell us much."

"Did you check on the guy who called you?"

Hawkins looked sheepish. "The cell phone in question belonged to some skinny jogging lady who was stopped by a homeless guy who asked to borrow her phone."

"Did she see the body herself?"

"She says that she didn't."

"That seems unlikely."

"I tend to agree."

"Can she describe the homeless guy?"

"He was apparently just a homeless guy wearing a bright-colored sweatshirt."

"That's not much."

Reggie nodded sadly. "I've noticed over the years that homeless people tend to get regularly overlooked by our regular citizens. They get looked right through most of the time. It's not done on purpose. It's just that the upstanding folks would rather not stare too long at people they would rather not exist. At least she did let him use her phone."

"So why was he called Nitro?" I asked.

Reggie smiled. "Ah, this you'll like. Art was pretty much a fancy beer snob. He only liked to drink the good stuff, like you guys make. The name came with him from L.A. They called him Nitro after the part of the brewing process. But you know more about that. How does it work?"

"You don't know?"

He looked sheepish. "I'm pretty much a Bud Light man."

"It's a way to pump the beer from the keg using nitrogen instead of carbon dioxide. It makes it taste a lot smoother and creamier."

"Does it taste better that way?"

"I think so."

"Could I tell the difference?" He grinned at me.

I laughed out loud. "Probably not."

I reached for my coffee. It was stone cold.

Then Reggie spoke. "How did it go for you on the creek yesterday?"

"How do you mean?"

"You were seen hanging out there." It wasn't exactly a question.

So I told him about the tarot lady and the fates and the sadness she had seen in Nitro. I told him she had mentioned the weed and the drinking and the charm and the ladies.

"There's a shelter called Lazarus that the homeless can go to?" I asked him.

He nodded. "There are several shelters in Boulder. Most of the homeless are pretty independent. Some are paranoid, and some are just bat shit crazy, so the beds are mostly empty most nights. I told you that Travers used them every night. He was unusual. When it gets really cold more of them go to the shelters at night. Lazarus is one of the places that they go to. Lazarus House is in the basement of Saint Andrew's Episcopal Church over on Arapahoe and Sixty-Third. They're real good people there. There's beds and hot food served every night and they send them off in the morning with breakfast and a packed lunch in a brown bag. A bunch of other local churches each volunteer to staff the place one night a week."

"Who does Sunday nights?"

He shook his head. "Not a clue. Last Sunday was a cold one so the place was probably full."

"They send a bus out for them?"

Reggie smiled. "Saint Andrew's owns a piece-of-shit old school bus painted bright blue. On the cold nights, some volunteer on duty drives the old bus to the creek and loads up the homeless. I think the capacity at Lazarus and the bus might be about the same."

"The bus only comes when it's cold?" I asked.

He nodded. "Temperature has to be at freezing or below for the bus to come out."

"How do the homeless get there other nights?"

"There's a bus service runs the length of Arapahoe and back for a dollar."

"The lady with the tarot cards said Nitro had stayed there on Sunday."

Reggie nodded again. "He'd have been crazy not to."

"Did he use the shelters the rest of the time?"

"No. Nitro liked to sleep out when it was warm enough."

"Not like Andrew Travers."

Reggie shook his head. "Like I said, Travers used them every single night. Travers had lived in Boulder for a few years. We're pretty sure when he got here because he registered for the shelters as soon as he arrived. He really kept pretty much to himself. We got next to nothing from the other homeless about him when we asked."

"So how did you find out about him?"

"We talked to the folks at the library. They were great. Travers spent every day there. He never bothered anyone. He signed up to use the computers there. Sometimes he slept, but mostly he read and researched stuff on the internet."

"What kind of stuff?"

"This probably won't surprise you too much."

"Try me."

"Okay. Travers had two big areas of interest. You can guess what they were."

"Eagle Equity."

Reggie smiled. "That's one."

"His ex-wife and daughter's charity work."

Reggie smiled again. "Bingo."

It all made perfect sense.

Reggie spoke. "At the end of the day, the library closed, and Travers slept at one of the shelters. As I said, Boulder has a few, and Travers tended to pick and choose. One or two of the librarians talked to him a little." Reggie smiled. "Apparently he liked to stay at the place that was serving the best meal that night."

"How did he get to the shelters?"

"That raises an interesting point. Travers spent his days in the library and his nights at the shelters. According to the librarian, he took the city bus to and from the shelters, so he usually had a little bit of money on him. But he didn't ever panhandle. He didn't beg on Pearl or on the Creek or anyplace else ever."

"So you're wondering how he had the money."

"Want to know what I think?" Reggie asked.

I answered for him. "The family sent him some."

Reggie nodded. "That's what I think. Not too much money, but just enough for him to get by."

It was an interesting theory.

I had nothing else to ask right now and we sat without speaking for a while.

Reggie broke the silence. "And I still don't know what the fuck Travers was doing at the creek in the middle of the night in the pissing rain," he said at last. Then Reggie stood up and made a pronouncement. "We'll be talking some more soon."

He looked hard at me. I said nothing.

"Because I can see you're nowhere near letting any of this shit go."

I still said nothing.

"But I want you to be very careful," he said, "especially when you deal with the homeless. The little hippy lady with the tarot cards was just eccentric. Some of the others are harmless, but some are pissed off and weirder than shit and strong and truly crazy, and they will fuck you up and go about their business. I know you can handle yourself pretty well, but I'm not sure how much crazy you are used to dealing with."

I tried to look noncommittal.

"When you were asking around did you notice any drug use?"

"You mean like weed?"

Reggie snorted. "Weed doesn't count in Boulder. Some of the homeless take all kinds of other shit. The favorite right now is cans of the aerosol stuff you use to clean computer keyboards with."

"What does it do?"

"You get a quick high where it hits you fast and you pretty much pass out for a second and lose half your fucking mind for the cost of a can, which last time I checked was about five bucks or less at CVS. Prolonged use of shit like that will scramble both your brain and your insides."

He spoke slowly and softly. "So let's be very careful out there." Reggie looked at me hard. "Okay?"

I caved under the pressure. "Okay," I said

Reggie turned to leave with a last sour look that indicated that he was far from satisfied with my answer.

Then he turned back.

"Can you play tennis?"

I wasn't expecting the question. "Yes. I mean I used to play. It's been a while."

"Are you any good?" he asked.

"Why?" I wondered where this was going.

"My wife needs a new partner."

"What about you?" I asked him.

"I suck at tennis, I keep getting hurt, and that was my painting hand I managed to fuck up the last time. Let me know if you want to play with her."

After he left I got out my iPhone and pulled up the latest Sunday magazine article on Reggie Hawkins, the painting policeman. The first image that went along with the text was of a murdered teenage girl. Reggie apparently paints all his figures in a style of graphic hyperrealism, almost like photographic still images. Then he superimposes the figures on garish pastel multicolored backgrounds that look deliberately crude, jarringly fake. The girl's throat is slashed wide open. She's lying on a big cloud composed of what look like huge marshmallows. Her skin is pale blue and lifelessly waxen. She's clutching in a death grip a giant lollipop with a kaleidoscopic pattern of swirling reds and whites. The series of contrasts were strange yet shrilly effective.

In a second image a small dog is hanging dead from the branch of a tree, trussed up and lifeless. Once again, the dog looks shockingly real but the tree's branches keep morphing into so many cartoon-shaped bones and fire hydrants and mailmen.

The title of the first work was *Candy*.

The second work was called *Good Boy*.

I stared at the two images for a long time.

SIX

That night it turned much colder. My iPhone rang as I sat inside my house and drank a glass of Pinot Noir from New Zealand and dutifully read the *New York Times* from cover to cover like a proper little liberal. I had swum and lunched at the Lookout in the afternoon and biked back home, taken a long shower, done all my laundry and, in truth, spent the next hour or so simply wandering around the house looking for things to do. But I had wasted my time. Everything was clean. Everything was put away.

I can effortlessly front load most of my days with copious activities, but my nights tend to be more barren and exposed in their dearth of social interactions. In the four years I've lived here, I've managed to sustain only about that many relationships.

I'm no longer young, and I don't believe I was ever particularly handsome. I'm a divorced man and no longer rich. As I ride my bike, I tend to run into the same faces, and I notice that many kinds of people choose to greet each other as they pass, like hearty middle-aged men squeezed into sports cars waving to each other. With some regret, I acknowledge that I've attained the age where I'm clearly both invisible and largely irrelevant to women under the age of thirty-five, and, as such, I am unilaterally ignored by that aloof subspecies. That would be just fine with me, but women over thirty-five are often married or already in relationships and are usually less than anxious to make my acquaintance.

At the falls, I've on occasion struck up conversations with

women I estimated to be comfortably south of that magic number, and, as I judge the situation to be promising—after all we both rode our bikes to a place we both clearly cherish—I often suggest perhaps continuing our chatting over coffee back in town. This has led to several cups of coffee, a handful of second dates over dinners, and four relationships that have lasted more than a month, but sadly, none that have lasted more than a year.

But I do continue to be optimistic.

Having said all that, it's in these early hours of the evening that I'm most aware of this yawning chasm in my socio-romantic calendar. The *New York Times* and a more-than-respectable glass of room temperature red wine are pleasant enough, but still a piss-poor substitution for the warm voice of an agreeable companion.

It goes without saying that I would like this to change. I tend to spend my nights alone, reading, listening to music, emailing or texting, all the while pretending to have an importance to either artworks.com and/or Belvedere that clearly doesn't exist.

I grab a sandwich or some food from the fridge.

I can always shop at Whole Foods, which is nearby. I can always sit in Cygnet and talk with Jesse, but at a certain point he often becomes busy, and I am suddenly exposed as a singular customer in a place mostly teeming with couples in their glaring plurality. I could look to date online but am loathe to take that desperate plunge. I could see a film in a theater and hide in the forgiving darkness, but I usually cop out and wait instead for Netflix.

During the day I bike and hunt for used books and swim and drink my beer with my lunch. At night I accept my lonely defeat and sit at home.

Occasionally I've chosen a concert and attended stag. This isn't as bad as it sounds, as I've yet to go to a gig and not spot a few other male loners. My music tastes tend to skew a good deal lower than my actual age and, as a result, I'm often the token oldster at the back of the house, a decent beer in my hand, a studied expression on my face, as if I'm maybe the hip music reviewer for a staid rag with only senior reporters on staff. Sometimes I wonder if the slackers in the audience think I might be the lead guitarist's proud dad.

I enjoy live music enough to make this shame-filled pilgrimage once in a while, and, by the second beer, I tend not to give much of a shit one way or another.

It occurs to me at this juncture of my dismal reverie that I have my two tickets to Admiral Fallow to deal with soon. Perhaps my former wife knows what a social dullard I am and is simply tormenting me. But I think not. She's just being insufferably thoughtful to a person who ill deserves such thoughtfulness.

My iPhone plays "The Blues Are Still Blue" by Belle & Sebastian to announce an incoming call. The voice on the phone is Nye, and he almost never calls.

"How was your birthday beer?" he asked me without any preamble.

I replied, "It was much appreciated."

"How would you feel about a business trip?"

"Why do you ask?"

"I'm sending you to Scotland."

"Why would you send me?" I enquired somewhat cattily.

Nye snootily ignored my question and began to explain. He had been talking to a small craft brewery near Aberdeen.

They wanted to partner up and make a beer with another brewery. This happens quite often, small batches of handcrafted beer in limited qualities, usually high in ABV, meant for sipping rather than sessional pounding. They had thought about Belvedere. Somehow they knew I was Scottish and wondered if we would be interested in a limited partnership, a one-off brew deal as it were. They wanted to use our porter, the Jolly Jack, and maybe make a barrel-aged smoked version of it, with some of their local highland waters, maybe a hint of peaty heather added into the hop balance, fermented in single malt barrels, that kind of thing.

So what did we think?

Nye confessed that he loved the idea, and I too could think of no reason not to proceed.

"You could go and meet with them instead," I offered lamely.

He openly scoffed. "Don't be ridiculous. You speak the language, and you haven't been back there in a long while, and you miss it, and you don't work very hard anyway. It's not like you'll be missed. They have already started making something they want us to try. You could be our official taster. It's virtually no work."

He made several good points. I cut to the chase. "Who's paying for this junket?"

Nye assumed an incredulous tone. "You mean will Belvedere pick up your tab for a week's vacation and about an hour of actual billable work?"

"Exactly."

There was a long disgruntled silence, which I took to be a bad omen for my chances of financial remuneration.

And Nye was correct. I did want to go home.

In September of the previous year, the nearby town of Estes Park had hosted their annual Scottish festival. There were wee dogs in tartan coats, rugby games featuring both sexes, bagpipes with or without folk music accompaniment, and frenzied bouts of highland games and highland dancing, which the casual observer might be hard put to tell the difference between. I'd driven over on an impulse, bought an authentically greasy pie and chips for lunch, almost let a plaid-bodiced lassie sell me a leather Celtic bracelet in all probability handcrafted in bonnie China, and after two lukewarm Belhaven Stouts, had stood to attention as the closing ceremony for the games took place, after a pageant-filled procession down Main Street, the massed bands droning and the batons twirling.

At the very close of the festivities, a professional singer had been co-opted to sing the American national anthem. He sang it beautifully. Bonnets and baseball caps were respectfully doffed, and there was the dutiful and cursory mumbling along. Then there was "God Save the Queen," which was performed to a shocking silence from the entire audience, and finally there was the singing of "Flower of Scotland," Scotland's unofficial anthem, in which the lone vocalist was helped out by a lone piper.

For the last, those of us who knew the words were asked to sing along, and I discovered two things: first, that I still knew all the words, and second, that I was unable to prevent several large wet tears cascading down my face as I began to sing.

My sense of patriotism has crept up on me late in life. I never cared about my heritage as a child. I lived there, after all, and very few of us who lived there in those days came from anyplace different. We were mostly born and raised there and doubtless expected to end our days not too far afield. Now I live a long way away from the country I grew up in, and I find that I miss the place much more than I ever expected. So I cried, and I sang.

The hills are bare now and autumn leaves lie thick and still.

Those days are passed now, and in the past they must remain.

O flower of Scotland, when will we see your like again?

But we can still rise now, and be the nation again.

"Can you go in a few days time?" Nye asked me. I told him I could.

We talked some more, but I barely paid attention. In amongst the talk, I was surprised to learn that Nye had heard of Reggie Hawkins' artistic work, his alter ego, his reprieve from long days spent keeping the peace in Boulder. As Nye pontificated on the relative merits of the Hawkins canon, I pulled up the local weather info on my laptop.

Boulder boasts more days of sunshine than most places, and the ten-day forecast offered up the next seven days as just such, the temperatures gradually rising then rising again, the overall numbers being well above average for March, but not excessively so. Also, for the first seven days, at least, there was no hint of any serious precipitation on the horizon.

The last few days of the ten-day forecast showed much warmer temperatures again and a greater likelihood of heavier rainfall. I took from this that little or no chance of flooding existed for at least a week, and somehow that thought came as a reassuring one to me, because, in a mind clearly made fevered and deranged by solitude, it was suddenly and irrationally important that I be back in Boulder in time for the next possible springtime flash flood.

So I had a day or two to get organized, a day to travel there, a day to travel back, and maybe two or three in the middle to spend cavorting in the highlands while pretending to work.

I canceled the *New York Times* by phone and graciously allowed my newspapers to be sent to a deserving school, my secret hope being to a deserving school filled with young Republicans. An email to the Boulder post office put a temporary hold on the paltry collection of junk mail I received each day.

After just one patient hour on the internet, I was flying coach, stopping over in Newark for two hours on the way out and two hours on the way back, and flying into and out of Turnhouse, Edinburgh's busy international airport.

I remembered pedaling my green Sturmey Archer three speed out to the motley collection of prefab huts that comprised Turnhouse when I was twelve or so. The bike path had followed the meandering course of a sluggish river for a couple of miles, then attached itself to the side of the train track as it rose up over a stone viaduct that you could lean against and feel ever so gently vibrate as the northbound passenger train rumbled overhead. The train would muster a last burst of diesel-powered speed before braking, then dawdling across the oxidized red suspended cantilever of the Forth Rail Bridge, down into the mysterious kingdom of Fife.

Close to the rail bridge, the path veered suddenly west, down through the harbor town of South Queensferry and then back up again, to the newly opened road bridge that stretched across the Forth. The old ferryboat was now in retirement, harbored directly across the quiet shore road from an inn celebrated in a justly famous piece of Scottish adventure literature. The squat, tug-shaped vessel seemed already aware of its own obsolescence, as it appeared to sulk rather than sit up against the high seaweed-covered harbor wall.

On days of light crosswinds, bicycles, and their brave riders, could cross the road bridge in those less paranoid and litigious times, although it provided for an altogether agreeable if vertiginous experience. Safely on the other side of the Forth, we rode our bikes down to the naval docklands and looked at the assortment of destroyers, aircraft carriers and frigates all spruce and ship shape and tied up.

The rest of my planning turned out to be a matter of more long hours on the internet, lining up cars and bikes and hotels and such. But not all: I had one old-fashioned phone call to make amidst my digital scheduling.

"Lazarus House." It was a kindly older woman's voice that answered the phone when I called.

"Hello," I said. "I was interested in volunteering at the shelter."

"Really? Well. That's good to hear." She paused.

"Do you need volunteers?" I asked.

There was a short burst of laughter. "Always. Have you volunteered before?"

"I used to volunteer at a soup kitchen in Chicago," I offered brightly.

"Really?" She seemed pleased. "Can I ask at which church that was?"

I told her.

"Who was the volunteer coordinator there?"

I provided a name.

"Oh, isn't she just an absolute angel?"

I thought she had been just an officious bitch of a woman but I refrained from saying so.

"Tell me your name?"

I did.

"What night did you want to work?"

"I thought maybe on Sundays, if that was possible."

"That's Faith Community's night to volunteer."

"Do they need help?"

There was another short outburst of ironic laughter. "All our volunteer groups need help."

She asked, "Are you a regular churchgoer?"

I answered her, "No. Does it matter?"

"Not at all. Were you one in Chicago?"

"No. Sorry."

"Don't be sorry. We need able bodies not saints. Let me just check something . . ." I heard computer keys clicking furiously in the background. There were databases of guests at shelters. I knew that from my soup kitchen days. Were there also databases of shelter workers? Especially godless ones not affiliated with any church? It seemed highly unlikely to me. But perhaps they needed to cover bases . . .

liability issues that required documentation . . . things like
that . . . so I waited patiently.

"Faith does need a volunteer on the first Sunday of the
month, specifically for the early shift. That's from six to
eleven. You need to get there at five forty-five and you leave
just after eleven, when the second shift arrives. We open
our doors at six-thirty and we serve dinner at seven-thirty.
You'll probably get served a dinner if there's enough to go
around. Actually you're very lucky. The first Sunday is Dora
Walters' famous meatloaf. It's very popular. Dora and her
son always make mountains. So please come hungry. And
be sure to bring something to read. It gets to be boring for
the last couple of hours. Do you know where we are?"

I told her that I did.

"When do I start?" I wondered out loud.

"That would be on April first."

"Okay," I hesitated. "Thank you."

"No, thank you, Tom," she said. "You have a blessed day
now, and we'll see you on the first." And with that she hung
up.

There were several possible ways to interpret the multiple
motivations that had inspired me to make that phone call.
Perhaps talking with Nye, a bastion of moral decency in a
blighted town south of Chicago, had suddenly alerted me
to the fact that I wasn't choosing to do anything charitable
in my life right now, and I had elected to fill up one night
in the month with something both generous and guilelessly
philanthropic. That was certainly taking the warm and fuzzy
view.

Alternately, I had engineered myself the chance to visit
the very place where an apparently distraught Nitro had

chosen to sleep a few nights before he died, and, while I didn't know if or when Andrew Travers had ever stayed there, it was certainly very possible that he had.

Two days later I drove from Boulder to Denver International Airport, which is about the same distance as Boulder is from downtown Denver. My flight left on time and was close to full. On the plane, I read a novel about Thomas Cromwell and since it was near enough to lunchtime, I drank a glass of overly chilled Australian Shiraz with the Half Fast veggie sub I'd brought along with me.

I sat for over an hour in Newark International Airport in a seat where I could see the New York City skyline.

On the transatlantic leg, the plane was again full. We flew into the night. I tried to sleep and failed. I chose the lasagna. I watched the movie soundlessly against my will. I passed on the breakfast sandwich. I finally fell asleep with an hour of the flight still to go and woke thoroughly disoriented. We arrived at Turnhouse in the middle of the night, which was the early morning in Scotland. It was misty and rainy as we shuffled across the runway and up the stairs to the immigration/baggage/customs complex. I cleared everything quickly and got my green North Face backpack from the baggage carousel. Unfortunately my main bag had chosen to fly on another flight, one that would arrive at Turnhouse two hours later. The airline offered to send the bag on, but I was travelling, and wasn't sure my rebellious luggage would ever catch up with me.

I was now starving and jet lagged. I found the terminal Café Nero which got me awake and the imaginatively named EAT, where I put away a giant fry-up of eggs, toast, mushrooms, tomato, black pudding, white pudding, bacon, and baked beans, all washed down with more weak coffee.

My bag showed up two hours later, looking decidedly unapologetic. I chose not to speak to it as I dragged my bloated frame toward the car hire counter and the next unscheduled hiccup in my spurious brew diplomacy mission as the Henry Kissinger of craft beer.

I was late for my car rental pick up. They still had a turbo diesel Passat, which was good, as that was the model I had specified when I booked online. Did I mind a manual transmission the young man with a Glasgow accent asked me with a broad smile and without the slightest trace of either sympathy or concern? The truth was that I rather did. I had learned to drive that way a long time ago and had then happily forgone the pleasure for as long as possible. Until now that is. They had other smaller cars available, a selection of boxy little Fiats and Renaults, if I preferred, and many of these were automatics.

As I stood there dithering, it occurred to me that the rigors of gear changing had to be easier now than battling the unforgiving clutch I remembered on my mother's old Hillman all those years ago. Also, the winding mountain roads up north might be more fun with a stick shift. So I signed all the papers with a tight smile and got the keys to my motor.

I was soon proved to be correct. Gears, and the changing of them, were a relative breeze these days. In twenty minutes, and after two multiple roundabouts negotiated slowly, I was as comfortable with my left hand poised and vigilant on the gearstick as I was barreling along on the other side of the road.

At the third roundabout, the abandoned remains of an old roadside hotel were fenced and boarded up. Grass and weeds fought it out for control of the front car park and a raggedy To Let sign had been imaginatively reborn with the simple addition of one graffitied vowel.

The Drystane Dyke Hotel had been the poignant scene of a distant cousin's wedding more than three decades ago, where I choked down several pints of Skol lager for liquid courage before attempting to get off with a bridesmaid seven years my senior, and several levels of sophistication beyond me, with my chin shaved and spotty, my rented morning suit barely concealing a loutish demeanor, and a solidly comprehensive school range of conversational topics at the ready.

The decision to pass myself off as a university attendee reading a subject I knew next to nothing about, and which she had recently graduated in, had been ill advised. We had danced together near the end of the night to Bowie's "Prettiest Star" which I had drunkenly attempted to execute as a slow number, complete with a tight clinch and possible necking. This maneuver had proved unsuccessful, and my reluctant partner was now in the consoling arms of her accountant boyfriend, who had shown up just as the house lights rose on the blinking, booze-pallid collection of tawdry night crawlers.

This had all gone quite badly, but miraculously the hotel bar was still open for business. An acute level of embarrassment clearly required the hurried consumption of still more lager and, as a direct consequence, a nasty spot of eye watering regurgitation was soon performed, down on my knees in the ill-fitting trousers, in the hotel car park, later that very night.

The Dyke had been, to all intents and purposes, a cheap drinking hole, a Formica-clad, burgundy-carpeted faceless brewery-owned shitehole of a place, tarted up periodically on the cheap to attract weekend getaway clandestine shagging. Having said that, it had come with two endearing virtues. The bar staff took a cavalier attitude to the serving of underage drinkers, and the premises were one of the first in the city to benefit from a recently discovered loophole in the Calvinist-inspired Scottish drinking laws and had subsequently obtained a Sunday license for the selling and consumption on the premises of beers and spirits to the general public. As a result the bar was filled to swaying capacity with teenage drunks capable of vacillating pathologically between maudlin happiness and murderous violence in the course of downing a warm pint on any given Sunday lunchtime or evening.

Ah yes, happy days at the Dyke.

I arrived at the bed and breakfast theoretically at lunchtime, had I actually been even slightly interested in eating lunch. I was staying in a large family house on the main road between Davidson's Mains and Cramond, both northwest suburbs of Edinburgh, a few miles from the city centre, close to the airport, but conveniently placed to head up north sharpish the next morning. The two children of the house were both at the primary school, Bill the father was at work at the bank, but Isobel, the wife, and Rory, the cocker spaniel, were home and happy to see me. Isobel graciously offered me a sandwich, which I declined, and showed me the bedroom and the bathroom, both located in the extension that the house had recently undergone. I could still smell new paint. She proudly offered their new conservatory as a place for me to sit in peace and apologized for the lack of a telly in that room. If I wanted to watch, I could always sit in the family room, although the children would be there at night and they were, in her estimation, a pair of right little terrors.

After she left me to myself, I lay down on the single bed in my room, closed my eyes for a moment, and woke up with a start four hours later.

At the local pub a quarter-mile down the road, the lounge bar was nearly empty at just after five. Madras chicken curry and chips was listed on the blackboard as the daily meal special, and Deuchars was the pick of the beers on tap. I ate and drank at a corner table beside a wood fire and sat for nearly an hour listening to preprogrammed music, an eclectic selection of Scotland's finest rock from a few years back: Del Amitri, the Proclaimers, Texas, Big Country, Deacon Blue, the Jesus and Mary Chain. There was absolutely nothing I hated, and a few I was more than happy to hear again.

In a big country, dreams stay with you. Like a lover's voice, fires the mountainside.

I listened to the words. Somewhere I had read that the band's singer hanged himself in a garage, somewhere far away from the Fife town he had come from. He had been struggling to make a comeback as a country singer.

Dreams stay with you all right.

I was in imminent danger of dozing off again so I headed back up the road, walking past the recycling bins outside the open supermarket and several padlocked greenhouses set far back from the road, part of a flower nursery closed up until the summer months, to the house. The children were on the floor of the family room, quietly watching the telly with Rory asleep at their feet. Isobel and Bill were eating their dinner in the kitchen with the radio on, a plummy BBC voice patiently explaining how to prune your roses properly. Their curry smelled much better than mine had tasted.

I got out of my clothes and, with the time not yet even seven o' clock, fell sound asleep once again.

In the morning, I showered and dressed and got myself together and, after another heaping fry-up only marginally smaller than the one served at the airport (Isobel skipped both puddings, the mushrooms and the baked beans, and doubled down on the rashers of thick bacon), said goodbye to her and Rory at just after nine and hit the road. There was a light misty rain coming off the North Sea that Isobel assured me would be gone by lunchtime. The shopping centre back toward the airport claimed to have a Starbucks. I found it nestled up against a Marks & Spencer and a convenient ATM and ordered a large coffee in a paper cup. Curious to see if the international exchange of technology was all it was cracked up to be, I tried to pay with a scan of my iPhone. It failed utterly, and I sheepishly handed over a ten-pound note and got a heaping load of assorted coins back in silent retaliation.

In the car park, I gave the iPhone a chance for redemption. Using an USB cord, I connected it to the Passat's sound system, selected AUX and shuffle, and, voila, James Yorkston began to sing "When the Haar Rolls In."

On the way out of the car park, I reflected on the notion of probability. There are, the last time I looked, close to one hundred albums loaded on my iPhone, maybe ten are by Scottish artists, and of these ten, only one has the word *haar*, a particular Scots term for sea mist, in the song title, which doubles as the title of the album. I drove back toward the derelict Dyke, turned left at the roundabout, and joined the light traffic heading toward the Forth Road Bridge, into Fife, around Perth, then further north up into the Scottish highlands toward Inverness, all the while conscious that I was driving through a light haar.

I ask you, what were the chances?

It took me about an hour to reach the outskirts of Perth, where I required a brief stop to tank up on more caffeine. This was a rare drive for me on diesel, and the fuel needle was either broken or pleasingly failing to register any activity after an hour or so of motoring.

At the next roundabout, I downshifted with the newly acquired finesse of Jackie Stewart, took the first left, and followed the signs to a crystal glassware factory/shop/coffeehouse. Inside, the coffee smelled of several hours spent painstakingly stewing. I added about a gallon of milk and sipped doubtfully at a truly awful beverage now stone cold, in addition to its aforementioned shortcomings.

There was a desultory children's play lot outside, and two prime specimens of that subspecies were listlessly pushing a swing back and forth in the gently insistent rain. The kids kept glancing sullenly through the windows of the restaurant, trying to catch a parent's eye, silently begging for a reprieve. The fact that they should by rights have been in school, and had additionally each been bribed with a bag of prawn cocktail crisps and a can of Fanta notwithstanding, they exhibited a clear desire to come inside and cease the dual-pronged torment of fresh country air and mild exercise. I spotted the odious parents at the next table, sipping at their teas in a carefree manner, nibbling on their sticks of shortbread, and giggling like truants. Neither one of them seemed much inclined to budge anytime soon. I assumed that it was going to be, or indeed had already been, a long car ride for this particular family.

I should have felt smug and grateful for my solitude. I wasn't. I like children. Well, perhaps not these two specifically.

Patricia and I didn't have any children of our own. I was in favor, especially toward the end, while, she, I suspect, was somewhat less so. It wasn't a topic that arose in our fifteen years of marriage, which perhaps tells you something. That she hasn't had a child in the years since, despite being happily together with someone, and someone younger at that, is, I suspect, indicative of something.

Meanwhile I have been divorced for ten years, childless for my entire existence, and now find myself edging close to the end of the first half century.

There certainly exist fathers of young children who are close to my age; they tend to look exhausted at little league games and wizened and sheepish as they pick up their offspring after preschool. But they also, in my experience, often look fairly contented. Maybe they left it late in life, when they were more mature and financially sound . . . maybe they took on demanding younger trophy wives, who made it a condition for allowing them a second crack in the nuptial arena with fresh blood . . . or maybe they find themselves unaccountably estranged from their first round of older children and simply want to get it right this time around.

Whatever the reason, I do envy them.

The town of Aviemore was my early lunchtime destination, and I was making good time. My travel app had predicted two and three quarter hours for the whole trip, but I hoped to do a little better. There were long stretches of divided motorway at first and then single lane roads as I got nearer to my destination. I had been lucky. All it needed was a touring caravan or ambling farmer on a tractor to slow my progress to a crawl. But it didn't happen. I'd been in Aviemore years ago for a spell in the summer. The weather had been glorious, and my visit had been agreeable. I knew March was a bigger gamble, but I was happy to risk it. There was a faster route from Edinburgh to Aberdeen, a shorter distance, hugging the east coast and skirting towns on a multilane motorway for the whole way, but I wanted to linger in a couple of places and take my time, since the parsimonious Nye had made it abundantly clear that this shameless boondoggle was on my dime.

In a past life, Aviemore had been a key player in Scotland's dourly determined ski industry, with vertigo-inducing lifts up into the nearby mountains, a train line to Edinburgh and Glasgow that also navigated several miles of daunting gradients, and a couple of quality hotels catering to Brits and other Europeans anxious to hurtle down hills in a hurry, or luxuriate in lodges over hot whisky toddies and pretend that they were. As a child listening to the transistor radio in the winter months, I found the long tedious ski reports were an irritating staple of my auditory experience. Over the years, that industry had faltered and all but died. The reasons were unclear, but I suspected that global warming had left the snow cover much less reliable and the plummeting cost of flying to places in Europe with more reliable supplies of the white fluffy stuff had put twin dents in the native skiing business.

After a spell of wound licking, the town had reinvented itself in the last two decades as a summer vacation destination, with pretty lakes and whisky tours and reindeer farms and indoor swimming flumes and golf/biking/hiking packages. Wisely too, Aviemore had clearly learned a collective lesson and not put all its commercial eggs in one basket. New hotels sprang up with annexed convention/conference centres, and they worked hard to attract businesspeople anxious to network in an undeniably picturesque spot.

It must be working. The main road through town was jam packed and the supermarket parking lot was almost full. The rain had stopped. The sun was coming out.

I bought two cheese and tomato sandwiches, some salt and vinegar crisps, and a carton of fresh orange juice. I kept the food for later and drank the juice as I drove a couple of miles out of town to the bike hire shop just yards across the river. The helmet was a retro black German stormtrooper affair and the bike was an eight-speed Genesis with solid front shocks. My Gary Fisher has twenty-four gears and about eight that I've actually used while riding in Colorado, so I wasn't too concerned about my reduced number of gear options. In the car park, I debated what to wear. It wasn't exactly warm. It wasn't exactly cold. There was little or no wind. The misty rain had ceased as promised. I put on shorts because my legs tend to stay warm biking, but a T-shirt, a long-sleeved T-shirt, and a sweatshirt seemed about right. I'd brought waterproofs with me, but the sky was now mostly blue with a few white clouds for contrast. I put my keys and iPhone and wallet and food in my North Face backpack and I got started.

I followed the main road southeast for a mile or so, mostly going gradually uphill, and then turning a sharp right into the nature estate car park. There was a posted bike trail around one smaller loch, then a forest path running across the bottom of a mountain range and around another larger body of water. At the farthest point of that loch, I planned to get back onto the main road and return back down the road to the bike shop. It was surely an easy circuit to follow. My rough guess was fifteen miles at most, which would take an hour on flat terrain, but since my Ordnance Survey map–reading skills were poor, I wasn't terribly sure how much hill I had to go up and down. If all these little lines close together meant a steeper gradient, it would probably take me longer, since I planned to sit at the side of the water at some point and eat what, after my second early-morning pig-out of a fry-up, I assumed would be my last meal of the day.

I didn't really care how long the ride took, as I had hours to kill. The hotel was another hour and a half away, and they expected me much later in the evening. If I made good time, I planned to take the bike back to town for a coffee or a pint or something, then promenade through the town and back, then return the bike after maybe another five miles and another misspent hour of indolent dalliance. So all told, maybe twenty miles or so on my bike today, a shorter distance than my creek ride up to the falls and back, but still pleasant, still accompanied by a profusion of running water and mountain air. Some things, after all, never change.

The fat mountain bike tires ground up the pine needles, grey stones, and red dirt on the path around Loch an Eilein. As I rode slowly, I looked out across the mirror-still water to an abandoned castle on a tiny island, and behind that to the pine- and fir-sheltered mountains in the near distance. A few birch trees lined the path on the lower sections and heather and gorse grew wild on the rocky thin soil between the exposed tree roots. Swift running streams of ice-cold water intersected the path and flowed down, feeding into the loch.

I rode much more carefully than I would at home. The views were breathtaking, and I wasn't altogether sure of the route.

The trail between the two lochs had several sections of scree stone pathway that ascended rapidly, and then fell away equally sharply. The thick tires were a blessing there, and the disc brakes did a commendable job as I skidded my way downhill to the shores of Loch Morlich, the second lake in my route. Morlich was easily twice as large as Eilein, and, judging by the number of abandoned sailboats stored at one end, it got plentiful use in the summer as a local sailing centre. There were plastic picnic tables and chairs stacked high, and a wooden café on two levels shuttered and boarded up for the season at the far end of Morlich, where the camping and caravan park stood nearly empty. I pulled a single chair free and sat there on the beach all alone, with my backpack and my sandwiches and my crisps and my bare legs growing colder as the sun retreated behind a cloud. I watched as the cloud shadow advanced across the forest-clad range of hills in the distance.

A man and a dog and a small boy got out of a car and walked across the beach. The man and I nodded to each other. The three of them walked to the edge of the water. The boy picked up a stone and showed it to his father. The man smiled and shook his head. The man found a flat stone and bent down in front of the boy and placed it in his hand. Then the man stood behind the boy and guided the youngster's arm as he tried to bend his body low to the water and threw the stone. The stone hit the water once and sunk. The man found another stone. The boy and the dog watched him closely. The man stepped toward the water and crouched low in one fluid motion. When he threw the stone, it left his hand low and flat against the surface and skimmed three times before disappearing under the surface. The boy cheered, and the dog bounded into the cold lake in a blustery but doomed pursuit of the stone. The man and the boy laughed, then the boy began to look for another stone.

The road back to Aviemore passed the bike hire, a fish hatchery, and the steel frame of a new hotel. A roadside café in the town centre played tracks from Nick Drake's last recording, his singing and guitar finger picking softly insistent, and offered ersatz bongo ambiance, free wifi, and huge hot chocolates doused in whipped cream and garnished with mini marshmallows and a single chocolate flake thrust like a dagger through the dense upper strata of softening cream and melting mallow. The waitress was a pretty Spanish girl with limited English, and she wordlessly offered a sprinkling of yet more powdery chocolate, which I mutely accepted. At that late stage, the notion of acting calorie obsessed seemed silly.

Later, fortified by sugar and chocolate, I rode the couple of miles back to the bike store and returned the Genesis eight-speed and my neo-Nazi headgear. As I pulled off my sweatshirt in the car park I stood for a moment in my Belvedere T-shirt. That brief moment of exposure was enough to elicit a spirited conversation with a young gentleman from the bike shop who had visited Chicago and, if you can credit it, had both drank and dined at Belvedere. Had I been there? Did I know there was a craft brewery outside Aberdeen that I should try to visit if I had the time? Telling him that I part owned the former, and was indeed on my way to the latter to do some less-than-urgent beer business, seemed like too much good coincidental stuff for my new much-inked acquaintance to assimilate at once, so I chose instead to smile, accept his sage recommendation, and get on my way.

My next ninety minutes of driving were spent crossing and re-crossing the River Spey, as I headed roughly northeast toward the challengingly named town of Fochabers, on the east bank of the river, just five miles from Spey Bay, where the waterway empties into the North Sea.

I was booked for one night at the Speyside Inn, a pretty two-storey whitewashed building standing at the far end of the quiet main street, with low plastered guest rooms, two cozy bars (one doubling in the morning as a dining room where my now ubiquitous and obligatory full breakfast would doubtless be served), and a red tartan–carpeted reception area where registered hotel guests bold enough to ring the desk bell and politely enquire could obtain timelessly adorable postcards and river fishing licenses at a gently discounted rate.

I checked in at the Speyside, got my key, unpacked my stuff, and took a wander up the main road.

In past years, considerable traffic would have ploughed right through Fochabers heading either west to Elgin or southeast to Aberdeen. Now a ring road circled the edge of the village, slicing through a section of prime unused farmland deeded centuries back to the local laird and leaving the small town well enough alone. When this happens, a state of suspended animation descends on places like Fochabers—a sense of relief for the townspeople, who no doubt petitioned long and hard for the alternative routing, tempered with the inevitable descent into an enforced calm.

The main street was huohcd; the supermarket where I bought a newspaper was brightly lit and empty. Across the road a combination Indian restaurant/fish and chip shop was open all day and late into the night. A shop selling hiking and sports equipment further up the road was surely close to going out of business. Inside, the ginger-haired proprietor struggled to maintain his comically dour exterior beneath head covering that scarily replicated the carrot-red Brillo pad hair/hat prank combination manufactured and derogatorily sold as a "See You Jimmy" getup in tourist shops. He had to be pleased to see me. I was a paying customer. Real-life Jimmy had a couple of good bikes for rent, and we confirmed my reservation for early tomorrow morning. I was getting a Scott Spark 29 Comp bike with more gears than this afternoon's Genesis, with which I planned to ride the five miles along the riverbank to Spey Bay and the same five miles back again.

Back at my room, I took a shower and afterward sat on one of two low stuffed velvet chairs at the lace-curtained window and read some more about Cromwell. Outside it was past five and almost dark. My previous summer trip to Aviemore had provided daylight that stretched until almost midnight and then evaporated into a subdued demi-twilight that never completely faded overnight and broke out into full morning sunshine very early. I remembered wondering how on earth tired parents could possibly coerce their youngsters into going to sleep at night without the soft lure of darkness. In March the reverse surely occurred. The nights drew in fast and early and lasted for fully two-thirds of the day. Locals left for work and came back home with the streetlights lit, the same parents surely having to resort to all kinds of persuasion to coerce their precious offspring off to school in the pitch-dark mornings.

Later that night I skipped dinner and sat in the tiny public bar at the back of the hotel with a pint and my newspaper. A few locals wandered in through a side door and chatted with Joyce, the barmaid. A few smiled in my direction and said hello. I did the same, but, after they enquired if I was here for the fishing and received my answer, I was gently but unmistakably ignored. This went on for a while. I could safely return to my paper if I wished. When Joyce brought a second pint without me asking, I felt much better.

By my calculation, I was still a few hours behind in my slumbers so I headed upstairs to my room early and once again fell sound asleep with indecent haste.

The next morning was cloudy and dry and not too cold. The Speyside version of the full breakfast came with smoked kippers, which Joyce, now in the role of my waitress, seemed steadfastly unwilling to let me take a pass on.

The ride to Spey Bay was short, barely five miles of

bumpy dirt path crouching at first under a high road bridge with towering concrete supports well covered in graffiti on the accessible lower sections. Apparently Sheena is a great ride and Wee Rab is a cunt. Past the bridge, the path wedged itself against the river for a swift-moving stretch where the waters leapfrogged rocks and foamed wildly before slowing and straightening, then dissecting a frayed-looking golf course neatly in two.

There's no actual town at the mouth of the Spey, and the river waters delta out into a flat plain with thick grass and harsh brown sand and smoothed gray stones at the termination, before the fresh river and the salt sea waters churn slowly and co mingle brackishly at the wide mouth of the estuary, the river suddenly almost coyly reluctant to get back home.

This was the spot I chose to stand at. The stony beach was steeply inclined all the way down to the water's edge, and large rocks stood sentry at the very top of the breakwater. The North Sea at that point is actually a wide estuary, the Moray Firth, less rough and battered than the main water, but still churning and white capped that spring morning. A makeshift fort of wood and dried seaweed had been constructed on the only available section of coarse sand. The wood was bleached a bone white and smoothed, and the seaweed was dried and brittle and cracked under your feet. On the top of the rocks, a small girl stood in a blue duffle coat with a bag full of broken slices of white bread. She threw the pieces onto the side of the car park as a growing contingent of seagulls ate and screamed out for more.

The youngster seemed pleased with the proceedings. The birds, too, were clearly happy. All the participants seemed certain that they were occupied in a contest they were winning.

Is there somewhere an unstated covenant that decrees that at every place I stop my personal space is to be shared with one or more small children?

Following the British rule of thumb, pretty much anywhere you go will have a spot to get a cup of tea. I found the bay café beside the stone beach car park, disguised as a wartime bunker covered over with lush turf. Surprisingly, given both the month and the time of day, it was open for business. So I went full tourist and had a pot of tea and a fresh buttered scone slathered with jam and sat in the warmth beside a log fire, before riding back along the path to the sports shop, returning the rented Scott bike to red Jimmy, and walking back to the Speyside to check out.

I was on the road to Aberdeen just before eleven and arrived at the brewery just after twelve.

What can you say about a small brewery famous for making some of the most potent brew available and then inserting said beverage inside the taxidermied remains of small road-killed animals like badgers and stoats? I am of the belief that nothing need be said, and that simply sitting back and admiring these near-deranged levels of dedication is the only course of action.

I met with Toby, one of the two owners, and willingly drank a sample of their latest IPA, reputedly brewed far below the North Sea in small underwater tanks and served in traditional brown bottles instead of nontraditional furry dead animals. It was inarguably great, but then so are lots of IPAs not brewed under the sea. I was clearly missing the purist point. I next got to sample their first try at customizing our Jolly Jack. It was dense and smoky and organic and had a palpable warmth that our lowly Midwest version sorely lacked. I noted that our humble 5.2 gravity had metamorphosed into a bracing 10.2. We would henceforth be encouraging genteel sipping rather than injudicious quaffing. I cautiously gave our corporate approval by smiling and demanding a second smaller sample. It was tasty, and as I tried not to chug, Toby produced a contract for me to take back to Nye. We did absolutely nothing of any consequence, nothing that couldn't have been handled by mail or text or email, producing a near-perfect example of the wanton corporate junket.

As we swallowed the last of the second glass, a photographer from the Aberdeen newspaper showed up all puffing and apologetic. There was supposed to be a reporter also, but he was delayed and wouldn't make it in time. We gave the photographer all the dull details of our beer, and the man took notes and accepted a small glass. He took several photos of Toby and me clinking glasses chummily and, in one idiotically posed one, the both of us stared long and hard at a beer keg as though all the secrets of life were stenciled in a perplexing cipher along the side. I just knew that this would be the picture they would choose to use.

Toby offered me deer stew braised in stout for lunch, but I declined. I wanted to stay and sup more, but I had to drive back to Edinburgh. Three hours allocated to the drive back south, using the coast road this time for speed over ambiance, left just over two hours to diesel up and return the Passat, get though Turnhouse, and board the plane bound for Newark, which would leave at six-thirty. It should be painless with time to spare.

And remarkably it was.

I was back in Boulder by two in the morning, dog tired and slightly disoriented, but smugly pleased with how much I had done and how little I had worked while doing it. It was early on a Sunday morning as I tried without much success to fall asleep.

I sat up in bed and checked the weather on my laptop. The forecast had changed for the next twenty-four hours. The last few days in Boulder had been warm and dry as predicted, but today was to be much colder, closer to freezing, and the temperature would drop again during the day. Snow would start to fall in the morning and continue into the afternoon. Two inches would likely accumulate in the city, with much more in the mountains before Sunday night, when the temperatures would go down to well below freezing.

This was to be a twenty-four-hour aberration, and the following days would revert to the original prediction: very much warmer, with significant rainfall scheduled to arrive later in the week, perhaps by Wednesday or Thursday.

Sleep obviously wasn't to be an immediate option. I was getting less tired by the minute. I sat by the window and watched the clear night sky over the Flatirons.

I checked my iPhone and realized I had forgotten to turn it back on after getting off the plane at the airport. I had been very tired then even if I wasn't tired now. I checked for recent text messages. Nye wanted all manner of details from my trip. What was the brewery in Aberdeen like? What was Toby like? And more importantly, what had they done to his beloved Jack Tar? At no point did he enquire as to whether

I had had a pleasant time on my trip.

I considered a quick text response to his queries, but instantly I found myself reconsidering. Nye would require a detailed recalling; he would need me to wax both wise and grandiloquent on the radical transformation of our porter at the hands of two wild Scots he had never met in person. He was right to be leery of people who inserted glass bottles into dead critters, whether the bottles were empty or filled with the finest ale. His reservations were not without validity, but I wanted to fully and articulately assure him that, in this instance, we could be both proud and confident that our Jolly Jack Tar was indeed famously reborn and boldly resurrected.

I would wait to text Nye back. I would use the time to painstakingly compose my thoughts, and I would drive him completely nuts by keeping him waiting.

The weather scenario was reminiscent of ten days ago, a cold/snow/rain/flood combination similar to the one that had flooded the creek and taken Nitro. The variables and permutations of that thought made me nervous, and I sat anxious, awake, and helpless at the window for a long time before reluctantly acknowledging my mortality, my confounding inability to do battle with the forces of nature.

I wandered back to bed for the last time just as the first dawn glow of morning light teased the sky.

SEVEN

The last few flakes had gently garnished the two inches of accumulated snowfall already covering the streets and gardens and rooftops of the downtown area by the early afternoon.

Outside my kitchen window, three underdressed students were throwing a yellow Frisbee, standing inches deep in the snow and almost knee deep in the tangled knot of high weeds choking the large backyard of the decrepit house that stood directly behind mine. Their breath clouded in the frozen air. They were sharing a plump joint in a dismal excuse for a game that only required that the person who dropped the Frisbee take a huge hit. I strongly suspected all three contestants of deliberate fumbling as the game proceeded to get sloppier and sloppier. At a certain point, the remains of the joint fell in the snow to a chorus of loud laughter and the game morphed indolently into scooping the snow up with the Frisbee and throwing it.

I stood and watched them play for a while and drank my tea. My iPhone weather app promised no more snow for the day but still predicted freezing temperatures for the night, slightly warmer ones early into the next week, then much warmer again by Wednesday and Thursday, when heavy rains were predicted to fall.

Several houses around mine operate as shamelessly overpriced year-round rentals for university students. The downside for me is shabby notions of property upkeep, and a fairly stagnant level of home equity. The upside is close proximity to the kinds of goods and services beloved of students, and a consistently high neighbor turnover. I get flyers pushed under my door for dj nights, an armada of bikes chained to my fence when there's an impromptu kegger thrown nearby, and once the abandoned keg itself, installed somewhat artistically in my front yard with a garishly painted garden gnome holding a fishing rod perched jauntily atop. Nye enjoyed the picture I texted him, Neal loved the gnome, christened him Trevor, and interred him permanently in amongst the flowers on his very own little stone seat. I returned the keg to the liquor store I frequented. It wasn't one of theirs, but I was assured the brewery would be more than happy to get it back. I received a small store credit for my trouble, but when I enquired about the deposit the kids had doubtless been required to pony up, the clerk merely shrugged in response.

Tonight would be a cold night, cold enough that the Lazarus bus would pick up the homeless from the creek and take them to the shelter for the night.

In the cold and logical light of day, there existed no sinister connection between freezing nights and buses and melting snow and rain and warm nights and floods and death by drowning and Art who was also known as Nitro and Andrew Travers who was once a very rich man.

So instead, I could only desperately tinker with so many slight and sinister half-truths, because I badly wanted there to be one simple connection to emerge logically and fully formed from my scattershot pattern of coincidences. But of course it didn't because there wasn't.

So what did I actually have?

I had been told that Nitro stayed at Lazarus House on a cold Sunday night days before he died. I did know that

Travers stayed in the homeless shelters every night, picking the ones that served his favorite meals. I did know that the people at Lazarus served meatloaf to the homeless on the first Sunday of every month. So Nitro had probably eaten meatloaf that Sunday when he stayed there. This of course assumed that he liked meatloaf. Did Andrew Travers like meatloaf? I knew that meatloaf was a cheap meal to make. I knew that Travers had been wealthy beyond measure, before he walked away from all his money, from both the cold hard reality of all that cash and from the moral and ethical detritus that it carried.

Do rich people even eat meatloaf?

If I could assume that they did, was it also possible that Travers stayed at Lazarus on the first Sunday of the month before he died? Was it cold that night? And if it was, did that mean that Nitro had stayed there that night also? Did they get to know each other on the bus there? Did they sit down at the same dinner table and eat? Or did they both sleep fitfully on thin mattresses laid out side by side on the church floor? Did Nitro shake his mismatched covers loose from his bony body during the night? Did Travers glance at Nitro's tattooed leg and ask him politely who Amy was? Did Travers speak the names of the Armstrong family as he slept and stirred uneasily? And did Nitro hear him and wonder who they were?

Even if I knew how to fasten answers to my wildest speculations, I would still have nothing, except for the enduring sense that something was wrong.

I wondered who would stay at Lazarus House tonight.

The base and inelegant truth was that all the homeless would someday die, as all the people with homes would someday die. And death, in the final reckoning, plays no favorites and favors no preexisting privilege. We would all die, with or without our homes, and with or without our trappings, the attendant materialist bells and whistles for which we paid dearly.

I wondered if any of them would die later in the week if there happened to be a flood.

The enduring certainty was that the creek flooded. The enduring uncertainty was that the creek either capriciously killed or chose to show mercy.

And so it was that I fashioned myself a gossamer-thin plan. I would sit in my car tonight with lots of clothes on, and the engine turned off, and drink lots of coffee, and I would watch for the Lazarus bus, all for perilously close to no good reason whatsoever.

Beyond the obvious question of sanity, there was also a logistic and geographic flaw in my cunning plan, namely that I didn't know where or when the bus would pick up.

So flying in the face of all reason, at just before four in the afternoon, I drove the main roads near the creek, and I searched for the blue school bus.

But I found the homeless first.

The creek path ducks under a series of roads that run north and south through Boulder, so I began crisscrossing them in a pattern of my own creation that started in the east and headed west a few city blocks at a time and took in each major creek crossing. I began at Folsom and Canyon by filling the largest coffee flask I owned at the corner coffee shop. I was well aware that I could just as easily have swung by Cygnet and gotten Jesse to load me up, but he would have relentlessly pried, and the scoops of sarcasm that would have come gratis with the order would have been too much. After all, I already knew how stupid I was. The shop was very warm, and I was wearing a lot of clothes. I had brought my Cromwell book to finish in the car, but I grabbed an *Onion* from the table by the back door as I left.

I didn't know where the bus would pick up from, but my sense was that the homeless were in much lesser numbers well east of Folsom. I did recall once seeing a few in the summer sitting and talking at the bench tables in Greenleaf Park at Pearl and Folsom, where a bone-dry creek culvert sat cracked and silent between the main road and the avenue of trees.

I thought of the crowded public parking areas and the concrete amphitheater on a busy farmers market day, or close to the two sections of the library building during the hours when the library was open, on the benches in the city parks in the summer, hidden inside the underpasses, especially when it rained or it snowed or it was later at night, or under the trees by the side of the water for shade when the sun was high during the dog days of summer.

I parked at the creek on Folsom. This would be my first designated stop. I left the keys in the ignition, turned off the engine, and sat there. There was no one on the path in either direction. I assumed that the bus would attract some kind of activity; either a number of people would be waiting for the bus or vice versa. First Aid Kit sang "Emmylou" as I started the engine and drove on.

I took Folsom to Stadium, which became University and

crossed over the creek again at Seventeenth. There were a few people bundled and walking the streets and on the path below. There was still plenty of snow on the ground, but the path was already plowed and clear. I parked at Seventeenth and turned off the engine. This would be stop number two. I was allocating twenty minutes at each promising stop to sit in the car, watch for the bus, and listen to the shuffled selection on my old 160 GB iPod classic plugged into the Pioneer car audio. Twenty minutes to drink my coffee and listen to maybe three or four songs out of almost sixteen thousand stored. I got "Baby, Baby, Baby" by the Jayhawks next, and I certainly wasn't complaining. The coffee was still piping hot. I was parked directly under a streetlight and I thought about trying to read. I sat and waited instead.

When "Love the Way You Walk Away" by Blitzen Trapper ended, I drove west. Seventeenth curved around and deposited me back on University again. I followed that until I hit Broadway and turned right. This was stop number three. I pulled over and looked around for a place to park.

There was a gray and immobile line of people standing on the bridge over the creek at Broadway. The line wasn't moving. I performed a quick head count. There were forty-four people. Some had backpacks. Some had plastic bags. All the bags looked full and close to bursting. Some wore heavier coats, and some were haphazardly layered in an assortment of thinner garments. Some were wearing gym shoes. Some had gloves and hats, but quite a few didn't. Were they all men? I thought they mostly were. There were a few visible faces and most of these were white. I couldn't begin to put an age to anyone.

The city buses run along the length of Broadway day and night, mostly moving students from school to home to bars to home to school. This could conceivably be a queue for one of these buses, but I was willing to bet that it wasn't. These people were the Boulder homeless and they were waiting for the Lazarus bus.

I studied the line again. If I hoped to identify the tarot lady, I was surely fooling myself. I scanned for smaller more feminine figures. There were a few, but they all looked somehow more substantial than the ethereally time-warped soul I remembered. Perhaps she was indeed standing there all toasty warm and bundled up in anonymity, but I remembered the scant threadbare skirt and blouse she had been wearing when we met, and I somehow doubted it.

I put the car in park as the fractured guitar intro to "Gimme Shelter" by the Stones burst serendipitously forth from the car speakers. I glanced to my left as a bus passed me and pulled in sharply a few inches from my front bumper. The city's buses are brightly painted econo-fueled modern vehicles with cute names, their destinations and bus numbers easily discerned on LED signs on the front, sides, and back. This bus was a blue and rusty and ancient smoke-belching anachronism, with no number visible anywhere, and the words Lazarus House painted on the side and the back in white paint that bled through to the blue underneath, the logo a kind of curved shawl draped symmetrically over a white cross.

When the doors opened, the bus began to fill. The process was organized but slow. I could see clearly through the bus window as the passengers handed something, a piece of yellow paper the size of a business card, to the bus driver, who studied it hard, handed it back, then nodded to the passenger who then continued to board. One passenger was handed his card back very quickly. The driver shook his head vigorously. I watched some discussion take place before the passenger stepped back and down. I watched another hand over a larger piece of paper. Again the driver shook his head and the second passenger also stepped aside. At the end of the line, things became more frantic as the bus reached capacity and people began to push forward. The driver shouted something, but the pushing continued. The driver began to wave his hands in front of his face with the last two people in line still waiting their turn to board. They held out their yellow cards to him, but he kept on waving. They stepped away from the bus as the doors quickly closed. Four people were left outside on the sidewalk, as the full bus pulled loudly away from the side of the road and ground its way north on Broadway toward Canyon, where it turned a sharp right.

I got out of my car with the engine still running and walked over to the remaining four.

They all looked seriously unhappy. It was piercingly cold and their breath billowed upward in the sharp clear air. A good portion of the evening's full darkness had sneakily descended in the last half hour.

"Why were you four left behind?"

One man spoke from deep inside the hood of his coat. "Bus takes forty. Church only got beds for forty."

I didn't fully understand the process. "What do you need to get a bed?"

The same man spoke again. "You gotta have your shelter ID."

"Do you all have shelter IDs?"

"Two of us do," he said. Then the hood pointed at another figure. "He don't have his ID." The hood pointed again. "And his been stamped."

It wasn't getting any clearer. "Stamped?"

"Daniel. Show the man your card."

The figure I assumed was Daniel looked up sullenly at me but he pulled out a yellow card with a tiny photograph and some information I couldn't read because the word BANNED was stamped diagonally across the card.

"Why are you banned?" I couldn't help asking.

Daniel didn't choose to answer me but the voice from the hood continued.

"Daniel got his self too many drinkin offenses for a bed."

"How many is too many?" I wondered out loud.

"Three." Daniel had a voice that crawled out of the deep.

"What if you don't have an ID?"

"They can make you one at the shelters. But folks with they ID gets a bed first."

"So where will you four sleep now?" I asked.

The hood answered. "Daniel, he gonna sleep out. Rest of us can use another shelter."

"Where?"

"South Boulder. At Infant. Takes two buses to get there. On Lehigh and Cripple." There was a measured pause. "Long ways." The hood was pulled back and two dark eyes watched me closely. I was unprepared for how young and how black the face was under the hood.

"Can I give you a ride there?" I asked the question on an impulse. There was no discussion as three of the men quickly moved toward me.

I asked. "What about Daniel?"

"Ain't no use in Daniel comin. He sleeping out tonight."

As if on cue, Daniel began to move silently away. He turned toward the path back down to the creek. I noticed then that he wore two unlaced gym shoes and carried two plastic shopping bags. One of the bags was splitting open, and he held it together carefully. Daniel moved with a heartbreaking solemnity.

As he walked, he mumbled something very quietly. A voice answered him softly. The only word I caught in the exchange was motherfucker, and in the time I spent wondering who had said it, Daniel had a knife in his hand.

He faced down the four of us.

"Say you sorry." He spoke this quietly but firmly. His eyes swept and fell on each of us in measured turn.

They each spoke.

"I'm sorry."

"Sorry, Daniel."

"Sorry."

His eyes fell on me, and he looked confused for a second.

"Why you out here with us?" He wanted to know. "What the fuck you want with us?"

"I don't know," I said.

He stared at me.

"You don't belong here."

"I know."

"You playin?"

I was confused. "Playing?"

He sneered. "Playin with us. Like we all lost? Like you on a mission to save us?"

"No."

"Ain't no game for us being here," he said.

And then the knife was no longer in his hand, as Daniel turned and walked away, and we four watched him go.

We said nothing as we got into my car.

When the traffic had cleared I turned around on Broadway and drove up toward the Hill. Inside the car, my new friend introduced himself as Devonte and the other two as Charles and Ed. Devonte was more than happy to talk for the three of them. He told me Ed could get himself a new ID at the Infant shelter, but because he didn't have it, he had lost his spot at Lazarus tonight. Lazarus was the best shelter, because the food was good, and the bus came for you when it was cold, and they had new showers installed last year, and the hot water never ran out. Devonte allowed as how he liked the meatloaf there just fine, but tonight was honey-baked ham and baby carrots cooked in butter and tater tots, and he was truly sorry to be missing that. Infant was serving sloppy joes and corn tonight, and they were just okay. Devonte and Charles had known they were at the end of the line for the bus and probably wouldn't get a bed, but strange shit surely did happen in the line, and you never quite knew. Someone was always losing his ID or getting banned. There were fights in the line on occasion. Devonte told me that Lazarus was always full when it was cold.

He also told me that Daniel was not someone you wanted to seriously fuck with, and I saw no reason to argue with him.

I was surprised that the bus had come so early, and I wondered what would happen for the hour or so until the shelter opened. So I asked Devonte.

"Sittin in the warm bus outside Lazarus be a whole lot better than standin outside in the cold." He clearly considered my question an idiotic one.

I thought again about Daniel.

"How else do you get banned?" I asked Devonte.

"You be banned for being high or drunk or else fightin," Devonte told me. "But I don't ever do none of that sorry-ass shit," he added proudly.

When we pulled in at the rear parking lot of Infant Savior Catholic Church there were already a dozen coated figures standing with their bags under a canopy. Again I tried to find the tarot lady in the shrouded line, and, again, as much as I willed it, I could make no one in the line come close to approximating her pixie-like dimensions.

"How many people can sleep here?" I asked the threesome.

Devonte answered, "They got themselves sixty beds here."

Then he asked me a question. "How come you so interested in our shit?" Unlike Daniel, he didn't sound particularly hostile, or concerned by my curiosity.

I told him I was just driving by, that I saw the bus, that I was going to be volunteering at Lazarus, and that I would be starting there next month.

"What day you gonna be workin?" He asked me.

"First Sundays."

"What shift you be on?"

"The first."

He smiled for the first time and several years fell tragically away from his face. "Maybe I see you then."

"Do you often stay there?"

Devonte smiled again. "Only if it be real cold, and I get my motherfucking ass in line early."

"Where do you go when the creek floods?"

"Get me some high ground then."

"But you stay outside? In the heavy rain and the floods?"

"Rain's okay," he said. "Cold be the serious motherfucker."

"You could drown."

Devonte shrugged.

"Two men have drowned in the last month," I told him.

"They was unlucky," he pronounced.

I suddenly thought of a question. "Did you know the two men who drowned?"

Devonte laughed at that. "Shit. Everybody know Nitro."

"What about Andrew Travers?"

"I seen his picture in the paper after he died. Maybe I seen his face someplace. I didn't know to speak to him. He didn't sleep out."

"How do you know that?"

"I would have seen him." Devonte again looked slightly pained at my display of stupidity.

"What about Nitro?"

Devonte smiled again. "Nitro be famous on the creek. Hung like a brother. Girls would get themselves drunk and all and ask to see his dick and touch it and shit like that. I heard some rich dude once paid Nitro to fuck his girlfriend so he could watch. Shit. Man got no respect for himself to be doing dumb shit like that."

I asked, "Do you want to wait in the car?"

Devonte shook his head. "We needs to get in line for a bed."

I had one last question.

"Were there any women getting on the Lazarus bus tonight?"

Devonte thought for a moment. "Two," he finally said.

"A thin woman who reads tarot cards?" I asked him hopefully

He shook his head. "She wasn't there."

"You know her?" I asked him.

He nodded. "Tol' me my fortune one time. Tol' me I gonna be a rich man one day." He shook his head. "Shit." He seemed faintly amused.

"Have you seen her recently?" I asked.

He thought. Then he answered. "Been a while. She a weird lady."

I let the three of them out of the car and drove back along Lehigh to Table Mesa, then north on Broadway to Arapahoe, then left on Folsom to Pearl. I made another left on Twenty-Second and parked outside my little yellow house and turned the car engine off. My car still smelled of old dirt and body odor and chain hotel soap and mouthwash and Vaseline and Febreze. I had driven all the way home in the cold with the windows wide open to try to get rid of the smells.

I was suddenly ashamed of myself.

On Wednesday it began to rain hard late in the afternoon. On Thursday morning, it rained even harder. I climbed up onto the rail of my front porch and reached up into the gutter without being able to see what I was doing. The opening into the downspout was completely blocked with a plug of leaves and small twigs. I pulled them all out in a dense sodden clump, and the water chuckled loudly and flowed unobstructed, instead of lapping over the edge of the gutter in a thin waterfall. I watched the clouds get darker and darker overhead, and by the middle of Thursday afternoon the sky was almost black. And the rain kept coming.

I remembered Jesse telling me where the flood closings were the last time, so I rode my bike west along Canyon, which became Boulder Canyon at the intersection of Broadway. I could have driven, but I wanted access to places either difficult or outright impossible to get to by car. The road had swift twin rivers of water several feet wide flowing down each gutter. The raised center of the road was the safest place to ride, as long as no other traffic came. It was possible to ride that way for the length of a city block, and I did so, not realizing that the lack of other vehicles meant that the road was closed off from the west.

It was unseasonably warm, and I wore my swim shorts and a waterproof jacket over a T-shirt, with my water shoes on my feet. I rode both carefully and extremely slowly. At Ninth, the creek path divided into two, and the river ran south of both. Now the rising water had fanned out across both paths, and spanned perhaps forty feet in width to lap menacingly against the base of the concrete overpass supports. I tried to calculate the difference in depth from where the creek usually was to where it stood now. I thought perhaps it was four or five feet higher. There were no flood gates to close at Ninth. I stood on the overpass bridge and looked both ways, up and down the engorged flood plain. I could thankfully see no one near the water. The runoff pools on either side were fully submerged. A yellow and gray backpack floated downstream with a broken branch clinging to it.

There was a snarl of cruel laughter from under the bridge. I sprinted, stumbled and half-fell down one side of the hill. On my wet knees, I peered up into the half darkness of the underpass. The creek was already halfway to the top, and a figure was lying facedown in a cocoon of old clothing and plastic supermarket bags barely two feet from the edge of the rising water. Two young men were standing over the figure. One had his back to me and was pissing on the outstretched body and giggling, while the other was capturing the event on a cell phone. I ducked and scrambled across the dusty concrete. The man with the phone was directly facing me but the phone blocked his view at first. When he did see me, he ran to the side of the underpass, onto the grass verge, and, stumbling a few times, took off over the bridge. The water got suddenly much louder inside the dark and echoing space. The other young man turned toward me, with a sly, questioning look on his face and his wet dick still in his hand. He looked too surprised to do anything as I lashed out at his groin with my foot and he collapsed to the ground and skittered downward, toward the water's edge. As he passed me, I kicked at him hard again. I aimed at his head but only managed to connect with his shoulder. He rolled away from me with his hand clamped between his legs. Then he began to crawl toward the grass.

It was hard to stay standing up. I was soaking wet. I hesitated. I wanted to chase the kid, but the homeless man on the ground would soon be submerged. I grabbed onto both of his legs and dragged him to the other verge and then up, through a descending wave of rainwater, to the higher ground, where the grass met the sidewalk. It was a lot like dragging a sack of potatoes through a cresting river. He slept blissfully on through my struggle, and I wondered if he was dead drunk, or if they had beaten him some first. He was soaking wet. He would get wetter still, exposed in the rain, but he hopefully wouldn't drown in the flood tonight.

The two young men were long gone. I hated them both and would have happily hit them again and again for their casual and unremarkable cruelty to a vanquished soul rendered sadly inconsequential by people arrogant enough to record the whole event and anticipate nothing in the way of retribution.

I looked at my sleeping charge as he lay on the ground. His hair was plastered by the rain to one side of his head. I examined him for signs of physical damage. His skin was an insipid color. His eyes were closed. He looked a little like a laboratory mouse, but he didn't appear to be freshly beaten.

I tried to imagine a righteously reworked scenario in which his two attackers would be proved dead wrong in their complacency. Their little performance would hit YouTube and go viral, they would be quickly recognized, and a powerful trial lawyer with a yawning gap in his pro bono calendar would have himself a field day trying them as adults.

It seemed a pleasant if highly implausible pipedream.

I pulled the sodden sleeper under a park bench and left him there. I texted Officer Hawkins and explained what had happened and where to find him.

After I sent the text, I stood in the rain and considered the possibility that I had just interrupted the killers of Nitro and Andrew Travers in the act of committing another murder. It would have been pleasant to make that scenario work. There was no logical reason why it wouldn't. Maybe there even existed a shaky ill-focused cell phone recording of Nitro being killed and dumped in the creek for the sick and the curious to download.

But I couldn't make myself believe that.

It was more likely that, after pissing on the man, they would have simply left him to either drown or not. Maybe they had even planned on doing just that. But somehow I doubted that second part. They were gutless little punks, opportunistic and spineless. The man's death, had it occurred, would have been an easily avoided event, and they would have been guilty of being creepy little uncaring assholes at best.

All they had wanted to do was publicly humiliate a helpless man.

That last pathetic possibility worked better.

When I got to the underpass at Sixth, the floodgates were pulled closed and padlocked in place. There was a loudly insistent siren sounding far away. The creek path was officially closed to the public.

On a piece of higher ground nearby, a boy and girl were dancing in the sheets of falling rain. She wore nothing but a red two-piece swimsuit, and a hula-hoop undulated without any effort at her supple waist. He wore a pair of wet cutoffs hanging off his bony behind. They were both barefoot and laughing, and a mixed-breed dog jumped up and down and barked loudly and happily at them. I realized that the barking got louder when they slowed down. After a while, the girl slowly worked the hoop all the way down to her bare feet and then stepped out of it as it lay motionless.

She put her hands on the boy's thin shoulders as his long arms wrapped around her still and tiny waist. The dancing slowed to a languidly sensual motion. The dog barked all the louder, but the dancers clearly no longer cared much about anything except each other.

There was a fracture of lightning that lit up the sky, and the rain poured down even harder in its immediate aftermath, rolling down the side of the bank and discharging into the swollen creek below.

In the sudden brightness, a figure in a red top moved quickly through the tall bushes on the other side of the creek, then disappeared from view as the darkness returned.

At Sixth, the overpass had two uniformed Boulder cops back to back directing a thin line of traffic crawling gingerly across. The water was close to the top of the bridge, and the cars were proceeding almost fearfully. When I got there, one of the cops glared hard at me but said nothing. The water streamed down my face as I looked in both directions. I could see nothing frightening. There was no one out there struggling and overwhelmed in the floodwaters, and there was no one out there unresisting and floating and lifeless; there was just a pair of dancing kids locked together in their mutually wet passion and an insistent mutt of a wet dog barking and cavorting on high ground a safe distance from the water.

Almost at once, the rain abruptly ceased, dissolving into the gentlest of soft taps as the stormy sky emptied out, and the last dark clouds gave up the ghost and sullenly moved on. A new breeze stiffened in the warm, wet air. For a moment, there was the anticipation of silence, only there wasn't; instead, the priorities of sound shifted—the loud rain had ceased, but the low hum of the rushing water under foot and under the bridge was newly more invasive and thrumming all the louder, and it would go on for the remainder of the night. And when the rushing water lost momentum, the flood sirens on the higher ground at the university would continue for a while until they too would cease in the early morning, and finally all the parts of the cacophonous equation were subtracted and there was instead a soothing silence.

EIGHT

The strewn leaves on the floor of my porch were still wet the next morning, and sweeping them off was a challenge, as they stubbornly wedged themselves between the cracks in the wood. As far as I could tell, my garden looked the same as it always does, but I anticipated a visit from Neal, who would look at me with doe-eyed reproach and then get to work doing whatever it was that he did, that I was utterly incapable of, that would make everything all fine and pretty again. The good news for my bike was that it had never been cleaner. The bad news was that the disc brakes had gotten good and soaked, and I wasn't sure if they would ever recover. I carefully oiled the chain and all the other places that looked like they could conceivably use it. I would doubtless miss a few spots, but a spring tune up was on the horizon, and the bike store on Pearl would soon put things to rights. I decided to give the bicycle a well-earned day off. The creek would still be a wet bedraggled mess, and I could find other things to do.

Nye had texted early to tell me absolutely nothing that I needed to be concerned about. The Lookout pool would easily survive one day without my patronage, and I would walk over to Cygnet later in the afternoon and chat with Jesse if he wasn't too busy or too cantankerous.

"I hear you've taken to directing city traffic." Officer Reggie Hawkins stood in front of me, a sudden materialization in the middle of my sodden garden.

I smiled at him. "Always happy to help out our city's finest."

"See anything interesting?" Hawkins asked me innocently.

I shook my head. "I was just out for a ride."

He raised one eyebrow.

"Would you like some coffee?"

"I surely would." He sat himself down gingerly on a dry porch chair and waited.

"Do they have you pounding the beat now?" I asked him pleasantly.

He snorted a little at that. "You're just lucky the wife makes me watch all that lame-assed public television English detective shit, so I actually know what you're talking about."

I ignored the nasty English crack, and, after I poured two cups of fresh coffee from the coffee press, we both sat on the porch. It really wasn't warm enough to sit outside, but the air was alluringly crisp, and the morning sun had set fire to the small section of the Flatirons visible from my porch, if you positioned your chair in just the right spot at just the right time.

"Your house is pretty small," he observed.

"I told you I was poor."

He sipped slowly from his cup. "This is very good coffee," he pronounced.

"I get it from Cygnet."

He nodded knowingly. There was a lingering silence after that.

He put his coffee cup down slowly. "Well, go ahead and ask me then."

I took a deep breath. "Did anyone die in the flood last night?"

He smiled at me. "Not so far."

"Well, that's certainly good."

He smiled a little more at that. "You sound like you're almost disappointed."

I struggled to laugh that off. "No, I'm really not. Is this why you're here?"

He shook his head. "No, not really. I just thought you'd want to know."

"I did. Thank you."

There was another faltering in the conversation. We both sipped from our coffees again.

"So how have you been?" He asked it a little too cheerfully.

"Good," I replied robotically. "And yourself?"

"Good."

The pleasantries thus doggedly dispensed with, I changed the subject. "You got my text?"

He nodded. "We found your package."

"How is he?"

"We took him to the hospital and dropped him off there. I'm not sure where passing out and being in an alcoholic coma begin and end, but he was somewhere in the bad end of the spectrum, so we figured medical help was needed."

I told Reggie about the two kids in the underpass. He didn't seem too surprised.

"The homeless are generally considered fair game for psychotic little fucks like that."

"I managed to kick one of the little fucks in the nuts."

Reggie smiled. "Well, good for you."

I decided to change the subject again. "I was on the creek on Sunday night, too."

He didn't look at all surprised. "It was pretty cold out that night."

"It certainly was. I saw the Lazarus Bus."

"I bet it was full."

I nodded. "It was. They couldn't take everyone."

He looked a little more interested at that.

"So what did they do?" he asked. "The ones that got left behind?"

"The bus parked and loaded up on Broadway. People were already in line waiting for it. They take as many as they can, and the rest have to go someplace else."

"Did they go to Infant Savior?"

I nodded in reply.

He considered this for a moment. "That's a much bigger facility, but maybe not quite so nice."

"I gave a few guys a ride there."

He looked up at me sharply. "That's probably not such a great idea." His voice was harsh.

"It's a two-bus ride to get there." I was defensive in turn.

"I know it is. Did you get them there okay?"

"I did."

"Good." He hesitated, and then he spoke again. "You should be careful how you deal with the homeless," he continued. "You said the bus was full?"

I nodded.

"I suppose that's a good thing, when all their beds get used up."

I asked a question. "Why shouldn't I give them a ride?"

He considered for a moment. "I can think of a whole bunch of reasons. You crash the car and injure or kill some people. You get assaulted by a homeless person. You assault a homeless person. They claim you coerced them into your car for whatever reason. If you give a ride and something shitty and unfortunate happens, it'll find some way to slink on back and make you very sorry you tried to help."

I listened to the reasons. They all sounded slightly plausible.

"So where are you now?" he asked.

"How do you mean?"

"Where does that leave you with your intuition?"

I was pretty sure the correct answer was nowhere and I said so.

He seemed somewhat satisfied with that.

"So what will you do now?"

I considered. In the last couple of months the creek had flooded four times, and two people had died. It was tragic but a long way from being an epidemic. The city was clearly far from caught in the grip of a killing spree, and federal disaster funds and a visit from FEMA were unlikely to be forthcoming anytime soon.

On the other hand, I still knew next to nothing about the two dead men, and I still had precious little else to do with my free time.

I decided to change the subject once again before I received another blunt lecture on the perils of being a dilettante vigilante. "I'm volunteering at Lazarus."

Hawkins looked at me curiously. "Good for you. What night?"

"Sundays."

"Which Sunday?"

"The first of the month."

Reggie smiled at me. "Why that's the famous Dora's meatloaf night."

I smiled back. "I've heard some talk. Is it that good?"

He shook his head. "I've never tried it. I was asking around the station about Lazarus, and believe it or not the subject of that woman's damn cooking came up. Some of the guys have eaten it. Turns out I was about the only person who had never even heard of it. The word is it's almost worth being homeless for."

"I'll get to try it when I volunteer there." I spoke boastfully.

Reggie Hawkins laughed. "That's good. You be sure and let me know what it's like." Then he stood up. "And thanks for the coffee."

"You're most welcome," I said.

Reggie turned to leave then changed his mind.

"You need to know that there are two rumors currently circulating on the creek." He paused then. "The first is that someone is out there trying to hurt homeless people."

"What's the second?" I asked quietly.

He looked hard at me and smiled coldly as he spoke. "The second is that someone is out there trying to save the homeless people. And just so you know, that guy they were pissing on was in pretty bad shape. They pumped his stomach at the hospital. You might have saved his life."

Reggie Hawkins then took his leave, just as Neal pulled up in his Subaru Forester and began to unload his rakes and shovels. As he did so, he dolefully surveyed the garden with the look of a taciturn midwestern farmer lamenting his umpteenth failed crop.

I have to say it all looked just fine to me.

NINE

Later in the afternoon, I found myself running out of self-assigned chores. Neal had left earlier, after we had shared a large sandwich from Snarf's, for which I felt duty bound to pay. I had surreptitiously watched Neal from the window as he tended to the garden, and I could see the telltale signs of a lonely person utterly determined to find busy work for himself. He labored slowly, and he tended to pause often in mid task and ruminate. At one point I'm pretty certain he meticulously dug up one plant and then equally carefully put it back. Maybe there was a minute adjustment to be made, or maybe he just changed his mind, but, then again, maybe not.

Neal and I had chatted over our sandwiches. Gus was apparently working long hours in the restaurant, and the two of them were seeing very little of each other. Neal had seen the real estate industry go into a state of recess, even in a place as affluent as Boulder, and had eased himself into a kind of semi-retirement. He still showed the occasional condo to well-heeled parents buying a decent place for their college kids to trash, and he had helped Anthem Branding, a North Boulder advertising agency, sell their small office and move to a much larger one. He hung out occasionally at Gus's restaurant, but most of the clientele were much younger men, men Gus's age, and Neal felt old and stuffy and uncomfortable there. Gus was a hip, fearlessly open gay man of the present day, Neal seemed an almost closeted character from yesteryear. He admitted to me that his elderly mother still had no idea he was gay. His was the fully repressed gayness of a previous generation. Neal had even been married once and had a son slightly closer in age to Gus than he was.

Neal loves to garden. He now owns a condo with a six-by-ten-foot balcony with two uncomfortable patio chairs and a small if undeniably healthy collection of plants wedged in one corner.

Neal loves to hike the Flatirons, but Gus seldom has the time to join him. Neal's last hike there was with me. We walked the three miles to Chautauqua Park and followed the Royal Arch trail a mile and a half in one direction, and over a thousand feet up. The best part of the hike is the hardest part, the sheer rock-stair section, which accounts for most of the difference in elevation. The trail turns around at a sandstone arch that overlooks the Boulder foothills and eastern plains.

As Neal and I had rested there, it occurred to me that Nye and Neal seemed more naturally simpatico than Gus and Neal. There's still a large age difference, but Nye was born older. I don't know too many gay people. I suspected my idle matchmaking plans might be perceived as ridiculous.

I was reminded of a movie a few years back, where a white character, the star of the film, had known precisely two black people, one man and one woman. Naturally, he had decided to try to bring them together. If I remember the plot correctly, his well-intentioned/subliminally racist plan had actually met with some limited success.

Neal still had puttering rights to my garden, but he long ago exhausted the actual practical demands my small wild yard could make on him. Now he was largely making work for himself. He certainly had my sympathy. I, too, was more than adept at spinning my wheels manically while pretending to move forward.

After Neal left, I rode over to Cygnet. Natalie was working behind the counter. Jesse was having his teeth cleaned, I was informed. Natalie was smiling as she evenly warmed a maple walnut muffin in what I assumed was some kind of a glorified, high-tech toaster oven behind the counter. Over the sound system, "Maybe Not Tonight" by Glen Hansard was playing very softly. Both the choice of a painfully earnest singer-songwriter and the gentle volume hinted strongly that Jesse had temporarily relinquished control of his domain, since Jesse favored reverb-drenched indie rock or organically retrofitted country, both played at high volume. I looked around suspiciously for other subversive tinkering, but everything else looked to be kosher, at least on the surface. So I kept looking. I did finally notice that the heat wasn't blasting for a change, because the huge door was pulled down all the way shut, and, Rose, the old Alsatian, had staked out her prime floor space on the inside. So maybe I had been naively wrong, and sinister changes were indeed afoot.

"Tom, how often do you get your teeth cleaned?" Natalie asked me out of the blue.

I didn't see that question coming, but I countered smoothly. "Every six months. I get a pithy reminder on a card from my dentist."

She nodded. "Me too."

"Why do you ask?" I wondered.

"Jesse hasn't had his cleaned in two and a half years."

I pondered this. "So why go now?"

She smirked evilly. "I told him if he wanted me to fuck

him again he had to go."

I smirked back. "That would do it," I curtly observed.

The man getting his muffin warmed was trying not to laugh. I drank my coffee quickly. Mr. Hansard was howling poignantly, and I badly missed Jesse.

One entrance to the Boulder Public Library is several red brick rectangular columns supporting a curving, vaguely triangular piece of glass perched on top. It stands on one side of the creek. The other entrance boasts a series of elongated stairways that lead into a large art gallery littered with huge sculptures of shiny painted plants, with loudly costumed cartoon figures scampering in Disneyesque delight between them. A carpeted ramp gently curves above the main exhibition area and offers the best way to observe the whole gaudy exhibit.

I use Boulder Public occasionally, mainly to check out movies on DVD that haven't made it onto Netflix yet. A system of reciprocal interlibrary loans and an iPhone app make ordering films simple. I get an email when the movie arrives, or is up for renewal. I can pay my fines online, renew a title, and search the catalogs of other libraries to place a hold on the films I want to see. Most of the books I read I discover as gently used specimens going for ten dollars or less in bookstores. I'm probably a few years behind the *New York Times* best seller list, but I like unearthing unread bargains in pristine shape, I like wandering through used bookstores, and I like sitting in cafés afterward and gloatingly fondling my prized purchases in broad daylight without shame.

There is a constant flow of people in and out of the

library and most use the south entrance and make their way purposefully to the section of the building they require. Older women enter alone with a popular title to return on time and the reserved copy of another to pick up. Mothers with small children unload large piles of picture books at the checkout/returns desk and sign up for story hour.

But my sense is that many of the patrons of the Boulder library are the homeless, and, again, my observations have everything to do with motion. The Boulder locals use the facility quickly and purposefully and then dutifully take their leave, while the transient population lingers instead in a safe place that was clearly designed to offer respite and to integrate seamlessly with the natural surroundings.

At the top of the ramp over the art gallery, an enclosed glass bridge allows both the creek and the creek path to pass underneath, right though the core of the structure. Chairs and desks line the glass walls of the bridge. Outside, concrete pillars hold the bridge above the creek. Inside there is thick twill carpeting and an attendant muted silence; a vending machine is stationed and sentinel at one end, tiny restrooms beckon at the other, and electric outlets are staged every six feet along the twenty yards or so. The bridge functions as a kind of raised and transitory mixed-media exhibit; assorted denizens of the creek pass freely through the hushed interior passage from gallery to library and back, or they brave the elements and use the path underneath, perhaps pausing to co-mingle with the nicotine-starved librarians who congregate outside under the transparent enclosure, the needy smokers doubtless serving as so many soft touches for the homeless to cozy up and bum a smoke from, assuming that librarians make enough to give away their cigarettes.

A frayed young man sat cross-legged on the carpet with a small Nokia cell phone plugged into the wall beside him and the last shaggy remains of a Mohawk perched on his quilly head. He picked up the cell phone every few minutes and stared long and hard at it. An older gentleman with long white hair and a long white beard sat in a long white T-shirt and read an old book at one of the tables, a frayed guitar case pushed under his chair. There was a red sweatshirt draped across the top of the case. His small pink fingers rubbed gently at his chin as he read. The early evening sun beat through the glass. A teenage girl in tight jeans and high sandals with one loose heel ate a sandwich while packing and unpacking the few unlikely possessions she had inside her small backpack: an under-stuffed teddy bear, a notebook with Britney Spears' flat tummy on the cover, a thin beaded purse, several pieces of notepaper carefully folded and rubber banded together. Outside the window and down below, two kids fished unfairly in the creek waters, with large nets brandished in their sneaky little hands. A table held a coffee machine, paper cups and various condiments in little packets and a gentle sign stating that, while coffee was free to patrons, only library staff could brew it.

"Can I help you with something?" Her voice was gentle, and her name was Eileen Arthur. She manned the library's bank of dedicated technology services computers, where questions were asked and answered, and the library's public computers could be reserved by people unable to use the library's online reservation system. Behind her station a room held thirty identical desktop Dell computers in six rows of five. There were two Brother printers waiting in the front of the room. Most of the computers were being used. The room was warm and darkened by closed shades blocking the windows along one wall. I was in a section of the library I'd never ventured into before.

"I wanted some information about a former library patron." I spoke up boldly to compensate for the hush of the surroundings, and the fact that I was convinced my mission was doomed from the start.

"I beg your pardon?" Mine was clearly not a run of the mill enquiry for Ms. Arthur.

I repeated my question in ringing tones. Eileen was perhaps forty, with long dark brown hair, and she was tall and pretty and not wearing a wedding ring and, sadly, would probably lose her temper with me in about five minutes flat if I kept this up. Libraries and, by definition, librarians wisely guard their patrons' various freedoms diligently and take a lot of pompous flack from loud right-wing windbags as a result. I was all for this well-meaning diligence in principle, except for right now, of course.

"What kind of information are you looking for?" I assumed there was little chance of her helping me, but she hadn't actually told me to get lost yet, so I still held out some slight hope.

"I really just wanted to know if he was here." This was meant to be a vague enough request and hopefully not an outright challenge to individual rights or national security.

"If he was here? You mean in the library? You mean here in the library?" Eileen Arthur was smiling at me in an odd way. Was my question either stupid or audacious? Would she treat me like a demented simpleton, or would she linger playfully, toying with her prey for a tender moment before casually administering the kill?

"Yes. But it was a while ago. I wanted to know if he was here a few days last month actually." I smiled brightly at her.

"Why would we know that?" It was a reasonable enough question.

"He would have been using one of your computers if he was here."

"I see." She looked thoughtfully at me. She was really very pretty. Her nails were short and painted a dark red. She wore several bracelets, nowhere near as many as Officer Hawkins, but then her job wasn't generally as dangerous. Her eyebrows were bushier than those worn by anemic fashion models. There was a blue Trek bike helmet on a table behind her.

I tried another big disarming smile. "You haven't said no yet. I'm actually kind of amazed."

"I haven't said yes yet either," she replied with a half smile.

I took a deep breath. "I'm going to say a name and some dates," I announced grandly. "And you're going to tell me if he was here."

She laughed challengingly back at me. "Well go for it then." Eileen was clearly enjoying this. Maybe most of her day was spent cataloging and telling patrons where the restrooms were. Maybe she had fallen in love with me at first sight and would do anything I asked, as she was already too hopelessly smitten and under my spell to do much of anything else. But I strongly suspected the former.

I took a deep breath and plunged in. "Andrew Travers. The dates would be from the beginning of February until the tenth of the month."

Her smile turned abruptly sad. "Was the tenth when

Andrew died? I knew him a little," she spoke these last words wistfully.

I told her that it was. And that I was truly sorry.

"You want to know if he was here on the days before he died," she mused out loud. She looked at me. She looked at the computer screen in front of her. She looked at me again. A decision was being made. My smile was starting to hurt.

Eileen Arthur spoke slowly. "I'm trying to think of what possible harm it would do to tell you what you want."

I could almost watch her mind keep on working as she spoke again. "So maybe you should tell me why I should?"

I thought fast. "He's not getting any deader. It won't much matter now. I want to know what happened to him. You're already hopelessly in love with me."

She giggled a little at that. "I am? Wow, that certainly happened quickly. You're not a policeman, are you?"

I shook my head. "I'm a private dick on a case." You can wait your whole life to unload a line like that. It had been said to me once. Now my moment had come. I seized it.

She giggled again. "No, you're not."

"I want to know all I can about his last days."

"Why?"

I looked hard into her eyes, which were green and large. "I just have a really bad feeling," was all I could say.

She spoke slowly. She was staring hard at the screen. "It's not exactly a secret that Andrew was here in the library every day. What day of the week was the fifth of February?"

"Why do you ask?"

Her hands flew across the keyboard and she answered her own question. "It was a Sunday."

She nodded to herself. "We open at noon and close at six

on Sundays. We stay open until eight every other day of the week." Was she talking to fill the dead air while she decided whether to help me or not?

"Did he stay until closing time most nights?"

"No. He usually left earlier to get his dinner at the homeless shelters. Unless it was a very cold night . . ."

I finished her thought for her. "When he needed to get to the shelters even earlier to make sure he got a bed."

"That's right," she said nodding.

"If the fifth was a Sunday, then it was the first Sunday of the month. Did Andrew ever go to Lazarus?"

She smiled. "He did go there sometimes. It all depended on the meal being served." She smiled again. "He had a complicated schedule."

Eileen Arthur anticipated my next question. "We talked sometimes," she said apologetically.

"Lazarus served meatloaf on the first Sunday of the month," I said.

She smiled. "Oh I know that. Andrew adored Dora's meatloaf."

It occurred to me that my fact-finding mission might have gone a lot smoother if I had mentioned the meatloaf first.

I spoke. "Andrew always took the city buses to the shelters."

She replied, "He did, except when he took the Lazarus bus. He took that on the cold nights when he went there. Can I ask you something?"

This was going a lot better than I hoped. We were still talking, and I hadn't been asked to leave yet.

"Of course," I said quickly, not wanting to lose any

momentum.

"Was the fifth a cold night?"

"Why do you ask?"

She smiled darkly. "You begin to interest me, vaguely."

She spoke to herself again. "Let me just check . . ." She typed for a moment. Then she waited. She looked at her screen. "I don't think it was cold that night."

"Was Travers here that day? I'd like to know for sure."

"If I tell you he was here, it's not necessarily certain where he went afterward . . ." Eileen's hands were still moving across the keyboard rapidly as she spoke and thought and typed all at once.

I persisted. "No. But he went to the shelters every night. He liked meatloaf. Lazarus would be quiet that night since it wasn't cold. He would get a bed there easily. You could look at what time he logged out and you could make a good guess where he went."

She was still reluctant. "It's still only a guess. You could ask the people at Lazarus if he was there."

"They wouldn't tell me if I did."

She nodded. "No. They probably wouldn't . . ."

I shook my head and I waited.

She looked at the screen. Her voice became suddenly softer. "All right. He was here that day. He logged off at just after five."

"Is the time relevant?"

She nodded. "I think so. It's the time he usually left here to get to Lazarus on the city bus."

I was surprised that she was helping me. And I was amazed at how much she knew about Andrew Travers. I said as much.

She shook her head sadly. "It's not just about Andrew. I know a lot about most of the homeless people who use the library. I know the bus schedules to the shelters. When they open at night and how many beds each place has. The meals they serve. We have a drawer with occasional bus money for those who need it. It comes from our overdue book fines. We've called the shelters to check on whether beds are available. We've called the police to help with someone who needed a ride. I spend a good part of my day helping the homeless. Andrew came here every day for a few years and he talked to me sometimes."

As Eileen spoke, it occurred to me that Andrew Travers and Nitro appeared to have the following in common: they were both homeless, and they were both dead, and they had both stayed at Lazarus House on a Sunday a few days before they died in the floodwaters, and they both had partaken of, by all accounts, the singularly greatest meatloaf ever baked.

And at that momentous point, I paused for consideration. Did I have enough motives and methods for suspecting murder most foul? I most assuredly did not come close. Did I have enough to continue my idiotic investigation, or at least to go on conversing with the decidedly not unattractive Eileen Arthur? I absolutely did.

An inconsiderate patron had a question for Eileen, and I had to pretend to wait patiently as she explained why color copies were more expensive than black and white ones. It made perfect sense to me, but then I didn't begrudge the extra ten cents. Was it possible that Eileen was in a hurry to get done with this customer? It certainly seemed so. Did she want to get back to our conversation? It seemed unlikely.

The disgruntled patron finally walked away with her

answer and we were alone again.

I struggled to explain myself. "I'm pretty certain that Andrew Travers was at Lazarus a few days before he died. So was the man who died in the flood this month. There's something strange about their deaths, and I don't have a clue what it is. The fact that they were both there is pretty much all I have at this point," I concluded sadly.

"You're not really much of a dick are you?"

I stiffened. "Some might argue that point."

She asked me, "What do you mean by something strange about their deaths?"

I tried again. "I think maybe their deaths are related in another way I can't quite see or understand yet."

She looked at me thoughtfully. Then she spoke. "I did read about the other death in the paper last week."

"His real name was Arthur Crowder. But he was known as Nitro." I had a sudden thought. Then I hesitated . . . oh why not? She still hadn't said no to me yet. "I was just wondering. Perhaps you could tell me. Was Arthur Crowder perchance a library patron?

"He wasn't," Eileen answered me much too quickly.

"How do you know that?" I asked her wonderingly.

She looked a little bashful. "I looked him up after I read the paper. What can I say? I'm a librarian. I was curious." She pointed down at the desk where her name was displayed. "We even shared a name." She smiled brightly at me, and without thinking I took a bold plunge.

"I wondered if you'd like to go out with me some time?"

She pretended to consider my question. "Is this going to be dating or detection?" she responded playfully.

I smiled. "I thought we could try a little of both."

She smiled back at me. "Good," she said. "Because they both sound like fun to me."

That night Boulder Public Library closed at eight, and Eileen Arthur was working until then, otherwise I would have begged her to meet me later that same evening. But I bit back my tongue and I didn't. I couldn't decide whether I wanted to see her because she was utterly adorable, and I wanted to wrap her up in my arms, or because we had talked, and I had revealed some of my crazy notions, and she hadn't rushed to find me a straitjacket, so that now I was free to unleash the full extent of my inner weirdness. Or maybe I was just taken with the deliciously exhilarating notion that adorability and arm wrapping and further unleashing said inner weirdness might all be within my reach.

Naturally I was well aware that, for someone terminally worthless in matters of romance, my expectations were ludicrously overextended.

So we arranged to meet the following day. Working a day and a half today meant that Eileen only worked until lunchtime the next day, and we were going to have lunch together at a place still to be determined. The blue Trek helmet did indeed turn out to be hers. She rode her bike most days, but not to work, because she lived in a small bungalow literally across the street from the library on Arapahoe. So we would ride to lunch tomorrow if the weather held up, and the birds were singing, and all was right with the world, and there was joy in the morning, as the inimitable P.G. Wodehouse would doubtless have it.

It was indeed warm the next day, and there was joy in the

morning. I was way early for our date, but in truth I try to be early for everything because I firmly believe that arriving on time is actually the same as being late. Please don't ask me why I believe this, but I do.

I don't much like riding in long trousers, but dating in shorts works best for men both under thirty and with well-sculpted legs, and I sadly fail both prerequisites. So I rode home from the creek in the morning and showered and changed into jeans and a shirt. My hair is still thick and graying and very short and thankfully doesn't naturally default to anything too frightening when I take my bike helmet off.

The creek by the library parking lot is officially designated a possible flood area. I sat down at a bench anyway. There are several posted hazard signs close to where the water forms a natural shallow pool, and tiny stone sculptures stand close to the shore. I think they're meant to be stylized renditions of a duck family, or little wine goblets sitting all in a row for no good reason.

I walked over to Arapahoe and tried to guess which house was Eileen's. I narrowed it down to a tiny gray frame ranch, with a line of pine trees behind it, at the corner of Arapahoe and Lincoln. Wrapped in warm shadow, the house had a false dormer window built into the oversized roof, and a mixture of bare patches and tufts of grass out front. In my head, I began to construct our common ground—our bikes and our biking and our little Boulder houses.

My garden is much prettier than hers, but I can take very little credit for that. It occurred to me that I could cut the woefully underutilized Neal free and send him over here to work miracles, but I suspect he has a sentimental attachment to my place. She's also much prettier than me, but again, that's not really within my control.

Eileen pushed her blue and white Trek racing bike out of the main library door right on time. Her bike was a fancier model than mine. Good, I reasoned, that meant she wouldn't be after me for my fortune.

"Hello, you," I said.

"Hello," she replied.

"You look fine," I said with gusto.

"I feel fine," she riposted with equal perk.

We stood then a little awkwardly. I had chosen a place to go to if she asked, and I assumed she had picked somewhere too. Being a chivalrous sort, I insisted that she pick first. Eileen chose a labyrinthine old student bar on Baseline in South Boulder where the house burgers were peerless, the service was solidly spartan, and a pitcher of Dale's Pale Ale was easily procured and consumed. The daytime soundtrack was a little heavy on the classic rock, but, all in all, it was an admirable choice.

How do you ride a bike on a first date? Pedal off ahead, set a ridiculous pace, and try to appear super fit? Or be a gent, hang back, and risk looking like a geezer on a less sporty model with a fit girl ahead of you who also happens to be younger? Or do you try to ride along together without crashing, and talk loudly? As I pondered the courting cyclist's dilemma, Eileen set off at a brisk clip that it was all I could do to keep up with, and I got to watch her rear end for most of the trip, which really wasn't so terrible.

We sat down to our frosty Dale's as Jackson Browne sang. There were all manner of cumbersome knick knacks covering the walls and ceilings. Close to where we sat, a stuffed badger had a good-sized salmon clamped in its mouth. It looked very pleased with itself—the badger, not the salmon. Opposite me, a small mirror on the wall showed my handsome features with the swaggering words *You Devil, You* stenciled rakishly underneath.

"What did you do yesterday?" she asked me as we sat down. Eileen wore a dark blue sleeveless blouse, skinny jeans and Keen shoes. There was a mole at the bottom of her neck and her skin looked darker in the bar than I remembered it being.

"The whole day?"

"No. I meant after we met."

"I rode along the creek for a while and then had some coffee, then I went home and listened to music and pined for you in my lonely solitude."

"Was I naked when you pined for me?" she asked.

"I don't believe that's any of your business."

She had another question. "What do you do when you ride?"

"Do you mean generally, or do you mean now?"

She paused. "Both," she said playfully.

"Generally I daydream most of the time and try not to fall over. Now I'm stuck thinking about floods and dead people and wondering how to get homeless people to tell me things, or how to get people with homes to tell me things about homeless people."

"And how is all that working out for you?" she asked coyly.

"I'm not very good at it. I did find a woman who offered to tell my fortune, and she told me she saw Arthur Crowder at Lazarus a few days before he died and that he was unhappy for some reason. And I gave three gentlemen a ride to the shelter in South Boulder."

"Is that the one at Infant?" Eileen asked.

I nodded. "They didn't really tell me anything. In fact, two of them never actually talked to me at all."

She shook her head and smiled at me. "You really have too much time on your hands, don't you?"

It was a fine example of the rhetorical question.

An amplified voice cut in on Mr. Browne and called out my first name. Our burgers were now cooked and ready, and we were invited to come to the rear bar and get them ourselves.

Eileen told me about herself as we ate and the late Warren Zevon sung to us of attorneys, weapons and cash. She was forty-two and had been divorced for three years. She was from Milwaukee, and her undergraduate and MLS degrees were both from the University of Wisconsin in Madison. She had met her husband Dave there, and they had dated all through her college years. Dave was a bluegrass mandolin player and played in various bar bands in Madison before they moved to Colorado, to Fort Collins at first, where she took a job as a young adult librarian.

Her husband made a little money playing around Fort Collins and seemed happy enough to be doing just that. After a while she wanted to have children, and Dave also said he'd like kids, but it never happened for them, and he didn't seem anywhere near as upset about that as she was. Then the technology librarian job opened up in Boulder. Dave thought he'd get less gigging work in Boulder, because he wasn't very good, and Boulder had better musicians.

"That's what he told me anyway," Eileen said as I poured

her a second glass of Dale's from the pitcher.

"Was there something else?" I wondered out loud.

She hesitated. "The something else was a fiddle player in Fort Collins," she finally admitted. "And Dave fell in love with her."

"I'm sorry," I said.

"Don't be," she said. "We dated all through college, and we lived together for five years. We were married for ten. It was a long time, and mostly it was good even if it ended up like a bad country song."

Eileen ate my pickle when I offered it to her. She proposed a handful of fries by way of recompense, but I waved her generous offer aside. Our legs bumped together under the scarred oak table and she made no effort to pull away.

She listened as I told her about Patricia and Nye and Scotland and Keith and artworks.com and Belvedere and Chicago and Boulder, about love and place and loss and work and place again, and, finally, after I had trivialized as much as I could and she had laughed at most of the moments I had hoped she would find laughable, I spoke about my last fortnight chasing down a handful of insubstantial nothings submerged in coldness and water. And when I stopped talking about that, we had finished our beers and Eileen spoke.

"What do you think now?" she asked me.

"I was going to ask you out again."

She laughed. "And I was going to accept if you asked me out again. No, what I meant was, what do you think about your two dead men?"

"I still think they died with more in common than I currently know about."

"Do you want me to help you?"

"I do," I said. "Very much." And I wanted it for all kinds of reasons.

She sighed. "I did tell you about how much of my day I spend dealing with homeless people, didn't I? It should be the biggest part of the job training, and of course it isn't at all. And I told you I talked sometimes with Andrew before he died? I talk with lots of other homeless people every day in the library. They really do like to talk."

So I asked her about Andrew Travers. Eileen agreed with Reggie Hawkins that Travers being on the creek at night during the flood didn't make sense. She also confirmed his suspicion that Andrew received a little money from his ex-wife when he needed it. Eileen also knew that Travers had helped his estranged family with their charitable investments; after all he understood his money much better than they did, and he occasionally advised them on the best places to invest it.

"Why do you think he walked away from his old life?" I finally asked her.

"I think that's simple," Eileen said. "He was deeply ashamed of it."

After our lunch we rode back to the library and then across Arapahoe to Eileen's house. It was indeed the little gray one, as I had first guessed. We stood outside and she apologized for the state of the front yard. I wondered again if Neal could be coerced into accepting another gardening project; with time on his hands he could even embark on a second career as a bespoke gardener for hire. God knows I would give him a gushing reference. I proposed we have dinner in two days time, and Eileen readily accepted. I was well aware that this was rushing things, but I didn't much care. We both agreed to think of a place before we met, and then without really meaning to, I kissed her goodbye.

I had impulsively leaned in to plant something short and chaste on her cheek by way of farewell. Eileen turned her head expertly and found my lips. As we kissed, her eyes closed then fluttered open for an instant and I glimpsed the whites inside. Her hand held the back of my head gently for a moment before we pulled apart.

"So long, pal," I said.

She smiled at me as I turned and rode away.

On my way home, I thought of something to add to our list of things in common; we had both wanted children, and we had both failed.

TEN

For the next two days I camped out on the creek path, constantly switching locations, sitting for a long while, standing for a shorter while, presenting myself shamelessly as an unheralded and unused sounding board for the homeless. Both days were sunny and pleasant, and both days were unsuccessful. I hung out at various places with an eager nonjudgmental look plastered across my face, which I hoped conveyed a gentle willingness to listen without either comment or condemnation. I considered my strategy to be not without merit: the tarot lady had sought me out unbidden after all, and Devonte had unburdened himself like a long-lost relation trolling for money and fleeting fame on a reality show. Surely others would do likewise and converse with me, unload their myriad anxieties, share sundry confidences and, I hoped, tell me all I wanted to know about Andrew Travers and Nitro.

I was aware of Reggie's warning words, and occasionally the more aggressively troubled of the creek dwellers wandered my way and I cut and ran. But in truth, when you subtracted those who might conceivably wish to do me harm, my list of the eagerly unburdening was grievously slight.

I had looked for the tarot lady on both days and been unsuccessful. Devonte, on the other hand, I had spied laid out on the grass in front of the Central Park bandshell on the first morning. I considered waking him, but he looked both comfortable and sound asleep. He was a sleeping dog, and I adhered to the oft-suggested maxim.

In the early afternoon of the second day, I stood at Fine Park staring at a cute if typographically suspect map of Boulder Creek attached to two pieces of ragged weathered wood, and I silently pleaded to the creek gods for inspiration. By way of answer, Eileen instantaneously texted with an invitation to the library to meet with two people she thought might help. One was Larry, a homeless man who claimed to know Nitro well, and the other was Timothy Hastings, a librarian colleague who spoke with Andrew Travers often. Could I be there in an hour? And could I possibly bring a large extra caramel macchiato for Larry as a bribe?

And what about for you and for poor Timothy, I facetiously texted back, what should I bring for the two of you?

Her next text informed me that Tim was just fine thank you, as he only drinks the organically grown coffee he brings from home, but, since I was so sweetly inquiring, could I please bring a green tea for her?

It served me right for asking; now I had to find myself an able barista. At least she had said please.

"You ever watch *House*?" Jesse asked me. His tone was combative. I knew he wasn't much of a television watcher, so I was justifiably leery.

"I believe I have," I ventured cautiously

"Natalie likes to watch it. It was a rerun last night. He's a British guy."

"He's English, actually."

"Whatever." Jesse was not about to be sidetracked with minutiae.

I said nothing.

"Is he supposed to be a sympathetic character?"

I wasn't actually too sure. "I suppose so," I gently expounded.

Jesse snorted then shook his head. "That makes no sense."

I foolishly took the bait. "Why's that?"

Jesse sighed and took a deep breath. "He's this guy who takes all the drugs he can get. He rides a fancy motorcycle. He plays a vintage Flying V. He gets to fuck a delectable piece of ass like Cuddy. He's an asshole to his buddy Wilson who's still his buddy. Can you explain to me why he's such a dick and why I should feel sorry for him?"

"His leg hurts?" I gently suggested.

"Spare me." The subject was thus firmly closed.

There was a wonderful song playing in Cygnet. I didn't know it, so I asked the erstwhile television critic.

"It's Chuck Prophet," I was informed.

"What's it called?"

"'The Right Hand and the Left Hand'."

"Is it new?"

"Yup. Want me to burn it for you?" he asked me shrewdly.

Not wanting to be seen actively contributing to the epidemic of music pirating, I said nothing but instead chose to look helplessly pathetic.

I had ridden back from the creek, dumped the bike at the house, showered, changed, and driven my car over to see Jesse with my drink order. I wasn't going to make it back to the library in an hour, but I would be close. After I met with Timothy and Larry, I could wait at the library for Eileen then drive us both to dinner. I hoped it was my turn to pick, because I wanted to go to a Mexican restaurant on Sixty-Third. The bike ride there was a manageable enough distance, but not particularly pleasant, past several industrial estates and car dealers and one very good brewery, along the side of a busy section of road going east on Arapahoe.

I would drive. Eileen owned no car. Given how fast she rode her bike everywhere, and how close to work she lived, it certainly made an unorthodox kind of sense, although, while you weren't actually required by law to own a Subaru in Boulder, it was certainly expected.

Eileen was waiting at the library door and kissed my cheek when I handed her tea over. I offered no objection.

It occurred to me that after one conversation and one lunch date we had already slipped into the kind of domesticated routine that people who had known and liked each other for a while fall into. The longest relationship I have ever had is with Nye, and he very seldom kisses me on the cheek. At one time, my former wife may have kissed me that way. Eileen kissed me with all the signs of an unforced familiarity, and I accepted her kiss in like fashion. It felt super, even as the cynic in me said it would surely never last.

She led me upstairs to a small conference room that was warm and stuffy in the afternoon sun. Larry was a great shapeless bear of a man decked out in what I barely remember was known as a kaftan, accessorized with dirty and voluminous cargo shorts and green Crocs, which looked surprisingly new and slightly small, wedged precariously onto his two huge feet. He took his drink in both hands, removed the lid, and started to slurp his way though the fast-shrinking layer of whipped cream on the top before even speaking one word.

"Gotta drink it fast before it all melts away." He murmured this to himself with a sneaky little smile, as he managed to coat his reddish beard and his chapped and sore-looking lips with a backsplash of cream, which he then licked greedily away.

Eileen had wisely chosen to pass on all this licking and slurping and had left us alone.

I looked around the room at the collection of posters of famous actors holding books. I recognized some of the older ones. The actor who played the apparently dickish House was holding *Treasure Island*, and I thought of Jesse. The young elf character from the Lord of the Rings movies clutched a hardcover copy of Tolkien. There were posters of even younger stars who I didn't know, and, quite frankly, I wasn't altogether certain any of them were old enough to read.

"This isn't Starbucks." Larry spoke in a surprisingly soft monotone and looked at me accusingly.

"No one told me." I tried to sound apologetic.

"Theirs is the best," he muttered.

"Maybe next time," I said insincerely.

He ignored me and applied himself some more to his clearly substandard beverage. I would be sure to inform Jesse of his shortcomings the next time I saw him.

"I hear you knew Nitro, Larry."

Larry wasn't going to be rushed. There was still some valuable detritus near the bottom of the paper cup that some combination of his dirty fingers and his long tongue could dig out.

"What can you tell me about Nitro, Larry?" I persisted.

At the second mention of the name, Larry began to snigger to himself. Then he spoke, his words a low chant punctuated by a series of rolling chortles. "He falls asleep one time, Nitro does . . . in the afternoon . . . hee hee . . . That fat bitch Sally she's always there . . . and Teddy . . . nasty little ugly hooker girl always there even though I can't fucking stand her . . . I swear to God one day . . . hee hee . . . the old Coach too . . . we wait some . . . Nitro's snoring real loud . . . like a croaking he's making . . . So Coach he shakes him . . . Nothing. Jesus Nitro . . . I swear to God . . . Coach pulls his zipper down and gets his johnson out . . . Sally says it's so big . . . hee hee . . . she has some sandwich she's got from a place . . . opens the bread up . . . puts the johnson in her sandwich . . . makes like she'll eat his meat right out of the bread . . . hee hee."

"What does Nitro do?" I asked.

Larry's got himself trapped somewhere between laughing and coughing. "The fuck does he do? Nitro goes right on sleeping, man. Dude's sound asleep.

Larry laughs too much to say anything more.

I wait a while for the laughter to finish. "What was he like?" I asked.

"Everybody liked Nitro."

"Was he ever unhappy?"

"I never saw him like that."

Larry was at the end of his drink. It hadn't taken him long. He paused. Somewhere inside his clothing he unearthed a napkin and pulled it out. It was neatly folded and looked spotless. He wiped his chin slowly and carefully.

Larry peered inside his finished drink and began to wipe at the last of the residue along the sides of the cup with his fingers. Afterwards he licked each finger, then wiped his fingers with the napkin as carefully as he had wiped his chin, then he placed the napkin inside the cup, put the lid back on, and left the cup on the table directly in front of him. He seemed subtly pleased with himself before he frowned and suddenly looked hard at me.

"You got yourself a nice car then?" He asked his question almost pleasantly.

I nodded uncertainly.

"A pretty new one?"

"Not especially," I answered him hesitantly.

"Got a nice house?"

"It's okay."

"Big or small house?" He wanted to know.

"It's pretty small."

"Got yourself a fancy bike for riding the creek and going where you sure as fuck don't belong."

I said nothing and stared at him.

"You like the librarian lady do you?" He sneered at me. "You all hot for her?"

I still said nothing, and Larry laughed to himself.

"You got everything you need then don't you?" he taunted me.

"I suppose so." Why was I even answering him?

"Me too," he said.

"Good," I said. "I'm glad for you." I must have sounded less than convincing.

He stared at me. "You don't believe me?"

"No, I do," I said, although I didn't. I stared at one of the posters on the wall.

"Look at me." His voice was intense and stronger.

"You've got nothing I need. You hear me. You've got nothing." He almost shouted the last word at me. He was huge and he was angry for his own reasons. I was half his size and mostly what I felt then was just sorry to be having this conversation.

Without another word Larry got up and left. His cup sat empty on the table. I looked at the back of his feet as he shuffled away. The straps on his new Crocs were cutting hard into the back of his heels.

I sat for a moment and then got up and left the overly warm room, throwing the empty cup into the garbage can as I went.

Out in the hallway, there was no sign of Larry. I wasn't sorry to see him go. He had cost me an expensive drink, and he had told me nothing. I felt the uncontrollable urge to head to the men's room and wash my hands.

I found Eileen in the computer room standing hunched over a library patron. An older woman was sitting at a computer. She held a CD case in her hand; it was Celine Dion's *Let's Talk About Love*. She wanted to make a copy for her friend. She'd tried at home with no luck. Could Eileen help her? Eileen could and would. There were a few clicks, a few minutes whirring and waiting, and two copies of Ms. Dion's most adorably histrionic moments existed when before there had been but one. The woman left the library smiling.

"Isn't that piracy?"

She didn't look happy. "How did it go with Larry?"

"He told me one dirty story, vacuumed up his macchiato, got a little weird, and left."

"How was his story?"

I shook my head. "Not worth the macchiato."

"He came to see me a moment ago. He told me you told

him something about me." She wasn't smiling.

"What exactly did he say?" I asked her.

"He said you told him that you fucked me in the ass last night and that I loved it."

I sighed. "Does any part of that sound even slightly believable to you?"

Eileen stared at me for a moment and then shook her head. "Not really. I'm sorry I mentioned it."

I reached out and touched her hair and she smiled at me. We stood there for a while.

"I'm sorry he upset you."

"I'm fine. Did you learn anything at all?"

"Not much."

"What time is it?"

I looked at my iPhone. It was close to four.

"You need to go see Tim now," she ordered. "He'll be having his late afternoon smoke and posing moodily under the bridge."

Timothy Hastings was indeed standing, his arms crossed, his elbow wedged in one hand—a ponderous study in neo-Byronic aloofness—all alone and pouty with his cigarette by the creek water. He was leaning against one of the pillars under the bridge. He wore dark narrow jeans and a dark grey V-neck sweater with a lighter grey T-shirt underneath. He was cadaver thin and aristocratically tall, and his glasses were around his neck attached by a cord. He wore new black Converse high tops in what was surely an act of studied irony. Even standing still, he radiated waves of tense poseur energy. From far away he looked no more than late teenage. Up close he quickly edged closer to mid-thirties.

"Are you Tim?" I asked him purely as a formality.

"You must be the famous Tom," he answered me with the arch look of a starchy English dowager.

We shook hands for a few seconds too long. The gaze he gave me was all the way down his long nose, hypercritical, sadly appraising. It plainly asked, "What can she possibly see in you that she doesn't see in me?" It affected disdain and bored indifference and pointed disappointment, but beneath that was the puzzled pain of someone bound up in unrequited love with someone else. I should have sympathized because, God knows, I've offered up the same hangdog look enough times.

When he spoke it was in rapid streams of fragmented consciousness. "I only allow myself the indulgence of five cigarettes a day. This is the third. I really need to get back soon. I understand you want to know about Andrew? I must say Eileen certainly seems to have taken quite a fancy to you." The last remark failed to hide his chagrined regret.

I chose the last subject first because I instinctively wanted to hurt his feelings. "I like her too," I said with a bright smile.

"How sweet," he replied drily.

Then I began to work backwards. "Did you speak to Andrew before he died?"

"We conversed the very same day. Andrew and I spoke often. You should know that Eileen and I went out once." Was he actually bragging?

"Why should I care about that?" I asked him bluntly.

He was instantly dismissive. "That's very true. It wasn't a fine romance by any means. A lovely girl though . . ." He tried to laugh at the absurdity of it all. Perhaps I was meant to assume that Eileen wasn't worthy of him.

Today was apparently my designated day to waste in protracted and worthless conversations.

I tried again. "How was Andrew before he died?"

Hastings posed in studied thoughtfulness. "I must say he did seem rather more at peace. Andrew used the library computers every day. He tended to be overanxious. He would get annoyed when there were other people using the computers and he could only be on for an hour at a time. Andrew wasn't by any means a happy man. He worried incessantly about his wife and his daughter. He thought that his money would destroy them. He dwelled all the time on what he'd done . . . about the lives he thought he ruined. You know of course about the last ones—the poor members of the Armstrong family?"

I nodded.

As Hastings continued to talk about Travers, I noticed that he had almost forgotten to be superior. He had clearly liked the man.

"He felt most guilty about them. He believed that he killed them. They were a family just like his, and he identified with them—a wife and a husband and a daughter, all about the same age as he and his family. Their deaths upset him greatly."

"You said there was something different about him at the end?"

Hastings looked intently at me before nodded slowly. "Andrew stopped using the computer for the last few days of his life," he announced.

"Are you sure?"

He smiled guilelessly at his recollection. His voice, when he spoke again, contained genuine surprise. "I found him sitting once in a section of the library he never ever used. It's just tables and books, no technology. The books there are fiction mainly, the old classics beloved of ponderous academics. There's a bay window that looks onto the creek and a stone patio with a few chairs left outside. I found him reading there. Actually, to be more accurate, he was sitting half dreaming with the book open in his lap. Thomas Hardy, *The Mayor of Casterbridge,* I believe it was. I remember asking him about it. I was curious at his choice. He'd paid little attention to literature classes in his college days, he told me. He was in too much of a hurry to go into business. But he remembered a professor whose lectures he enjoyed. The class had been reading Hardy. He had paid little attention then. Now he had decided he would try again. I asked him if he was enjoying it. He said he was. He seemed quite surprised and quite happy."

"Happy?" I asked.

"Perhaps content would be a better word."

Hastings changed the subject abruptly.

"Do you read fiction at all?"

"I try to."

He mused. "Strange to imagine choosing not to read for most of your life. I read all of Hardy's books before I finished high school. From your accent, I imagine his works would have been something you'd have been required to read in school."

I nodded. I remembered we had read *Tess* in my third year.

"I grew up in Shaker Heights, Ohio. I can confidently claim to have been the only boy in my graduating class who was reading Thomas Hardy."

I saw no reason to argue with him.

Hastings was now talking without much encouragement.

"Can you imagine reading Hardy for the very first time as an adult? I envied him that. Maybe not very much else. When I remember Andrew now, I remember him sitting in the sun by the water with the book open and his eyes shut. It was like he was at peace, in repose, finally content, or at least a little more content. It was almost as if he had been forgiven for something. As though he had been absolved of his sins. Am I making sense?"

I told Hastings that I thought he was.

He looked at me with some surprise. I realized his conversation had been mostly for his own pleasure, but that he hadn't actually resented my presence for the extent of it.

Hastings glanced at his wristwatch. It was an expensive antique Raymond Weil. I had once owned a similar model.

As he had begun to talk, I had watched him carefully grind out the remains of his third daily cigarette on a flat stone then hold the dog end in his hand delicately, as if it were something singularly unclean. I was certain he would later dispose of it very carefully.

"I must get back to work now. I do hope you find what you're looking for."

And with that, his flighty and supercilious tone returned in an unpleasant rush.

"Andrew Travers wasn't nearly as terrible a human being as he thought he was. Be nice to Eileen. She's a shockingly needy girl. But I trust you'll find that out all by yourself."

Did that last remark come with a slight smirk?

I had no response to his first and third and fourth comments, but "I'll certainly try" seemed to address the second one just fine.

At that, Timothy Hastings turned away from me. The gesture was an oddly theatrical one. He was, I chose to imagine, Angel Clare heading back into the wilds of Wessex, this time stalwart and pious and painfully alone without his besotted and surely much wronged love, without his abandoned Tess.

"I think Timmy is still sweet on you," I told Eileen. She was closing up her computer and getting ready to leave work for the day.

"No one ever calls him Timmy." She was smiling and I could tell she was a little flattered.

"That's probably why I said it."

"He was too young for me."

I smirked unpleasantly at that. "So what is he then, about fourteen?"

"No." She grinned teasingly back at me. "Tim's thirty-seven."

We each had tasty margaritas in big glass jars and blisteringly hot plates of Mexican food laid out in front of us. The place was busy and the small square tables were pushed close together.

I hastily calculated. "He's actually slightly closer in age to you than I am."

"I like being younger than you," she responded playfully. "It means you'll need to work harder to keep up with me."

"I'll bear that in mind." I replied in what I hoped was suitably curmudgeonly fashion.

"His mother still does his laundry."

"I thought he was from Ohio."

"She moved here to be nearer to her little darling."

"That must be nice."

"Your mother is still alive?" Eileen suddenly asked me out of the blue.

I nodded. "She's . . ." I hastily calculated in my head . . . "seventy-two."

"Does she still live in Scotland?"

I shook my head. "Nope. She lives in Spain with Bill, her new husband."

"Really?"

"Yup." I was starting to laugh now.

"What's so funny?"

So I told her.

My mother suddenly entered her second stage of youth about four years ago. She had lived alone in a small house with her television set and a shrinking collection of friends and relatives. My father had died many years ago. She retired with a small pension from years spent cooking and cleaning at the local comprehensive school. She bought her small council house a number of years ago.

Her quite remarkable transformation began quietly enough. She took road trips to Cornwall and York and other places she had never visited. She dyed her hair. She checked Man Booker Prize–winning books out of the library. She read all about Spain. She bought a computer and emailed me proudly to tell me she was flying to Palma on a senior singles charter trip to Majorca in the off season.

S'Arenal is a resort town with palm trees and white sand beaches and young German tourists in the height of summer.

In the autumn it is much quieter and the beaches are still pretty. My mother met Bill on the second day of her trip. They both signed up for the bus trip to a series of brightly lit underground caves, with a stopover at a brandy distillery on the way back. My mother drank too many free samples of banana and apricot brandy, and Bill stood silently with her in the dusty parking lot by the side of the road as she spewed her load and the driver/tour guide looked on with a sour and jaded expression.

Bill and Mum had been inseparable for the rest of the trip. Bill was Scottish, a retired newsagent from Falkirk, and a lover of the Rolling Stones, German food, and warm weather (he had chosen the resort town of S'Arenal for its sunshine and sauerkraut) who had recently lost his wife to cancer. He was two years younger than my mother and had a daughter who dressed like a tartan goth and sold organic concert T-shirts on the internet.

Bill bought the beach-view flat before the end of the fortnight. In his defense, he was already planning to find a place there before the trip. The hasty lovers returned to Scotland, sold their respective houses, visited the registry offices in their Sunday best, and were back walking along the quiet sands after a gassy bratwurst-and-beer dinner as husband and wife well before Christmas.

Bill's daughter sent my mother a vintage Keef T-shirt as a wedding present, which she wore the next time the Stones played in Barcelona, after Bill slapped down a stack of Euros for two exorbitantly priced tickets.

"Is she happy?" Eileen wanted to know.
"As a pig in shit," I replied.

Eileen returned to our previous subject. "You and I are six years apart."

"I'm well aware of that." I tensed. Where exactly was this leading?

"So when you were a teenage boy, I was just a little girl."

"Are you deliberately trying to make this sound dirty?" I laughed.

All the talk of my mother made me think back to Scotland. I reflected that the time spent in high school lasted for six years, so that I would have been in the sixth and final year, and Eileen would have been in her first year, and unless I was planning to endure piss-taking from my classmates, there would have been no interaction between us whatsoever. Six years would also have been the possible difference between a young schoolteacher and an older high school student and a matter of both criminality and disgrace.

Eileen spoke again. "Do you realize that one day you'll be ninety-seven and I'll be ninety-one?"

"What makes you think either of us will live that long?" I wondered out loud.

"My family all live that long." She spoke these words proudly.

"Well, mine certainly don't," I replied ruefully, although my recently rejuvenated mother might well prove that last rash statement to be a falsehood.

"So if we do get to be that old, our ages won't matter much at all. We'll both just be really, really old people in our nineties."

I held up my margarita glass.

"A heartwarming thought. Here's looking at you, kid."

We clinked our glasses together.

"I'm going to pretend to be deaf when I get old."

"Why would you do that?" she asked.

"Pardon?"

"Very funny, you old fart," she snorted.

After dinner we went back to my house and sat bundled snugly together on my porch in two thick wool blankets, and Eileen got to sample her first-ever Belvedere beer. It should have been, by rights, a historic event, replete with hanging bunting and volleys of fireworks. While it wasn't anything like that, it was, however, a rather wonderful moment.

She sipped at it hesitantly. "This is the brown ale?"

I nodded and struggled to stop myself from grinning like a proud parent. "The Daphne and Hen. Did I mention I named it all by myself?"

"You did," she chirped. "It's very good." She pretended to swoon. "And such a lovely name."

I was hopelessly proud of Nye at that moment and was even, in a moment of hopeless delusion, able to wallow in a bathtub of self-administered kudos. I reflected that things were looking up. Eileen was going to spend the night. Her work day was to begin tomorrow at lunchtime and end at eight in the evening. We would be able to breakfast together and I would drive her home before she had to go to work. Things were going quite swimmingly.

"You need to know something, Tom." We had pushed our two chairs together and she was all but sitting in my lap. Yet the insertion of my name at that instant boded, I felt, quite poorly.

"We've only been out a couple of times."

"Very true," I expansively concurred.

"It's been wonderful."

She would certainly get no argument from me on that score.

"But I'm going to be in the spare room tonight," she said.

"I assume from that statement that I'm not getting any tonight," I concluded with badly concealed ill grace.

Eileen nodded solemnly.

She gave me a long and bitterly cruel kiss on the lips.

Then she spoke.

"It's too soon. I'm too drunk. Do you think you can wait a little longer for me?" she asked tentatively as we slowly pulled apart.

I responded stoically. "I suppose so. I might choose to have a wank."

She giggled out loud. "Were you hoping I wouldn't know what that meant?"

We kissed again and held each other under the blankets for a long while before retiring chastely to our separate bedchambers.

The restaurant on Pearl served thick crepes, and we both partook. Hers had all manner of fresh fruit and whipped cream. Mine came with ham and cheese and onions and green and red peppers. They both came with heaping home fries, and, since I was planning to loaf for the rest of the day, mine came with a half-price Bloody Mary.

"Did I smell burning hairs sometime during the night?" she asked me innocently.

I sneered at her. "No one thinks you're funny. You do know that, don't you?"

Eileen just smirked and ate a single strawberry with her hands, an act that came, I considered, with a little too much overt sensuality for my liking.

"Did talking with Tim help?"

I nodded. "More than talking with Larry did. And he was cheaper. They were both strange, but Larry was a lot stranger. I know much more about Travers than I know about Nitro."

"Is that a bad thing?"

I considered for a moment. "I suppose not," I finally admitted.

Eileen asked, "What do you know now that you didn't know before?"

I thought for a moment. "It seems that Andrew Travers was a sad man who might have died a little happier, and Nitro was a happy guy who maybe died a little sadder."

"That's something."

"True."

"Do you know why?"

I shook my head. "Not a clue."

"What's next?"

"I'm volunteering at Lazarus on Sunday night."

She looked at me but said nothing.

"Maybe someone there will tell me something new," I mused aloud, mostly unconvinced.

"Someone sleeping there or someone volunteering there?"

I shrugged. "I really don't care. Either. Perhaps both." But I spoke this without much confidence. Perhaps neither, I thought to myself.

We lingered for a while over our food. Later, after I dropped her at her house, I drove over to the Lookout, grabbed an *Onion*, sat down at the bar, idly cast my eyes over the assorted beer taps, and experienced a brief moment of heart stopping panic.

"Where's the Old Chub?" I managed to keep most of the quiver out of my voice as I spoke.

"We're serving Claymore instead," the young bartender cavalierly replied between cursory wipes at the counter with his towel.

After he stopped pretending to clean, he poured me one, which, cleverly noting my street duds, he served to me in a regular glass. I sniffed and then sipped at it suspiciously. It was very good. He looked at me in silent enquiry, and I slowly smiled, as the planet lurched back onto its rightful axis.

Later that same afternoon, with my frayed nerves largely salved, I rode along the creek path as the final glow of the early spring sun crouched down behind the Flatirons. I stopped at several places and hunched, still and chilly, once again eminently approachable and once again largely ignored.

At a point near Boulder High School, one of the many manmade culverts detoured under several low-hanging willows and passed alongside the ornate, lush green sculptured vegetation of the teahouse garden. From there the water dropped down, past a steep set of ten concrete steps, to a circular sitting area with tall wooden benches and wooden tables and a dull metal barricade holding the creek waters at bay.

The afternoon was rapidly siphoning away its slender reserves of residual heat as the early-spring darkness descended.

It was getting cold, and this would surely be my last stop of the day. I happen to like this particular spot. It's singularly manmade—concrete and water and metal and sidewalk—and feels urban and canal-like instead of elemental and nature-formed.

I heard him before I saw him.

"It's the last great adventure left to mankind." The voice was close behind me. It boomed, strident and painstakingly articulate, the words spoken slowly and clearly, the accent the kind of upper class mock-English accent that American actors employ in period movies to sound classy.

I turned in surprise toward the dark figure speaking. He wore a large flower on his head. Or rather, his head was encased in a large flower-shaped hood or hat or bizarre combination of both, which left his face bare and absurdly round in the center. The effect was weird and deliberately theatrical. The face was made up and pale and the eyes were paint rimmed a very dark shade. The body beneath the flower headdress was tall and thin and shrouded in a reddish brown robe that wrapped around him loosely, and was tied and gathered at the waist.

"Who are you?" I asked him.

There was a significant pause before he answered, "A giant hogweed."

"Do you have a name?"

"Rael."

"Did you say Real?" I wasn't sure if I had heard him correctly.

"Rael Imperial Aerosol Kid," he said, his tone becoming a little impatient.

"Should I just call you Rael?" It wasn't actually meant to sound facetious.

He nodded his head slowly and the giant petals flopped up and down. "It's the grand parade of lifeless packaging."

None of this made much sense. Yet the flower face stared at me expectantly.

Then Rael spoke, "And as his strength began to fail he saw a shimmering lake . . . "

There was a long pause. I waited. Then he began to chant again, "A shadow in the dark green depths disturbed the strange tranquility." Did the words sound as if they were memorized, as if they were being recited? Was this a famous speech? Should I recognize it?

"What does that even mean?" I was tired and growing colder by the minute.

"The two are now made one . . . by our command the waters retreat."

The words two and water drew my attention.

"What are you trying to tell me?"

He spoke much more loudly now, his baffling words evoking both an incantation and a plea that was passionate but still beguilingly elusive. He lifted both arms to the sky.

"There's an angel standing in the sun . . . and he's crying in a loud voice . . . this is the supper of the mighty one . . . Lord of Lords . . . King of Kings . . . has returned to take his children home . . . to take them to the new Jerusalem."

And with that last cryptic burst of quasi-apocalyptic prose, the flowered figure left me; I was alone, and the creek was a somber dark and the wind gathered strength and whispered melodramatically through the willow branches hanging low in the mannered grounds of the teahouse.

I felt as though I had received a warning, obscure and convoluted. I thought about water retreating and angels returning. The phrase lifeless packaging sounded like another way to speak of a body and a death. Some of the words were biblical sounding; some were less so. I didn't know what the flower man meant exactly, but his language was foreboding, and it left me feeling troubled as I pushed my bike along the path back toward home. It was too dark to see clearly, and I suddenly feared riding through the growing blackness.

It was a surprise to recognize "The Boys of Summer" by Don Henley playing loudly in Cygnet when I entered. I suspected some form of musical compromise between Natalie and her husband had been reached. She got to pick the song, and he chose the volume?

I raised a sardonic eyebrow at my barista.

"Best fucking song ever written about California," Jesse informed me curtly and defensively. I considered bringing up Randy Newman but decided against it. I also considered cattily asking if his wife had chosen the selection, but again the path of least resistance both beckoned and prevailed.

There was no question that Jesse was either mellowing or sucking up. He was getting his teeth cleaned and playing songs by ex-Eagles. What lay ahead, and more importantly, what did he think was in it for him?

I sipped my coffee and told Jesse of my encounter by the teahouse. "That was the Watcher of the Skies." Jesse poured my drink and simultaneously solved the mystery of the flower man for me.

"What was he wearing?" Jesse wanted to know.

"A flower hat, or a flower mask. Some kind of a flower. Something like that." I was clearly struggling.

My server smiled knowingly at my feeble powers of description. "He has three costumes . . . the flower hat . . . a fox mask and a red dress . . . and a kind of warty series of big round lumps that make him look like a cross between the elephant man and the Michelin Man."

"Why have I never seen or heard of him before?" I wanted to know.

Jesse shrugged. "You haven't lived here all that long."

"What do the words mean?"

"They're song lyrics."

"From real songs?"

Jesse nodded. "Do you remember Genesis?"

"The English rock band?"

He nodded again.

"The Peter Gabriel version or the Phil Collins one?"

Jesse smiled. "Gabriel. They were better then."

"I wasn't much of a fan of either," I confessed.

"Me neither. Before my time." There was a smug half smile to accompany that statement.

I ignored it. "The Watcher clearly was," I observed.

Jesse made no comment.

I asked a question: "Where does he keep his stuff on the creek?"

"What do you mean?"

"All his costumes?"

"In his place, I guess." Jesse looked a little puzzled by my question.

"He's not homeless?" I was momentarily surprised.

Jesse shook his head. "He lives in that cute little trailer park on Folsom in North Boulder. His name is Greg something. He's a former junior high English teacher."

"How do you know all this?"

"He's kind of a local character."

"What else do you know about him?"

Jesse took a deep breath. "He's close to your age. Maybe he's a little older. He was almost fired after an eighth grade kid, a boy, accused him of sexual abuse a few years back. The kid's parents threatened to sue. The school district began criminal investigations. This was a while back. The boy who accused him was apparently a nasty little shit, but his allegation was initially widely believed. Then his story began to fall apart. Remember it was a small town where all this happened. There was a hasty retraction, but by then Greg had had his name dragged through the mud. The school offered him his job back. He turned them down. They offered to make him the assistant principal. I think he planned to sue them but they finally offered to settle, to let him retire early, with all his benefits and his pension in place. So he took them up on the offer, he came here to Boulder, he buys himself a trailer home where he lives quietly and gets to creatively indulge his abiding passion for constantly quoting pretentious progressive rock lyrics from the mid-seventies."

"You mean Genesis?" I asked

"He was a really big fan back in the day."

"Clearly he still is."

Jesse nodded. "He's pretty much harmless. When he wasn't teaching, he used to sing in a Genesis tribute band. They were called Trespass. Apparently he can sing just like

Gabriel if he wants to. Ever seen a tribute band play?"

"I saw Lez Zeppelin at the Double Door in Chicago once."

"Some of these bands are as good as the originals."

I had to agree with him.

We both said nothing for a while. I had my hands wrapped around my coffee cup for warmth.

Then Jesse spoke up again. "What did you make of the things he said?" He looked at me shrewdly as he spoke.

"Why?" I asked him carefully.

"There are two schools of thought in Boulder on the Watcher. Some people think he's some sort of a savant who utters deep and abundant truths wrapped up in enigmatic ambiguity. Some people think it's just so much wordy bullshit that desperate people want to find meaning in."

I paused and considered my two options. "Some of the words . . . "

Jesse finished my thought for me. "Maybe made some kind of sense?"

"I wouldn't quite go that far."

"Weren't a load of total bollocks?"

"Wherever do you pick up these expressions?" I smiled archly.

Jesse said nothing but he smiled back nastily.

"There was some mention of water and endings and beginnings."

"Was there anything else?"

"There were also references to plants and shadows and lakes and two becoming one and something at the very end that sounded an awful lot like the Book of Revelation."

"So let me ask you again. Did it make any kind of sense to you?"

I thought hard. "I'm not really sure," I finally had to concede.

Jesse left me then to serve a man who wanted to know if Cygnet would honor a discount coupon from another coffee store. Choosing not to gawk at the tempting spectacle of an ugly train wreck in progress, I sat down at a table with my coffee far from the counter, and tried not to listen as Jesse tersely explained in some detail his policy vis-à-vis the honoring of competitors' promotional offers. He would win high marks for his succinctness and a decidedly low score in the areas of diplomacy and entrepreneurial acumen.

When he had finished and yet another Boulderite had sworn never to enter Cygnet again, Jesse came to my table and handed me a CD in a plastic case. I tried to read the writing on the disc, but it was impossible. I must have looked a little confused.

"Temple Beautiful," he said.

"I beg your pardon?"

"Chuck Prophet. You said you liked it."

Now I remembered. "Thank you."

"You are very welcome."

I thought of a question.

"Does the Watcher quote lyrics from solo Peter Gabriel songs?"

"You mean after he left the band, stuff like 'Sledgehammer?' That was a great song."

"It certainly was."

"Nope. Only Genesis songs with Gabriel. You gotta stay true to your convictions."

"Like not honoring competitors' coupons?"

Jesse smiled. "Exactly."

ELEVEN

On Sunday night I parked my car in the handicapped spot behind St. Andrews Episcopal Church on Sixty-Third at close to five-thirty. It was an officially sanctioned offense. I had been called the previous day and, amongst other instructions, I was told to park there. There was considerably more to this call; I was reminded that I was assigned to work that first shift on Sunday, and I was also informed that parking my car on Sixty-Third for a long stretch at night would very likely get me a ticket.

I hadn't realized until then that Lazarus House was situated so close to the Mexican restaurant where Eileen and I had recently dined.

Wylie was our shift leader, and he graciously let me in the back door of the church when I knocked. He had turned on all the basement lights and already set up an industrial-sized urn of grim smelling coffee. The basement was warm. There was a second urn filled with hot water on the counter, along with paper cups filled with plastic utensils, sugar packets, salt and pepper, teabags, stacks of plastic cups and plates, and the biggest bottle of Louisiana hot sauce I had ever seen.

The basement was partitioned into two uneven sections. The front, near the kitchen, was the smaller section, and was taken up by eight round tables with six folding chairs at each table. Or at least it would be, once Wylie and I got started laying them out.

Wylie was close to seventy, but he moved and talked at least a decade younger. He would get us started tonight then head on home for a while. He lived very close by, he told me, and was a retired American Airlines pilot who had never gotten around to getting married when he was a younger man. He would come back at the shift change at eleven and check in on us. Before he left he would also administer the breathalyzer test to the guests when they first checked in. The homeless were always to be referred to as guests, Wylie told me. The tester he used on them was, in his words, "a goddamn finicky piece of cheap crap," from which he claimed only he could obtain an accurate result.

Wylie's views on the test itself were also singularly blunt. "It's a goddamn waste of my time, and I've been stuck doing it for two straight years now, and trust me: I can spot a shitfaced drunk just fine without the help of science."

I was certainly inclined to believe him.

As Wylie and I pulled the tables and chairs from a closet, a small black woman materialized at our side and began to help. She told me her name was Shirley. I realized that she had let herself in at the back door, and that regular volunteers must all have keys to the place. She pulled a long rectangular table over to the side of the room and began to cover it in towels and soaps and deodorants and razors from another nearby closet. I noticed that every item of toiletry seemed to be in a really small size.

"Every good church member knows to borrow as much of this stuff as they can from hotel rooms when they travel," she explained with a sly smile. She had brought a brown paper bag with her. Inside were several packets of brand new white tube socks, all in size large.

"Everyone needs fresh socks," she said simply, as she tore open the plastic and made a neat pile of socks on the table. She wrote the words old socks on the brown paper bag and placed it on the floor nearby.

David arrived with a chunky Sony laptop tucked under his arm. He smiled at me and whispered his name and then wordlessly began helping me with the last of the tables and chairs. Wylie had meanwhile vanished. David kept on smiling gently as we worked. He was perhaps in his middle twenties and skinny thin with pale skin and badly thinning hair. After we pulled the last table out from the closet, he rolled out a cart with a boxy old television on it and plugged it into the wall.

"We get very basic cable," he whispered to me softly.

"Wylie, you need napkins out front!" David's shouting voice was surprisingly loud. "He always forgets something," he instantly reverted back to a default whisper.

"Got it!" I heard Wylie shout back from somewhere.

"And hot chocolate packets too!"

"Got it!" Was there a slight tone of exasperation I could hear emerging?

David and I finished the dining area and moved to the other side of the partition. A long storage room held single-size mattresses stacked on their sides. I pulled them out one by one and inexpertly began sliding them out onto the floor, where David and two other men I hadn't seen arrive began to arrange them quickly in four rows of ten.

David whispered to me and pointed quickly as he maneuvered the mattresses expertly. "That's Bruce and that's Michael." I wasn't sure which was which. I assumed it could wait. They both nodded to me and I nodded right back.

Michael or Bruce moved to another closet and pulled out

boxes of pillows and blankets. I helped with the blankets—one good blanket or two ratty ones per mattress. Shirley came over and told me this formula after she had got her toiletries table into pristine shape and she began to work on the sheets.

Bruce or Michael smiled at me and spoke quietly. "If Shirley does the sheets, they match, and each guest gets a nice fitted sheet for their mattress. If we do them, they don't ever match."

"Do they get a fitted sheet?" I asked.

"Their chances are pretty good."

In less than twenty minutes, forty mattresses stood in straight rows with all the bedding piled neatly on top. And everything matched, thanks largely to Shirley.

Michael introduced himself. He was stocky and thirtyish and very fair. He shook my hand. "Our guests like to make their own beds," he explained.

Bruce and I met Wylie at the side of the room where he had dragged another rectangular table close to the door. Under the table was a giant box, and Wylie was pulling documents and other stuff out of it. He extracted a huge white plastic binder, a stack of brown paper bags, a bottle of hand sanitizer, a selection of cheap ballpoint pens and three thick Sharpies held together with a rubber band, several sheets of plain white paper, and a very basic ten-year-old Fuji digital camera. Outside the door was a hallway and stairs that led, I assumed, to the outside of the church.

Wylie moved the stuff around and spoke as he worked. He pulled his cell phone from his pocket for a second and looked hard at it. Then he put it away quickly.

"It's a cold one today, so Wes went and took the bus over

to the creek. He's outside the church now. The bus is full, so we're going to be full. I'm going to let them in. You can come with me, Tom."

Wylie and I got to the top of the stairs and opened the door. It was very cold outside, and the blue Lazarus bus was parked only feet from the door of the church. There was a handwritten sign taped to the door.

ONLY GUESTS ARRIVING ON THE BUS WILL BE ADMITTED TO THE SHELTER TONIGHT.

Underneath, in smaller print, were the names, addresses, and phone numbers of several other Boulder shelters.

Wylie made a thumbs-up gesture to the bus, and the door swung open. I looked with some surprise at the bus driver.

"That's Wes." Wylie said. "We're twins," he added somewhat unnecessarily.

The bus emptied quickly. Wylie and I held the church door open as the guests filled the stairwell. When they were all inside, we pushed our way back down the stairs, with Wylie feverishly counting the assembled heads as he went.

They were mostly quiet as they stood on the stairs; they were bound and submerged deep inside their coats and hoods, but a few bare and scruffy heads began to surface as I elbowed and bumped my way past them. The smell was old clothes saturated with dirt and sweat. Most of our guests were white men. I spotted one older black gentleman with impossibly thick eyeglasses that left him bug-eyed and blinking in perpetual surprise. Then I spotted another. He was much younger, and he grinned at me. It was Devonte. I smiled back.

We got back inside the basement and left the guests standing outside in the hallway. Bruce sat down at the table and opened up the binder. Wylie pulled a Rolodex holder from the box and opened it up on the table. David went behind the counter where the twin urns stood and grabbed a huge bunch of keys then headed toward the locked bathrooms. Wylie sat down. Shirley walked over to the table and grabbed a pen and one sheet of paper. She sat down. Wylie pushed the Rolodex over to Michael who was standing close to him. Michael sat down. Shirley found a big fat brown Sharpie and arranged a pile of brown bags in a neat stack in front of her. Wylie looked at his watch before heading toward the side door. Then he turned around and came back. Bruce smiled and handed him the breathalyzer kit and he left again.

And I stood stupidly watching all this.

The guests entered and formed a single file line at the table. They were tested first by Wylie. Two guests failed. Bruce took the tester from Wylie and tried them both again. They still failed. Bruce introduced himself to me and asked me to get two cups of black coffee. When I returned, the two men were sent back into the stairwell to sit in seclusion with their coffees to wait and get themselves more sober and try the test again in half an hour. I noticed they were both highly amused by the whole process.

Bruce was thirtyish and stocky and dark. He watched them go. "These two have failed this plenty of times before. We're supposed to make a note of their names and send them away. Three times and they're supposed to be banned from the shelters, but Wylie is a ridiculously nice guy."

"Will they pass in half an hour?" I asked him.

Bruce nodded. "They always do," he said.

Those who tested positive for sobriety had their ID cards

taken and read and their information and photographs compared with duplicate entries in the Rolodex file. Their names and ID numbers were then written down on a master list in the binder. Each list was dated and saved. Underneath the sections for guest information was an area with a list of that night's volunteer names, their addresses, and their email and phone numbers. There was also a box at the bottom of the page where the shift leader could make his or her shift incident report.

I watched carefully as the information was recorded and the identification cards were returned. None of the guests offered banned cards. Everyone had their cards in order. Everyone got a bed, although two still stood empty, waiting for the drunks to lower their numbers with the application of time and black coffee.

Once the guests were given their cards back, they passed along the table. They were asked if they wanted a shower, and, if they did, at what time. Showers lasted for fifteen minutes and ran from eight until ten-thirty. Shirley recorded this information on a sheet of paper. They were also asked if they wanted a bag lunch tomorrow. This was two ham and cheese sandwiches, a banana, a bag of chips, and a can of soda. If they said yes, their name was written on a brown bag, again by Shirley, who informed me that the early morning crew had to prepare the bag lunches. When one guest requested no cheese, Shirley silently nodded as she made the appropriate notation on his bag with her Sharpie.

I asked her about the camera on the table.

Shirley answered me. "Guests with lost cards or no cards need to get themselves new ones. We take down their particulars and take their photo, and the cards get processed during the next week or so. But we never have to do this on a bus night."

After Shirley was done with them, the guests were free to head over to the beds or to her toiletry table and grab a pair of fresh new socks. One guest turned on the television and selected the football game preview. There seemed to be no objections to his choice. The volume was very loud, and Michael walked over and quickly turned it down. Most guests chose to get in line for a new pair of socks, and Shirley left quickly to police their distribution. I noticed that no one tried to take their socks until Shirley was at the table and ready to do business.

Wes came in through the back door, and he and Wylie wandered the room and helped guests find the last of the available mattresses. Wes went to the kitchen and pulled a huge plastic bottle of generic fruit punch from the fridge and began filling plastic cups, which Bruce carried to the tables. Wylie called the local police station on his cell phone and told them Lazarus House was open tonight and was completely full. David let a woman in at the back door. She brought a selection of new wool gloves in a large box. Shirley hugged her and took the box from her. The new socks were long gone, and Shirley laid out the gloves where the socks had been. The guests eagerly clustered around Shirley's table for a second time. Michael helped a young woman make her bed and found her a thicker blanket. Halfway through the process, she asked him something and he nodded. Michael and the woman picked up her bed and her bag of stuff and carried it across the room. Shirley sent me to look for more facecloths in a closet, and I came up empty. She told Wylie, and he made himself a note to request donations of more facecloths. Bruce carried two enormous hampers to the showers for the used towels.

I still felt utterly useless.

There was an alcove section of the room where three mattresses had been pulled over. All three were occupied, and I realized that the three beds in that section all had women sitting on them. Michael arrived with the fourth woman and her mattress. When the mattress was placed on the floor, the woman threw herself down on it. Michael knelt beside her and held her softly by her shoulders. I could see that she was silently crying.

"We usually try and make that part of the room a little more private for the lady guests to sleep there." Wes was talking to me. I wasn't really listening to him. I was studying the four women, looking for the tarot lady; but as much as I wanted her to be one of the four, she simply wasn't.

I turned to look at Wes. He really was in every aspect identical to Wylie.

"Do you always drive the bus?" I asked.

He nodded happily. "Usually I come in the late afternoons and drive the bus on all of the cold days the shelter is open. I only stay and work on the nights that Wylie and I volunteer for the first shift. Other times I just go home after I drive the bus here and get up early in the morning and drive the guests in the morning."

Wes was happy to talk some more about himself. "I taught high school science before I retired. I sub now at the elementary school for as many days as I can each school year without messing up my pension. Neither Wylie nor I got around to marrying when we were younger men. When I retired, they asked me what I wanted. Maybe a gold watch, they probably figured I would ask for. But Wylie and I talked about it and I figured what the heck, so I asked the school district to donate a bus to Lazarus House. Wylie and I have helped out here for years. It was way too much money, they told me at first. But some of the parents and kids heard about it. To tell the truth, I blabbed about it to pretty much anyone who would halfway listen. There were donations and there were car washes and bake sales, and we finally got the bus from the bus company, although, between you and me, they were pretty damn cheap about the whole thing. I like driving more than Wylie does, so I usually end up driving it."

Wes hustled away then to get three cakes out and thawing from the freezer section of the giant church refrigerator. When he returned, he told me they had been dropped off on Saturday by the fancy confectioners on Walnut who showed up virtually every day with a van filled with all the items ordered and not picked up for whatever reason: wrong name spelled out in the icing, too expensive a cake, not nearly expensive enough a cake. The guests at the shelter presumably cared little that the fine gateau they devoured at the end of their meal had been intended for Our Son Rueben on the Proud Occasion of his Bar Mitzvah.

And then, with little fanfare, the illustrious meatloaf arrived. There was a beautiful blonde woman and a pasty young man. They entered from the back door with flat trays covered with lots of little meatloaf tins. This tray cavalcade happened four times, and I was commandeered for the second trip onwards. Following the meatloaf procession came three deep pots, each filled with mashed potatoes, then came the green beans in two smaller pots, and lastly one pan filled with thick brown gravy.

I looked at Dora Walters every time she entered and left the kitchen. Why had I imagined a doughy amalgam of Mrs. Butterworth and Julia Child, or to be more accurate, Dan Ackroyd playing Julia Child?

Dora was perhaps forty and tall and stunning in tight skinny jeans stuffed into high-heeled brown leather boots. All her food came from the back of a shiny red BMW sport utility vehicle. The youngster helping her was perhaps twenty, runt-like and neo-gothic, and painfully shy.

There and then I experienced a singularly horrible thought. Perhaps Dora's attributes were purely physical rather than culinary. Perhaps we were all simply besotted by her perky sensuality and rendered incapable of accurately divining good vittles from bad. I prayed that this was not so, and the marvelous blend of aromas now emanating from the kitchen area seemed to back me up.

I looked at the kitchen clock as I put a meatloaf tray down. Ten minutes remained until dinner time. I turned back around. Dora and her son, later introduced to me as Dennis, had most of the counter not taken up with urns and condiments and utensils now covered with paper plates full of food.

I held my breath and licked my lips as Wylie bowed his head and mumbled a short prayer in the sudden silence before announcing, "Ladies and Gentlemen, dinner is served."

While it was all mouth-wateringly fine, the gravy was simply unsurpassed. It was piping hot, and I placed it in an artificial lake set deep inside the potatoes, where it served as a reservoir and dipping source for the green beans and the meatloaf. Dora's meatloaf was firm and contained, I believe, some strong hint of both red wine and Worcestershire sauce. The green beans were buttery and soft. The eating took place in almost total silence. Dennis got himself a plate and joined the volunteers around the same table where we had checked everyone in. Dora watched over us, folded her sculpted arms, and smiled. Our two drunks had pulled themselves together and were rewarded with heaping plates of food. Seconds were offered to everyone, and few passed.

I sat beside Shirley and watched her pack it away with palpable relish.

"Are you having seconds?" I asked her.

"No room," she replied sadly. "Also we try and hold back and let the guests eat more." She sounded for an instant almost resentful.

David was pulling multiple loaves of bread out of a freezer and setting them out to thaw. They would be used to make the lunch sandwiches in the morning. Shirley explained that on some mornings they would have a group of morning volunteers show up and cook a full breakfast for the guests. Other times cereal and milk and coffee and toast and juice were laid out by the morning shift. On nights where the guests ate well, cereal was usually offered. Meatloaf Sunday was just such a night, when most guests woke up still solidly stuffed. Either way, all breakfasts were served at seven.

Bruce cut up the last few meatloaves into thick slices and was walking around the room offering seconds. I picked up the gravy and a big ladle and followed him. I was learning. Bruce smiled softly at me. Michael followed us with the mashed potatoes. The green beans were apparently long gone.

After everyone had eaten, Dennis and Dora washed their

pots and pans in the kitchen. The rest of us threw all the plates and cups and utensils away, and Bruce wiped down the dinner tables. Shirley swept the floor, and at fifteen-minute intervals she shouted out the names of the next two showerees. The basketball game began, but a surprising number of guests headed straight to bed. Michael turned the lights down on the sleeping side of the partition. David made himself a hot chocolate and started writing his geology paper on his laptop at the check-in table. I pulled my iPhone out and was surprised to be offered free wifi, courtesy of the church. Perhaps that explained why so many guests were on their cell phones at various times during the night.

I asked David for the password. "Saintandy. One word. No caps," he softly whispered.

Wylie had left us without my even noticing. Bruce sat down at the table and watched the basketball game with Wes. Dennis brought out one cake, but got few takers. I put the rest of the cakes back in the freezer. Two guests in adjacent beds were shouting at each other and Michael moved them apart quickly. He also found another blanket for the crying girl and he sat with her for a moment. When the kitchen was spotless, Dora and Dennis left with a slight smile from Dennis and a big wave from Dora. There was a round of applause from the television watchers.

I tried not to watch Dora's rear end as it glided toward the back door, but failed miserably.

By nine o' clock the game was over. It was quiet.

Shirley only worked until nine, when her husband showed up to pick her up. Bruce, David, Michael, Wes and I were left with two more hours of the shift to go and not much left to do. A few guests sat and watched the start of a crime show set someplace hot and steamy in the Deep South and waited for their shower time. The hot chocolate was proving popular. The coffee urn stood barely touched.

At eleven, we would be relieved by two volunteers who would fire up a few laundry loads of towels and sit around until four. At four, the morning shift would arrive and lay out the breakfast, do more laundry, prepare the lunches, put all the bedding away, and get the guests onto the bus at eight-thirty if the temperature was still below zero. Wes would make several stops along the creek and across Pearl to let the guests off. He would also stop at the library. His ultimate destination was another church, this one in south Boulder, that housed a daycare facility for the homeless, with ping pong tables and television and bingo and no cooking facilities, hence the provision of the brown bag lunches.

When the last showers of the night were taken, Michael locked up the shower rooms and brought the towel hampers into the back of the kitchen where the washer and dryer were located. Wes checked the fridge inventory, discovered we were a gallon of milk short for the morning, and headed off to the local drugstore. Bruce turned the TV volume way down on the crime show that he and three guests were still watching without much interest. David kept right on working.

I sat at the table and opened the binder. I skimmed though the pages, moving backward through the past three months, to the beginning of January, and the very first page with an entry. Reluctantly, I closed the binder and moved away from the table.

At eleven Wylie returned, along with Dan and Alice Jones, a very elderly couple who relieved us. They arrived with two old battered thermoses, a thick paperback of Sudoku puzzles, two sharpened pencils, and the Sunday edition of the *New York Times*.

We gave our report. Two guys had been drunk. Now they were sober. We were full tonight. There were four ladies staying. Two guys had argued and been moved apart. Everything was now fine. There was a long pause. For some reason Dan and Alice looked a little concerned. They needn't have been, because, unbeknownst to me, Dora and Dennis had set aside two large plates of food for them to microwave later. At this news, the Jones's looked very much relieved.

We were now free to leave. Wes and Wylie lingered to chat with the two swing-shift volunteers, and the four remaining early-shift team members took our leave, waving to each other as we got into our cold cars in the church parking lot and drove away. Everyone thanked me for volunteering. Everyone told me they looked forward to seeing me there again next month. I said I would try to be a lot more helpful next time.

I began my drive home, but the brewery on Arapahoe, while nearly empty, was still open for another forty-five minutes.

I bought myself a brown ale and sat alone in the spartan taproom, which felt a little too much like Belvedere, and which therefore made me automatically think of Nye, such was the tactile process of free association. Nye had texted me earlier in the day to wish me well in my newest philanthropic endeavor. Eileen had also texted and told me to have some fun and not snoop too much.

I had met the volunteers at Lazarus, and no one had readily admitted to being a vicious hater and stalker of the city's homeless. I had dined with the guests and several had been clearly unhappy, but none had confided in me that a killing jag concentrated on their lowly compatriots was making them feel a whole lot better about themselves. I had wanted to peek longer in the big binder and finally confirm that Andrew Travers and Arthur Crowder a.k.a. Nitro had both been there on occasion and perhaps even on the Sunday nights before they had died. I had several other wildly untested theories that a serious perusal of the binder would surely illuminate. But sadly, none of this idle speculation had been possible to test.

I had hoped to encounter a discernable strangeness about Lazarus. Or to be utterly reassured by the wholesome spirit of charity that engulfed the place. I could then either fine-tune my sleuthing deductions or tuck all my misplaced fears away. All the evidence pointed strongly to the latter, but, unaccountably, or perhaps simply perversely, I still wasn't quite ready or able to walk away.

My beer was almost gone. I finished it, briefly considered another, and then talked myself out of it. I was tired and I wanted to go home. As I drove down Arapahoe, I looked on the bright side; I had now set eyes on the truly delectable Dora Walters, and partaken of her justly legendary meatloaf.

A text to Reggie Hawkins and a good gloat over both seemed like just the ticket.

TWELVE

I had spent my four-plus years in Boulder biking the creek path more days than not, but my last few weeks there had been somewhat more intense, if also more sedentary, largely a process of sitting and watching, always unrealistically hopeful that someone would break ranks and talk to me. I had always sensed that the place and the people operated by a series of unspoken rules that didn't quite apply to me. I was an outsider and would surely remain that way. I also assumed that my more focused presence of late had gone largely unnoticed by the denizens

I was quite wrong.

STAY AWAY FROM THE CREEK. STOP ASKING QUESTIONS.

The message was clear enough; written in painstakingly neat and anonymous capitals on a piece of clean white paper, folded carefully in four, it had been slipped under my front door sometime earlier that night, before I had returned home from Lazarus. There was a third and final sentence written underneath.

THE LIBRARY LADY WILL GET HURT IF YOU DON'T.

Naturally, there was no signature.

An hour later, all my attempts at sleep were fatally thwarted by a recurring loop of disturbing logic. They knew about Eileen. They knew where I lived. They knew what I was doing. They knew about Eileen.

In the morning I sat at my kitchen table and blearily stared at the email Nye had forwarded first thing. Somehow I was expecting some equally dark variation on last night's note. Perhaps they had my Belvedere email address, and more overt threats were winging their way across the internet to Chicago.

Once again I was hopelessly incorrect.

A young woman in Scotland had seen my picture in the Aberdeen newspaper after the beer trip and had contacted Belvedere. Nye answered most of the more general brewery electronic correspondence and had quickly forwarded this one to me. The reason, he informed me curtly and mysteriously, would soon become very clear.

The original email was a letter addressed to me. It was from one Lesley Cowie, a young woman of twenty-eight living in the town of Elgin in Scotland and working for the Scottish Forestry Commission. Her mother had recently died of liver and lung cancer. Alison Cowie had attended university in the south of England with me. We had stayed on the same coed floor of the same coed residence hall for our second year. Lesley had somehow verified all of these facts.

I had only put in two years of study there, left for America that second summer for an undergraduate extension course at a Chicago university, met my wife Patricia and her father Ben, and never returned to finish my studies.

Lesley Cowie informed me that Alison had become pregnant during her second year, had her baby girl, who was of course Lesley, stayed on, moved to the dorm rooms assigned to young single mothers, graduated with a first in some convoluted aspect of physics, and became first a postgrad student and then a lecturer in a university in the north of England, where Lesley had been brought up.

Alison had never chosen to marry. She had never

mentioned me by name. She had been unwilling to discuss the subject of Lesley's father. Lesley said her mum always laughed the subject away and described herself as a randy little slut in college and said that her dad could be anyone of the roughly five hundred inept but eager college men she had shagged silly. Lesley's email ended abruptly with her asking me to reply to her, either by email or phone. Her mobile and home phone numbers were both listed at the bottom of the message.

She had included an attachment to the text.

I clicked once, and I waited. A photo soon filled the screen. What was I expecting? A picture of Alison either as a college student or as a much older woman? But it wasn't her. Instead it was a young woman leaning against a tree, in dark woods, smiling broadly. She wore a T-shirt, and the straps of a heavy backpack cut into her shoulders. Her hair was long and curly and not quite blonde and not quite brown. She was freckled and outdoorsy and tan and grinning at the camera. I stared at her face for some minutes in disbelief.

I experienced two thoughts simultaneously. Either the Scots were adept at cloning more than sheep and had surreptitiously siphoned off a sample of my genes to use as a subject a few decades back, or someone had gone to the trouble of photoshopping an old picture of my face onto the body of a young woman forest ranger out for a woodland stroll one warm summer day.

Neither explanation seemed especially plausible.

There was therefore only one likely scenario.

I had a daughter.

Eight o'clock in Boulder translated to three in the

afternoon in Scotland. Ms. Cowie would be at work, perhaps analyzing pieces of bark or practicing putting out forest fires. I would wait three hours and call her at home. The landline connection would be free of echo and clearer, and I would not be disturbing her at a place where she might not be able to talk easily.

For a moment I indulged myself that this was all a laughable coincidence, a haphazard throw of the genetic dice that would pleasantly evaporate in the course of a charming conversation between two people, who just happened to look ridiculously alike, with one of the two being the daughter of a woman I had once known intimately enough for the likelihood of me being her father to be a perfectly rational possibility. Who was I kidding?

Alison Cowie and I were the only two Scottish kids on a corridor full of English university students. As if that geographic ostracization hadn't been enough, we were both also dejectedly aware that we possessed a lot less disposable income than the rest of the scholars on our floor. We both came from humble beginnings and had both benefited from the well-intentioned and soon-to-be-discontinued largesse of a Labour government, which, in more carefree economic times, had offered university attendance at close to gratis, paying the tuition fees and most other sundry expenses for students with the requisite number of higher qualifications and little chance of any parental financial support. My father was long dead and my mother worked two low-paying jobs. Alison's dad was a single parent and an importunate drunk, part of the second generation of unemployed ship-industry workers in the hushed urbanscape of the Greenock docks.

The town of Greenock had been wretchedly reborn as a haunted urban backdrop littered with tall cranes and acres of deserted factories, a sprawl of industrial wasteland once only a freight train away from the nearby Clydeside ports, which now stood in solidarity grim and silent and derelict. Her mother had died from cancer when she was young, and most of Alison's formative years were spent with her aunts and her grandmothers in a gloomy rotation of unrelenting charity when her dad chose to hit the bevy especially hard.

The other floor residents, indeed most of the student body at our university, were Oxford and Cambridge rejects, long in old money and overstated social grace while lamentably short in the requisite number of bona fide academic qualifications these other two venerable institutions had the sheer gall to actually require of the young and much-landed English gentry.

Alison and I were simply a sorry looking pair of clogged and lumpen proletariat, highland swine set before so many low-country pearls.

The first week of college was designated as freshers time. During the day various societies requisitioned the gym halls to recruit the newest students in tennis and rugby, anti-blood-sports societies, and clubs for those interested in young conservatism or creative anachronism. I had chosen tennis and squash in my first year and saw no reason to alter course now.

At night there was half-price beer in the student-run bar and all-night film shows, earnest retrospectives on Woody Allen and Humphrey Bogart. I opted for Bogey.

On Thursday night, the Clash rocked the packed student union long and hard. On Friday night we were treated to a disco, and at midnight Alison and I kissed each other tentatively, as the wily DJ offered the lust filled a slow song, the languidly dreamy, studio-smooth wash of 10cc's "I'm Not in Love."

We slept together the very next week in the thin wood-framed bed in my dorm room, with Robert Smith of the Cure staring gothically and nonjudgmentally down. I had persuaded two girls to sleep with me in my first year, while Alison had labored at hanging onto a long-term boyfriend named Mark back in Greenock, who was a plumber and lived at home and wrote her long serious letters that arrived every three days with depressing regularity. Alison informed me she was on the pill and I took her at her word.

We became an undeclared couple. Alison read sciences and I helped write her occasional class papers and patronizingly gave her books by Mervyn Peake and George Orwell to read (and doubtless despise). I read literature with a minor in history, and she guided me through my two required economics classes. She cooked and I washed the dishes when we ate together alone in the tiny kitchen we theoretically shared with the other students on our floor, who on rare occasions brewed up their imported teas there, but who mostly preferred to take their meals in town in one of a number of handpicked bohemian urban boites they thought deliciously grotty. Her father sent her next to nothing to supplement her grant. My mother sent me a generous check when she could, so I became the occasional sugar daddy; I bought most of our beers and our cigarettes and the lion's share of the food.

Alison studied much harder than I did. She applied early each year and obtained a study carrel in the sciences section of the university library, and she attended more lectures in a week than I slept through in a year. I sat in her room, which was tidier and much cozier than mine, and I waited for her to come home most evenings. Sprawled on her bed, I read and reread Mark's letters and tried to feel superior because there were numerous spelling mistakes, and his feelings came rushed and unencumbered by any collegiate coolness. He loved her and seemed quite certain that she loved him back. He was proud of her for going to the uni and was saving his money when he could. He had been to the building society and had enquired about a house and a mortgage. Mark was a year older than Alison and I, but his letters managed to vacillate between drippy adolescence and preternaturally dull adult sensibility. Feelings of smugness thus came both easily but cheaply.

I relished the notion of being a thief in the house of love.

Near the end of our second year Alison went back to Greenock to see Mark and to visit her dad in the hospital, where his liver was solemnly protesting its steady pickling in a lethal blend of Dewar's Whisky and McEwan's Export.

Alison and I had made no promises to each other.

I not-so-secretly fancied an ever-so-well-bred girl named Elsbeth Philpott from my agrarian history class; she invited me to a party in a remote village, where a trio of her second-year girl chums chose to rustically slum and live out, near where their horses were stabled. I should of course have known better. I stumbled like a plodding farmhand in a Victorian novel through a pretentiously ratty cottage with dark plastered rooms full of chinless tossers named Jeremy or Trevor who did something terribly tiresome in the city that was reputedly too dull to mention but that nevertheless was all they were able to talk about for hours at a time.

I spent the first part of a long night being ignored and supping hard from the keg of Adnams that graced the pitted oak table in the kitchen.

I never discovered whether Elsbeth was on a charity kick or there was some kind of scavenger hunt in play, where each big-toothed society girl had to produce a genuine prole for the night, to be revealed like some kind of party piece. Most of the party attendees were decidedly well heeled, but a smattering of riffraff like myself was on hand to provide rustic color.

In a gathering snit I stormed off to the local pub and played some serious darts in a tiny smoke-filled room, where mushy peas in vinegar were served in paper cups to several young men who were surely, in the view of Jeremy and Trevor, a better socioeconomic match for a young man of my questionable social standing. At some point in the beery evening I achieved an ideal alcoholic equilibrium of ease and accuracy, and three darts all somehow landed in the triple twenty spot to a chorus of loud cheers.

Drinks were henceforth declared to be on the house, and, for me, the night deteriorated pretty rapidly.

I came shakily to in a nearby field many hours later, dew-cold and hung over and faced with a bracing and solitary walk back to town.

Perhaps Alison learned of my foolishness while she was home and wordlessly disapproved. Perhaps Mark pitched his troth that little bit more forcefully in Greenock that weekend. Perhaps her father's declining health brought about the realization that our ill-defined relationship wasn't worth much of an investment. Whatever the cause, Alison and I drifted apart as our second year came to an end.

I applied for a summer exchange program to a university in Chicago, which improbably required only average grades, plus a well-written supporting essay that I was somehow able to generate.

I never came back to my studies or to Alison Cowie.

As I sat in my house in Boulder, at my table, and thought back nearly thirty years, it occurred to me that Alison may well have known she was pregnant by then. She hadn't said anything. In the years since, she had, as far as I knew, never tried to get in touch. Even when on her deathbed, she had told her daughter nothing. She had never married, either Mark or anyone else. She had told her daughter that she was promiscuous, but I seriously doubted it.

We had been two lonely and scared eighteen-year-olds, and we had liked each other very much for nearly a year.

But, as the song said, we weren't in love.

"Is this Lesley?"

It was six in the evening in Scotland when I called her. I had biked and swum and planned on lunching but was much too nervous for the last activity. I rode home quickly and picked up the phone and punched in the numbers before my nerve failed me. Lesley hadn't provided the international codes but I knew them from long years of transatlantic calls to my mother.

"Speaking." Her voice was lower than I expected, much lower than I remembered her mother's being.

What on earth should I say?

"Hello. This is Tom. I got your email. The one you sent to Belvedere."

"Oh." There was a long pause. "Good . . . I wasn't sure if it would reach you there."

"It did."

"Good."

This wasn't starting too well. I tried again.

"How are you?"

"I'm fine. Did you enjoy your trip to Scotland?"

"I did . . . yes. You live in Elgin I understand?"

"Yes. You were quite close to there."

"I was . . . yes." By my calculations I had only been about half an hour away when I was biking in Fochabers and I told her so.

"It would have been nice . . . " I ventured at that point.

" . . . for us to have met." She finished my thought for me.

I was surprised at that. "Do you want us to meet?" I asked her.

"Actually I do."

"You really do?" I must have sounded both tentative and absurdly pleased.

"You are my father." She spoke this fact simply.

"I must say the likeness is rather remarkable," I ventured cautiously.

She laughed. "It's a little more than that. Several people saw the paper before I did, and they all remarked on it. Did I know there was a man in the newspaper who was the spitting image of me? Had I seen it? Naturally I was curious."

"Naturally."

"You and my mum were lovers at university." It wasn't a question.

"We were together for most of our second year."

"But not as lovers?"

"I'm not quite sure."

"You were friends with benefits then?"

I bristled. "That phrase is a newer concept."

"But is it accurate?"

I thought for a moment. "I suppose it is, yes," I finally admitted.

There was a pause then. I wanted to say something that wasn't going to sound trite.

"Lesley, I never knew about you."

"Would you have wanted to know about me?"

"Very much."

"Do you have other children?"

"None."

"That you know of?" Was she teasing me?

"That's a little cruel."

"My mother did die last year from cancer." Was that to be the rationale for her harshness?

"I know. I'm very sorry to hear that."

"Her mother died very young from cancer, too."

"Yes. I remember her telling me that. Is her father still . . . ?"

"My grandfather died a long time ago from cirrhosis of the liver."

"I'm sorry." I seemed to be spending most of this conversation apologizing.

"So my genes would seem to indicate a rather short lifespan. That being the case, I thought we should know about each other." She paused. "Do you mind?"

"No. Not at all. I'm very glad. My father died young, too. I'm afraid my lifespan may not be too long either."

"Your mother?"

"She's still very much alive, and she lives with her husband in Spain."

"So I have a grandmother." She sounded pleased. I was oddly glad that she was.

"You do," I said. And she would be almost overcome with happiness to know that you exist I thought to myself, but didn't quite say it out loud.

"You live in Chicago?"

"No. Close to Denver. Much further west."

"But the brewery . . . " She was clearly confused.

"I'm more of a silent partner there."

"I see . . . "

"Would you like us to meet?" she suddenly asked me.

"Yes. I would. Very much."

"So what are you doing in May?"

Lesley explained that she was flying to Seattle for a conference then travelling for pleasure afterwards. Her plan was to fly to Seattle, then take a train ride after her business was concluded down through California, along the Pacific coast, then east across the country, through the Rocky Mountains, to end up in Denver, where she would fly back to Scotland via London. She already had her plans and her ticket.

"So you were already coming to Denver before you even knew I was here?"

"I'm afraid I was." Did it sound like she was smiling at the coincidence?

"Can you stay in Denver for a while and let me see you and show you around?" I asked impulsively, breathlessly.

"Are you sure you want to do that?"

I was. "Absolutely. You could stay with me."

"You might hate me."

"I'm willing to take that chance."

"The thing is, I already have my return ticket from Denver. We were only going to be there for a day."

"We?"

"I have a partner."

"You're married?"

"I'm a lesbian. I have a partner. Her name is Theresa."

"Can you both stay?"

"Don't you mind?"

Did she mean about two people staying? Or about them being lesbians?

I took a chance. "I'm just glad you have someone." And I truly meant every word.

She considered this. "We could try to change our return date."

"Please. Do it if you can. And if they charge you more please let me take care of it."

"We can afford to take care of it ourselves."

"I'd still like to. How long can you stay on in Denver?"

"I'm not too sure. Perhaps five more days?"

"I'd like that very much," I said.

"You know I think I would too," she said.

Our conversation ended with Lesley promising to look into changing her travel plans, and my promising to call her again in a few weeks. We said our goodbyes and hung up.

I sat for a while at the kitchen table afterwards, grinning inanely at nothing and everything.

THIRTEEN

The next few days passed uneventfully. There were no more notes pushed under my front door, and Eileen laughed when I continued to express my fears for her safety. When I offered to sleep close to her purely for protection she accused me of having shamelessly transparent ulterior motives. I naturally took slight umbrage at this.

The lady from Lazarus House called on Wednesday and asked me to work the second shift that Sunday. It was generally a two-person gig, but both the scheduled volunteers had canceled at the last moment. She had already made several calls and, so far, she had no other takers. I said yes without any hesitation, and she sounded quite relieved.

I asked her what the second shift entailed.

"It's really just babysitting, Tom," she told me. "You run a couple of loads of laundry, and then you just sit around. You can watch television with the sound down low, or you can read. We have wifi at the church, so most of the younger volunteers bring their computers and get some work done. You can listen to music on headphones. Sometimes guests get up during the night and sometimes someone gets upset about something, but most of our guests just sleep right through the night, and you have nothing much to do. The weather forecast is for warm weather that night so the place should be very quiet. The team captain will be there at eleven to check you in, and he can answer any other questions you might have. The morning crew will be there at four to relieve you and you can go home then."

I told her I would be happy to help out. She thanked me

and, as before, she told me to have a blessed day.

Nye called me later that day. We had texted back and forth as usual, but my sudden exposure to fatherhood had yet to be broached. That he was calling rather than texting hinted that serious conversation was in the offing.

"She looks very much like you," he volunteered after a few awkward attempts at pleasantries.

I snorted at that. "That's putting it mildly."

"How do you feel?"

"I'm pleased. I think."

"What is she like?"

"She seems very nice. She's a lesbian. Did you know?"

"How would I know that?"

"Some form of gaydar?" I knew I was being mean.

Nye sighed loudly. "That's largely a myth."

"Really?"

He signed again. "And if there was any truth to it, I certainly wouldn't admit it to a gabby breeder such as yourself."

I told him about the note.

"Were you aware you were being followed?"

"I don't think so."

"Are you worried about Eileen?"

"Yes."

There was a long pause. "Is this something serious?"

"She'll never replace you."

"That's very sweet. Tell me. Does she care for our beer?"

"She does."

"Then you have my approval. Endeavor to keep her safe at all times."

"Will do. How goes the hunt for the perfect stout?"

"If you must know it goes quite badly."

"Why don't we just shamelessly rip off Left Hand?"

"The thought had crossed my mind."

"Persevere Noble Nye."

"I shall certainly endeavor to do so, Gentle Leader."

We both hung up at the same time.

Both the pool and the hot tub at the Lookout were closed for heater repairs that were supposed to be completed in one day, but the young man behind the front desk was not terribly optimistic.

I rode my bike to the Hill and ordered a burger at the Sink and read the dated cartoons and graffiti covering the low ceiling in the back room while I waited for my food to arrive.

After lunch I bought a Mountain Goats CD in the basement record store across the street then went upstairs to the concert box office and looked at the list of live acts coming to the Fox Theater. I realized I still hadn't asked Eileen about Admiral Fallow. I certainly should. The rare opportunity to have a partner at a concert shouldn't be squandered.

When I moved my eyes away from the chalkboard list of bands to look out the street-level window, a figure in a red sweatshirt moved quickly and furtively away. Had he been standing there watching me? What else could he be looking at? Had he been there for very long? Was this my phantom note writer?

Out on the sidewalk he or she was gone. I ran half a block to the corner and looked to my left. A red-hooded figure was descending the steps that led to the Broadway underpass that in turn led to the CU main campus on the other side of the busy road.

My bike was still chained up outside the Sink. Should I run down to the underpass and probably lose him, or go back and get my bike, give more leisurely chase, and lose him for sure?

Neither option offered much possibility for success.

I tried to think. Perhaps I was quite wrong. The man in the red sweatshirt was so far guilty of nothing except looking in a shop window that I happened to be standing in.

But I wasn't at all convinced of his innocence. The window in question faced onto a set of stairs that led all the way down to the record store and all the way up to the box office, and it had offered a choice view of nothing except me. I had been recently threatened, and something about the color of his clothing registered on the distant edge of my awareness and left me suddenly uneasy.

I walked quickly back to the bike.

Both of my tires were completely flat. Kevlar tires are pretty hard to puncture without using something seriously sharp, but letting the air out through the finicky Presta valves is a piece of cake, and a lot more innocently done on a crowded street, in a town chock full of rabid bike lovers attuned to every conceivable possibility of cycle cruelty.

Two blocks from the Sink was a bike shop. In fairness, two blocks from pretty much anywhere in Boulder is a bike shop. I walked the bike there and they quickly pumped up my tires well past the recommended high pressure point. We waited for the tires to deflate. They didn't. My offer to pay them something for their trouble was waved away, and

I was on my way, fully inflated, but with growing concerns.

Back at the Broadway underpass the figure in the red sweatshirt was nowhere to be seen. I stood impotently for a while before I crossed under the road and took Broadway back down the hill, past a crowded Starbucks located in a former gas station, a small chalet-style motel that had always been a small chalet-style hotel, and a pricey outdoor gear shop that had once been the site of a cheap takeout pizza restaurant, to the creek.

I rode back home without stopping.

The next morning dawned warm and sunny and fresh and infinitely better right from the start. No new threats had slithered under my front door. I still had fully inflated bike tires and a shiny new daughter to think about, and the ever-lovely Eileen was sitting on my porch looking disgustingly fresh, wearing a fetching pair of short shorts, drinking one of two coffees procured from Jesse, reading an *Onion*, and giggling girlishly to herself.

I kissed her. "Did you plan on announcing yourself at some point?"

"I had you figured for an early riser." She kissed me right back.

"I might have been entertaining," I admonished her firmly.

"I elected to live dangerously," she responded, handing me one of the coffees.

I fired up my laptop, found Lesley's email, opened the photo attachment and clicked. Her picture opened instantly and I repositioned the computer so Eileen could see it better.

"I apparently have a daughter. This is her. Her name is Lesley Cowie. She lives in Scotland. She loves trees and a woman named Theresa. She's coming to Denver in May. I never even knew that she existed. And now I do." I was quite breathless.

Eileen stared at the photo for a long time. Then she smiled at me. "You have a daughter." She spoke the words softly.

"I do. Her mum and I went to university together when we were very young. She was supposed to be on the pill. She's dead now."

"You really do have a daughter." Her tone was marveling.

"I just told you that."

"You always wanted to have children."

"I did. I do." I sounded momentarily cretinous.

Her face turned unreadable. "This will sound stupid."

"I seriously doubt that."

"It will. I can't even say it."

"Say it."

"No. I can't."

"Say it."

She smiled. "Must you pry?"

I smiled back. "I must. I must."

"Okay then." There was a pause.

"Don't you dare laugh." There was another pause.

"Will you share her with me? When she comes here to stay? Even if we're not still together? I want to have a daughter for a while."

I answered. "We will still be together. Don't you think so? Why on earth wouldn't we still be together?" I was drifting from idiocy to a slapdash bout of insipid dithering.

Eileen countered with some verbal meanderings of her own. "You never know. I hope so. Perhaps we will. So will you share her if we're not?"

"Do I have to?" I pretended to whine.

Eileen was suddenly firm. "You absolutely do."

Eileen had the beginnings of two large tears escaping from her eyes as she hugged me. The hug was clearly designed to stop me from seeing them. It was a pleasant diversion, and I was more than okay with it.

My hands somehow tangled up in her hair and we kissed and held on to each other for a long time. When we finished she pulled away and she spoke seriously.

"I do want to share your daughter with you if you'll let me."

I said nothing but I nodded and pulled her close again, kissing her hair, and the top of her head, smelling her shampoo, which was orange citrus and sweet.

"I did tell you I wanted to have children."

"You did."

"Is she nice?"

"I can't really tell yet. I think so. There will be two of them coming to stay. We could have one each."

Eileen said nothing but squeezed me hard in annoyance. She looked at me and her face offered up all of her exposed need.

"Promise me you'll share," she spoke quietly.

"I will."

"Say it."

"I promise."

"Good."

I wasn't quite sure how to interpret the last minutes of our conversation. It had all sounded simultaneously playful and serious; as if some sort of major relationship milestone had been hesitantly but successfully navigated, without too much serious injury but also without full disclosure or complete clarity. I had the overwhelming sense that I had committed to much more than I was aware.

Unsure whether I should let the moment linger or try instead for lucidity, I told Eileen about the note and the figure in the red sweatshirt and my belief in their correlation.

She didn't seem all that surprised. "The people on the creek are a little society unto themselves. You're stirring things up in their world, so naturally someone has noticed and doesn't like it much."

"Is that someone the killer?" I asked her.

"What do you think?"

"I don't know." I spoke truthfully.

Eileen shrugged. "Me neither."

"I'm sorry I got you involved."

"Don't be."

"I'm worried about you."

"Shut up," she said. "Let's run through all the dismally pathetic conspiracy bullshit you have concocted so far."

I laughed. "That's my girl."

Eileen took my laptop away and I pulled out my cell phone and we sleuthed away in silence for a while. She accessed newspaper articles for this year and last, and I played with a weather watch website that tracked past weather for this and last year. We both made electronic notes, saved everything we could, and sent copious copies to each other. Both our coffees quickly grew cold without us noticing.

"You get to go first," I said, after a long silence broken only by flurries of furious typing.

"Okay. A grand total of two deaths on the creek this year so far. Both were flood related. Both were homeless folks. Both were accidental, according to the police. Your turn."

"Four major creek floods reported this year."

"So why not four deaths, Sherlock?"

"Beats me. Any cunning theories, Watson?"

"Nope. Want to hear about last year?"

"Oh, I surely do."

"There were three deaths on the creek in total last year. One was a heart attack on a bike. One teenage girl was raped and strangled. One homeless guy was beaten to death by another homeless guy after they argued over ownership of a sandwich."

"Must have been a good sandwich," I observed.

"No flood deaths?" I asked.

"Not last year."

"Reggie said they do sometimes happen."

"He's right. They do. I've read about them before."

"Did you check further back?"

She nodded. "The year before that the creek flooded only twice. Once was pretty major, and a homeless old lady passed out drunk and she washed away. Plus a young local guy on a bike slipped and fell, hit his head, and he drowned too. His wife said he really liked to race his bike really fast in the rain on really warm stormy nights."

I spoke. "The creek is flooding more times each year."

"Global warming?"

"That's pinko commie talk," I countered.

"Four floods so far this year averages out to more than one a month. That's way more than usual." She did have a point.

"Two flood-related deaths already in a year are also above average."

She nodded but said nothing.

"Are we crazy?" I asked her finally.

"The guy in red writing you nasty notes doesn't seem to think so," she answered.

"The note writer and the guy in red may not even be the same person."

She conceded my point. "That's very true."

"The note writer, the guy in red, and the homeless killer may not even be the same person."

She again conceded my point. "That's also very true."

Eileen continued. "Do we have any more bullshit theories to consider?"

"The two dead guys both stayed at Lazarus House."

"That probably true. But then most of Boulder's homeless have stayed there at one time or another."

"The place seems nice enough."

"Do you think the cold weather is a factor?" she asked.

"You mean beyond making it snow, so that the snow eventually melts and makes the winter floods that much bigger?"

"Right."

"Probably not."

Eileen changed the subject abruptly. "I hear Meatloaf Dora is quite the babe."

"I hadn't noticed."

I employed a diversion of my own. "Don't you have work

today?"

"I start late."

"Good. Breakfast?"

"Maybe later." She hesitated. "You could take me upstairs now if you like."

I was pleased but curious. "Why today?"

"I don't know. I was thinking about the other night. I'm not sure what I'm saving myself for. Also . . . " She hesitated.

"Also?" I pressed.

"I don't know. Maybe hearing all about threats and surprises like children you never knew you had. I suddenly feel a lot more fragile. And a lot more alone. And you never know," she smiled, "maybe you'll get me pregnant, too."

"It was a long time ago," I smiled back.

She replied, "Stop making excuses."

Eileen stood up then and took my hand. I followed her up the stairs.

"You realize I'm wearing my booty shorts?"

"I hadn't noticed."

FOURTEEN

Cygnet closes its doors at eleven-thirty most nights and ten-thirty on Sundays. The café was almost empty when I arrived, just two women on cell phones sitting at separate tables, with less than ten minutes left until closing time. Natalie was behind the counter with her laptop open and Jesse was nowhere in sight. I was relieved. I had smelled the coffee they brewed at Lazarus House, and I wasn't ready to force it down anytime soon. I needed my thermos filled for a long night on the Lazarus second shift. It was an old-school Starbucks model, more exposed metal than the original dark blue paint, but the ubiquitous mermaid logo was still visible, and Jesse would have been more than happy to seize my battered flask as a prop for a nonconformist rant against the sins of the corporate world.

In retribution, I couldn't wait to tell Jesse what Larry the homeless guy thought of his macchiato.

Jesse wasn't really being fair. It was a very old thermos. I bought it before coming to Boulder. I was a much younger man then. It still worked fine.

I had already prepared all my possible lines of defense, and I was almost sorry he wasn't there; almost sorry.

"He's not here." Natalie was listening to "Million Dollar Bill" by Middle Brother. "He's home nursing Rose."

"What happened?"

"She had glaucoma surgery on one eye on Friday."

"They can perform that on dogs?" I was blissfully unaware.

"They can even perform it on old dogs for stupid-as-shit

owners who enjoy throwing away their money."

"You weren't in favor?"

Natalie slowly shook her head. "Rosie's old and has another good eye that the vet isn't too worried about. She sleeps most of the time and doesn't need to see all that much. The pressure in her eye can be controlled with drops, so she isn't in any pain. It cost us several grand for the operation. Putting an old dog under anesthetic was a big risk even though she came out of it just fine. They can't even tell yet if the operation was a success or not."

She abruptly brought her cascading rationales to a halt and finished filling my thermos. She expertly topped it off with a dash of milk and a little brown sugar. She looked at me to confirm that she had the proportions right. I nodded sharply once and she nodded once back. She screwed the thermos tightly closed and handed it back to me.

"He's a big fucking softie," Natalie said, and abruptly burst into tears.

Takes one to know one, I thought to myself.

It was clearly time to leave. She tried to wave one arm in some kind of feeble blubbery protest as I put ten dollars into the tip jar and began to beat a hasty retreat.

The two women had already departed.

I looked around as I left.

Cygnet was empty, and suddenly it felt even emptier, without the large presence of Rose, her massive chest unhurriedly rising and falling, her big soft body flopped inconveniently under several tables either inside the café or out, and even, on several occasions, hopelessly wedged somewhere in the no man's land between both.

I hoped she'd be okay.

Lazarus had only eight guests on this warm Sunday night, and the room with the tables and the television set stood empty and quiet at just after eleven. The first shift left just as I arrived—two men and two women who looked bored but waved and smiled at me as they headed for the back door. The shift leader was an elderly black gentleman named Eric who hung around to help me get organized. We threw a load of towels into the Maytag washer in the back of the kitchen. Eric unwrapped the chili, the macaroni and cheese, and the huge slab of cornbread left in the fridge, and we microwaved it for my late dinner. The lady on the phone had instructed me to come hungry. There was some diet Pepsi and ginger ale left from the earlier dinner, and he obligingly poured me a large paper cup of each.

When Eric left, I plugged my laptop into the charger and used the church wifi to access the internet. As I ate the hot chili, which I moated in the center of the homemade mac and cheese, I pulled the big binder across the table and began searching through the past three months in the life of Lazarus House.

I began with the guests. I looked first for full nights and matching guest lists, and I pulled weather records up on my laptop. Andrew Travers stayed at Lazarus often and seemingly at random, unless choosing the days when meals he liked were served could be called a logical pattern. The site reports didn't mention what food was served, although they did list the names of the meal servers for each night. Andrew's last stay at Lazarus was on the Sunday before he died. Dora Walters and Dennis Walters were the meal servers that night. There were ten other guests sleeping over; three volunteers worked the early shift, two on the second shift, and three in the early morning. I wrote all their names down. The report for the shifts listed no major events, although one guest had reportedly stayed up most of the night, unable to sleep. He was identified as Andrew Travers.

My weather website recorded a low temperature of only fifty-one degrees that night. More than warm enough for most of the creek dwellers to stay out and sleep rough, and more than warm enough to explain the low attendance that night, even with the promise of meatloaf.

Using the same website, I pulled up a list of all the nights with overnight lows below freezing in the past three months. Ten evenings were listed in addition to the last Sunday when I had first volunteered. None were Wednesdays. The other days of the week were represented by three Mondays, three Sundays, one Tuesday, one Thursday, one Friday, and one Saturday.

I wrote down all the dates of the freezing nights and tried to cross-reference them with the Lazarus reports. Arthur Crowder a.k.a. Nitro showed up on two occasions; both were Sundays, once just before he died early in March, and once before that, in the middle of January. Andrew Travers wasn't there on any of these nights. He was already dead by March, and the meal servers in January weren't the Walters, and presumably their vittles weren't worth him getting on the Lazarus bus with Wes behind the wheel and the doomed Nitro somewhere onboard.

I thought suddenly of the cold night I had driven Devonte and the other two guys to the South Boulder shelter. I found Devonte's name listed on several cold nights but on none of the Sundays. His last name was Williams, and he had managed to miss Dora's meatloaf all year so far.

A small plastic box held a Rolodex file of guests' photographs, which I remembered were checked against the ID cards when they entered the shelter. I found Devonte's card. He was smiling in the photograph. I even found Daniel, the guy who was banned. His card was rubber banded with several others and placed in the back of the box in an envelope with the word BANNED curtly written across it. I found Andrew Travers and Arthur Crowder. Their cards were still active. Neither man was smiling in his picture. Travers looked worried in his shot, whereas Nitro simply looked stoned beyond belief.

I went back to the entry for the last Sunday of Nitro's life and read through the list of other guests that night. There were three women's names, which I wrote down. The first name matched the photo of a black woman who looked very old and weathered but who might be considerably younger than I imagined.

I hit pay dirt with the second. Evangeline Tully was the tarot lady, and now she had a name.

I had also noticed something. Working the soup kitchen in Chicago with Nye, I had met the same customers over and over again. Nye said the same thing happened in the suburban shelter where he now volunteered. The same people in terminal need, over and over again. The transient were remarkably and tragically permanent. But in Boulder, the names kept varying. Andrew Travers had been about as close to a regular as Lazarus House got. The other names kept changing as people presumably moved on.

It would have been pleasant to imagine that their situations improved—a new house to live in or a new job to work at. But perhaps they didn't. Perhaps poverty only took their misery and relocated it.

I chose to focus on the three cold Sundays and then added, on impulse, the one warm Sunday when Andrew had stayed and last Sunday, another freezing one, when I had worked the early shift. I wrote down the names of the volunteers for all three shifts for all five nights and read the incident reports.

I already knew about the sleepless Travers in February.

In January one drunk had repeatedly failed the breathalyzer all night, and the Boulder cops were eventually called and asked to provide alternative accommodation. This they had willingly done. The offender's name was duly recorded. It meant nothing to me.

The notes from the night in March mentioned that a guest was crying and very upset right before dinner but that he had recovered by bedtime. There was sadly no name recorded.

I remembered Evangeline the tarot lady and her recollection of Nitro's inner sadness. I thought about Dora's wonderful cooking and wondered at its possible redemptive powers.

Last Sunday's report merely stated that two drunks had gotten their collective shit together in time for meatloaf. I thought some more about my first night at Lazarus House and tried to recall if there was something else I was missing.

I was left with more questions than answers as I opened my flask and drank the first hot cup of coffee of the long evening.

Fortified by caffeine, I began to concentrate on the volunteer lists.

Again I was struck by the level of transience. People were simply too busy and stretched too thin to be able to volunteer consistently. Yet they all still managed to help when they could. I went though the list starting from now and working backwards until the start of the year. I saw no discernable pattern. I focused again on my cold Sundays. I added Andrew Travers' last Sunday and a few names did begin to repeat.

On my laptop I found the flood dates for the past three months. I matched them up in their close proximity to Sundays, both cold and otherwise. I pulled up a calendar app on the iPhone and electronically circled floods and deaths and Sundays and below freezing cold. I wrote down the names of volunteers for each Sunday and I underlined their names in different colored pencils that I found in a drawer in the kitchen.

I had the last of the chili and sucked the flat dregs of the ginger ale from the plastic bottle and threw it away. Then I stared at my circles and calculations and papers and screens for a very long time.

Then I had a thought.

Actually I had two thoughts, but the first one was desperate and quite clearly insane.

The second thought was to take a break from conspiracy and search for references to my newfound daughter.

There wasn't terribly much—a presentation made to a government agency in London and a co-credit for a paper on deforestation in the Scottish highlands that was cited extensively at a conference in Bruges. Still, I found myself obscenely proud of her for both.

While she lived in Elgin, her office was located close to the village of Findhorn, on the coast of Scotland.

Findhorn showed up in two searches. It was the site of a new age lifestyle convention center year-round and a thriving sailing club operating in the summer months.

Findhorn also brought back memories of the time I had escaped the clutches of Jesus.

The beach at Findhorn extended a long way, with white shells coarsely ground into the harshest sand, a protracted crescent of naturally occurring harbor, and the deepest water for fifty miles in each direction. The camp had been run by an organization called the Wayfinders Mission, who were a rotating fifteen or so indifferently Christian young people from Milngavie, a snooty suburb of Glasgow, who chose a different Scottish seaside town each summer for their operation, putting up a half dozen tents and ministering to heathen campers aged thirteen and fourteen.

My mother had seen the Wayfinders sign under yellowed glass outside our local church and, on an unlikely religious whim, had signed me up for a week in August, at the tail end of the school holidays. I was to be a very reluctant fourteen-year-old camper.

In addition to the marginally wholesome fifteen there were also co-Camp Leaders Katherine and Kevin Ogilvie, the dementedly evangelistic parents of two of the campers, and Mrs. Temple and Sandra Temple, her resplendently crimson-haired slag of a daughter, who cooked and cleaned up in the one big tent where we ate three solid meals of lumpy consistency, held a dull-as-dishwater daily Bible study, sang the few simple love songs to Jesus that Eddie Ogilvie, their lumpen galoot of a son could just about play on an unforgiving Eko twelve string, and played cards and listened to music when the contrary highland weather turned against us.

There were about fifty campers, evenly split between boys and girls. There were six tents, three for each sex, with eight or nine kids in each tent and two young Wayfinders assigned to each and acting as tent leaders. In our tent we were blessed with Eddie and Malcolm Chisholm. In a time and a place predating any attempt at correctness, we quickly and cruelly consigned Eddie to the lowly ranks of the simpleminded. He was hideously cheerful and never wavered In his simpering doe-eyed love for Jesus and his insane conviction that our swearing, farting, smoking, tent-pole-shagging selves were ultimately glory bound. Malcolm knew better. He plundered our fag stash and told us in graphic detail what he planned to do with that barry wee red-heided ride Sandra Temple the first chance he got.

Malky soon made good on his lurid threats, and we caught him getting the finger outside our tent late one night. He had Sandra captive in the tent ropes with her back to the front of the tent and her jeans and Top Shop underpants down around her knees. Malcolm saw us over her shoulder and he winked at us. When he was finished he told Sandra to pull his cock out of his trousers and gie him a wank.

Thankfully Eddie slept the sleep of the sinless through the whole performance. He was a back sleeper and his loudest snore managed to coincide with Malky's low grunt of release as he shot his load on the dew-wet grass.

Malky let us listen to his tape recorder when he wasn't

using it. He had cassettes of late Mott the Hoople, post-"All the Young Dudes," some pre-"Ziggy" Bowie and *Houses of the Holy* by Led Zeppelin. I had brought a paperback of Tolkien's *Lord of the Rings* in one thick daunting volume, and I walked into town and bought apple juice and chocolate bars with raisins from the seaside café. I read on my sleeping bag at the end of the day in the dawdling twilight, after hiking and playing, but before gospel studying and singing along with ten-thumbed Eddie in the evening, before piss-weak cocoa at bedtime and volleys of midnight farting and the whispered mucky tales of Don Juan Malky soothing us into a sordid slumber.

Our days were long games of hiding and discovering, long nature treks over field and stream, long football games on a flat pitch as much cow shit as grass, telling camp girls we fancied them in elaborately staged affairs of meaningful looks and secret notes and proxy messengers of desire that always dissolved into nothing. Meanwhile Malky bragged in the darkness of getting a good gamming from Sandra while thick Eddie slept on.

I never did find Jesus in Findhorn, although, to be fair, the beach is one of the prettiest on the planet, especially when the orange-red sun finally sinks down below the flat water horizon, and the masts of the sailboats point straight and still and black into the darkening sky, like a charred forest of empty crosses.

A fortnight after coming home from the Wayfinders Mission I dreamt about Sandra Temple, and my mother changed the sheets on my bed that next morning and washed them, hanging them on the clothesline in our tiny garden on a windless Thursday morning before she left for her cooking and cleaning work at the school.

My mother never washed on a Thursday, and the sheets hung wet and limp in silent rebuke all day long.

It was long ago.

Now I was somewhere between awake and asleep, between the teenage lips of Sandra Temple and the beach at Findhorn at the dimming of the day, watching the gulls scream and scavenge at the low stern of a returning fishing boat, listening to Eddie sing and cry all at once, with his true moronic faith, his two pathetic rivulets of dirty tears slipping down his shiny smooth cheeks.

Can it be true the things they say of you? You walked this earth sharing with friends you knew.

When the morning crew showed up at four, I shook myself fully awake and reported a night without incident. They thanked me for helping out and I stumbled off home soon after.

Half an hour later, unaccountably wide awake and simultaneously dog tired, I lay on my couch in the darkness of the early morning, staring at the living room ceiling, and waiting for the sun to come up.

When it did, I revisited my first thought—a shiny, newfound theory on the occasions of madness and related death on the creek. While it was unquestionably leaky and spurious and, until the next flood, utterly impossible to prove, I had nothing else. I considered revealing my slight suspicions to Eileen, who would be sympathetic and a good sport, and/or to Reggie the cop, who would be disbelieving for all kinds of rock solid reasons and would be more inclined to make good sport.

The basic iPhone weather app could do none of the retro digging I had performed last night. But it would tell me when the next flood might happen. Today was the ninth of April, and very heavy rain was predicted for the night of the twelfth.

So, to test the validity of my conjecture, I needed to be patient and wait until then. It should be possible because, if I was right, the killer had waited even longer.

FIFTEEN

Goss Street was waterlogged and empty in the driving rain that had poured down for most of the past twenty-four hours and was growing even stronger as the day ended. I turned on the car engine to charge up the iPhone. I also checked the weather forecast. It was unseasonably warm. It had rained all yesterday. It was raining now. It would rain all night, and the creek was scheduled to flood at around eight o'clock. It was just after five on the afternoon of the twelfth and it was already dark.

His house was small and unremarkable on a quiet road of mostly student rentals—anonymous multiunit buildings and scruffy stand-alone bungalows with peeling paint and wild unkempt yards filled with weeds and wildflowers and rusted bike parts. His house was a sunburned antique white and stood on the left-hand side of the street. His car was a white late-model Honda Civic anchored in the mud of the circular driveway at the front of the house.

An empty Yakima bike rack was attached to the roof of the car. The fence on one side of the house needed painting, but the last of the wood color matched the house next door in both shade and condition. There was a hairline crack on the back bumper of the car and a sticker for a winter blues festival in Aspen.

The house was better tended than most of the others on the street. Two tall fir trees stood side by side and formed an acute angle where they intersected in the wet dirt, obscuring the view of the property from the street. There were three windows facing onto the street. Two were small and square and set high on a part of the structure that looked to be converted garage space. The third was a large bay window that opened at an angle onto a porch where two Adirondack chairs were painted to match the house and sat on either end of a low wooden table with an empty vase in the center.

It had been dark all day and there were lights on in the front of his house. I had seen him look out of the bay window twice in the forty-five minutes I had been parked there.

My bike was fastened to the Yakima rack mounted on the back of my car. I had brought no coffee to drink, and I had been unable to eat anything for lunch. I had been far too nervous to eat or do much of anything else except think and worry and then think and worry some more. With my bike and my car and the clothes I had carefully chosen, I was ready to follow him to the creek, by whatever mode of transportation he chose.

I had composed and recomposed a short text to send to Reggie the cop time and time again. Each time my message got more abrupt. I had read and reread and abandoned each version just before sending. Finally I decided that when I needed him I would simply text him to help me—a two-word plea of blunt succinctness. I was going to text him at the official police number. They would be able to accurately pinpoint my location. He or someone else would come quickly.

This was my naïve assumption.

I chose not to dwell on whether they would come quickly enough.

As I thought over my electronic distress signal I had once again considered letting Hawkins know my theory in advance. My motives were nothing if not selfish and self-serving.

I could use some help.

But I still hesitated. My theorizing remained no more than a slim notion, which happened to point to a particular person in a particular way. It was purely and simply an intuition that needed to be played out.

Before I left the house, I had researched my suspect online. Little had been revealed. His name was a common one, and there were several gentlemen who shared both his first and last name. One was an aspiring actor in New York who had landed a part on a reality show about aspiring actors in New York. Another had written a book about clay pigeon shooting and owned an outdoor shooting facility somewhere in downstate Illinois.

As I read about both men, it occurred to me that, if my guess was accurate, my suspect would soon leapfrog ahead of his namesakes in fame and notoriety. His name and his life would surely appear first, suddenly both famous and famously horrifying, his star easily able to surpass youthfully petulant self-indulgent whining on prime time cable or, however efficient, the blasting of so many flying clay discs to oblivion somewhere in the rural heart of the Midwest.

At just before six, he emerged from the side of his house, pushing a mountain bike, in a long brownish-red waterproof jacket with the hood up and grey shorts and running shoes underneath. The jacket was large and baggy and shapeless enough that the backpack he was carrying underneath would have been barely visible as a formless lump underneath had the rain not plastered it against his thickset frame.

So the pursuit was to be on bicycles.

We were both dressed strangely alike. The hunter and

the hunted; the seemingly innocent and the very possibly insane.

He climbed onto the bike and pedaled slowly to the end of the street where he turned right toward the creek. He was riding a bike a little big for him, or at least he had the seat positioned a shade higher that I would have had it. He was shorter than I was, but younger, and much more powerfully built. When I could no longer see him, I got out of my car and pulled my bike down from the rack. I zipped up my keys and my iPhone in the front waterproof pocket of my jacket and rode quickly to the corner.

The rain was falling hard. The air was warm against my wet face. I braked hard at the corner of Folsom. He was gone. I wasn't too concerned. He was heading to the creek and he was going to a place he had already chosen. I wasn't exactly sure where on the path he would be. It would have to be upriver rather than down, I reasoned, because he would want the water there to be high and powerful rather than low and more widely dispersed.

He and I would have the place to ourselves. The floodgates would be closed, and wiser citizens would have been moved, or be in the process of moving, to higher and drier ground.

But I was forgetting something.

There would be a third person there.

Because he had arranged to meet someone.

And I thought I knew who it was.

The path dropped down toward the churning water, and a barrier was already padlocked and in place on the near side of the creek. A bench set close to the bank was already several feet under water, with only the top half of the backrest still visible.

Some floods materialize with an unexpected violence, while others are telegraphed days in advance and arrive with a wrenching precision. For the man I was following, the latter was surely a far more welcome scenario.

In either event, he was following the proven methodology he had employed at least twice before.

Amazingly, a lone bike and its rider passed me exiting from the creek path and up onto the road. A man in a yellow T-shirt and black shorts was going much faster than the flowing lakes of water on the road would safely justify. He grinned at me as we passed each other. Boulder bikers aren't an especially gregarious breed, and he presumably took me for a kindred member of a cycling subspecies—the flood-surfing daredevil.

I thought of the unfortunate young man Eileen and I had recently discovered, who had chased the floodwaters on a whim and lost. He had left his wife behind when he slipped and fell and struck his head and drowned over a year ago.

The path was empty and quickly became a swift river to navigate upstream. I got off my bike and pushed against the water. I saw no one. The rain hammered down on the plastic corrugated roof of a bike shelter that stood close to the university football practice fields. I passed under one bridge and pulled my iPhone from my pocket. Thankfully it was bone dry. I tried to turn it on, but the battery had run all the way down. I realized my nerves had betrayed me in the car. The USB cord hadn't been connected properly. I hadn't even noticed.

Now I was alone.

I was able to ride my bike for some stretches on the

path. Each underpass was gated and sealed off. I heard the flood sirens howling in the distance. The lights were on in the library, and several steam-clouded faces were pressed against the windows of the glass bridge looking down as I passed underneath. I looked for Eileen but I couldn't see her.

Most of Fine Park was transformed into Fine Lake, with two feet of standing water to battle through. Past the park, the path climbed uphill, clinging to the side of the road as it curved out of town. The gradient was steeper and the water flowed much faster downhill and I struggled to walk uphill quickly. I stumbled once and fell into the bitter cold water. The bike went fully underwater. The brakes would be worthless by now. I lifted it up and kept on walking.

A hundred yards later, on the left of the path and the road, the ground suddenly dropped down several feet to a drainage lake in front of a large log house set some ways back behind a line of tall oak trees. The house was dark and the driveway was empty. At the far end of the lake a stone wall stood with a metal grate set inside it. The wall was normally six feet above the water and the sound of water trickling through the bottom of the grate was a gentle rhapsodic murmur. In the floodwaters, the wall was overwhelmed as the creek ran down into the lake and the lake rushed through the grate and the beating rain created a misty haze over the surface of the water.

And standing in the middle of the haze, in four feet of icy water, was a man in a white robe.

The last time I had seen Michael John Duncan he had waved goodbye to me across the Lazarus House parking lot as the first shift of volunteers had got into their cars and headed home two Sundays ago.

Now he stood with his head raised toward the sky, his face, in demented ecstasy, pummeled by a cleansing torrent of rainwater. His eyes were tightly shut, and he was speaking words I was powerless to hear or understand. Both his hands were thrust deep into the water. Out of the corner of my eye I registered a bike, presumably his, hanging safely from a high branch with an empty backpack tied neatly to the handlebars.

When he raised his hands from the lake, a woman's head broke the surface. Her eyes were closed. She opened her mouth and took a slow, unhurried breath. Her eyes opened as she looked into his face and she smiled. One of his hands rested gently on her forehead and the other gripped her shoulder awkwardly. He was still saying something to her.

I remembered Michael at the shelter, helping the homeless woman make up her bed and settle down for the night. She had been crying and he had held both her shoulders. He had even brought her a warmer blanket later in the night when she was cold.

I had looked up the names of the women at the shelter that night. I had matched their pictures with the girl crying on her bed. There had only been a few women in the corner of the room. Two were much older. One was much blacker.

The woman in the water was younger.

Her name was Tess.

She closed her eyes again, smiled a last slow smile of heartbreaking sadness, and gently sunk back under the water. Michael held something in the hand that touched her shoulder. I couldn't see what it was

Michael began to speak to her again.

I stood there, momentarily transfixed by the serenity of the image and the baffling juxtaposition of tableaus—what looked at once to be both sweetly and ethereally sacred and horrifyingly sinister—in the churning heart of a maelstrom of swirling and beating forces of nature.

I began to walk into the water toward the unholy baptism.

The cold of the water was instantly numbing while the rain felt wrongly warm. Lightning sheeted across the inky sky for a few fractured seconds. The quickening water through the grate was loud and insistent.

The woman under the water had begun to struggle. As her face came closer to the surface, Michael lifted the hand that had held her shoulder and I finally saw the large stone he had been holding. He hit her once. I screamed again as his hand rose above the water for a second time.

Then he turned to me.

He was no longer speaking.

His face was pale and wet, his features transforming from joy to confusion to a sudden hatred. He pushed the woman loose and began moving toward me. The water was getting deeper for both of us, yet he seemed somehow to be much more fluid and mobile in it than I was. I stumbled and went under. As I surfaced he brought the rock down onto my shoulder. The pain was sharp and one arm lost all feeling. I went under again and my other hand found the bottom of the lake and I tried to find something to either grip onto or use as a weapon. But there was nothing. I came back up to the surface defenseless.

He hit me again.

A sickening pain exploded in the top of my head and then transformed into a dull numbness that spread out across my body. For a second I might have heard a muted noise, a cracking sound somewhere far off, but it wasn't worth considering, hardly even relevant, as I began to lose consciousness and sink.

I woke up at the side of the lake with the rain splashing on my face and Reggie Hawkins standing over me with a gun in his hand.

"How did you . . . " I began to speak slowly. My head hurt more than my shoulder did.

"We've been watching you."

And for a second the image of the watcher's flower mask blossomed in my head.

"That sound I heard before he hit me?"

"That would be me shooting the little fuck in the shoulder. He'll live."

"The woman in the lake . . . "

"She's got a sore head. Just like yours. But she's going to be fine. She got the second ambulance. We had to give him the first. You'll get the third one when it shows up."

"Her name is Tess."

Hawkins said nothing.

"Like Thomas Hardy."

"How do you feel?"

"My arm is sore."

Reggie nodded and smiled. "His is a whole lot worse."

"That's good."

"You should have told me what you were doing," Reggie said.

"Would you have believed me?" I asked him.

He considered this. He began to smile. "Not sure . . .

maybe not. But hunches are always worth following."

Reggie was drifting out of focus rapidly.

"You should close your eyes now," he said.

And I did.

SIXTEEN

Have you read about the Baptist killings in the newspapers?" Reggie asked me.

I nodded. "His middle name is John. I suppose it was inevitable."

It was three days later and I was sitting on my porch wrapped in wool blankets. I felt somewhat better. Eileen had been over in the morning to deliver a thermos filled with chicken soup, and the hospital's generous supply of codeine-laced Tylenols was still going strong. I didn't feel much like eating solid food. I thanked her for the soup.

"I'm your girl," she said as she departed.

"Wouldn't be bad," I replied.

Reggie had shown up at lunchtime bearing two coffees. We drank them and split the still-hot soup between us. My shoulder was bruised and felt a little stiff. I had thrown up in the hospital due to drinking a gallon of unpurified rainwater and/or receiving a mild concussion. There was a small knot on the top of my head but otherwise I was fine.

"How are you feeling now?" He asked me.

"My head still hurts." It was sadly true.

"He did hit you hard."

"My shoulder's okay." I rolled it slowly to prove my point. He nodded encouragement. "Good. We found your bike."

"I don't even remember what I did with it. How is it?"

"It travelled a good ways down the creek, so it's pretty much fucked up beyond repair. But I have some good news."

A final, fatal voyage down the river it had spent most of

its life being ridden alongside seemed an apt way for my Gary Fisher to depart. I observed a moment of silence for a good and loyal bike lost in action.

Then I said nothing and waited for my news to arrive.

"We're giving you a special reward."

I was instantly suspicious. "What kind of reward?"

"I ordered you a police bike."

That was unexpected. "One of the fancy Cannondales?"

He grinned. "Yup."

I grinned back. "Sweet. What color?"

"You can have any color you like as long as it's black."

I considered briefly. "Black would be nice. What size did you order?"

He looked slightly offended. "Do we look like idiots? It'll be the same size as your old bike. We get them from the same place you got yours."

"Thank you, Officer."

"You're very welcome."

"Do I get a siren?"

Reggie chose to ignore me.

As we had our soup and coffee, I offered Reggie some of my Tylenol stash. He looked slightly tempted.

"You found out about Duncan before we did. So what did we miss that you found?"

"There was nothing."

He persisted. "But you found him first . . . "

"Through an insular piece of logic," I stated enigmatically.

"Explain it to me."

So I took a deep breath. "I started from a place that made very little sense. There had to be a million suspects in the world who were more likely. But all I had was Lazarus House, so what you have to do is think of Lazarus as a possible means or a probable cause. So then you have the facts: two dead homeless men drown in floods and both had been at the shelter on the Sunday before they died. That fact didn't need to be important but since I had nothing else it was all that mattered to me. It was all I knew that they had in common. It turned out that Michael worked there on both of the Sundays before they died. Almost no other volunteers did. Well, actually three others did—the two older brothers and Shirley—but the brothers have been working at Lazarus forever, and I couldn't imagine Shirley as a killer, so that left me with Michael John Duncan, in my blinkered world of probable guilt, as the only suspect I had. He was a new volunteer. He was also working there last week when I did. When he was there, he talked to a girl who was upset. Again, in my myopic worldview she would be his next target. Michael made a connection with his victims. They were hurt in some way. And that was what I had to go on. Either I was right or I was utterly full of shit and would end up chasing an innocent man in the rain."

Reggie interrupted me then. "You were mostly right. Michael John Duncan started volunteering there in December. He moved to Boulder not long before that from New Castle, Indiana, and rented the house on Goss with some money he inherited from a dead uncle. He worked part-time at the big hardware store on Folsom. He liked to read the Bible during his lunch breaks, and he listened to jazz music on headphones all day long. He's thirty-one and has never been in any kind of trouble before."

"Is he religious?" I asked Reggie.

"He regularly attended a seriously fundamentalist church back in Indiana for a while. Then there was some sort of falling out. Michael has strong views on the Bible and what to do with sinners, but he's decided that regular churches aren't for him. He's also dead certain that he's been personally chosen by God to perform baptisms. He's on a mission."

"Has he talked?"

Reggie's laugh was more like a bark. "Oh my God, has he talked? He's done pretty much nothing but. He's on a personal undertaking for God. He's finding repentant sinners, forgiving them, and cleansing their sins and absolving them of all their guilt. He's a busy man."

I was curious. "And how does all that work?"

"It works like this. At the shelter, God shows Michael a sinner who feels real bad about him or herself. Michael knows this to be true because, soon after God shows Michael the sinner, He sends down the floodwaters for the cleansing. Michael takes them to the God-sent waters and washes their sins away and, once they are washed, he sends them back to God all nice and clean. He's a kind of divine laundering service."

"Why do they have to die?" I wondered.

"Michael says it's because they're in a pure state. If Michael let them live, they'd get themselves all impure again, and God wouldn't want them that way."

"How does he know that?"

"How do you think? God told him."

"God must be pleased with Michael."

Reggie smirked at that.

I changed the subject. "Andrew Travers talked with Michael."

Reggie nodded. "Andrew Travers was the first to die because that was the first flood God sent Michael to do his baptizing with. Andrew was seemingly tired of being a sinner, and Michael cleansed him and sent him home."

"Michael didn't kill anyone in December. He worked at Lazarus on the third of the month. That was his first time volunteering there."

Reggie barely paused. "God didn't send down any floods in December."

"I wonder if Michael had got himself a sinner for that month just in case the floods came."

"Michael told us that he had found someone. But God didn't want them yet." Reggie shook his head in wonder. "When you talk to him it has a crazy kind of logic."

"There was a second flood in February."

"Michael only chooses one likely candidate per month for his baptisms or God only shows him one a month. It works either way."

"Don't serial killers have to keep on killing?" I had read this fact somewhere.

"I don't think Duncan sees himself that way."

"Do we know how Michael got Andrew to agree to be baptized?"

"Michael said Andrew was more than willing to be cleansed. He said he was eager. He wanted to be made clean and he wanted to go home."

"Did he know he was going to die?"

Reggie hesitated. "Michael said that Travers was at peace with himself. That may well be true. Whether he wanted to die . . . I'm not so sure about that. He may not have given a shit one way or another."

"So what about Nitro?" I asked then.

"Michael had way more trouble there. He talked to Nitro at the shelter. He said that Nitro was really sorry about something that had happened in his life but it turned out that he wasn't sorry about the same things as Michael thought he should be sorry about."

"My head's starting to hurt more and I'm not quite following you."

"It turns out Nitro used to act in porn movies when he lived in Los Angeles. Michael wanted him to ask for forgiveness for doing that and for all the weed he smoked. The problem was that Nitro didn't especially feel bad about either of these things. He liked to smoke weed and he liked to fuck and get paid for it. But he did feel bad about something else."

"What was the something else?"

"Michael never actually managed to find that out. He got Nitro to meet him at the creek during the flood by promising him more weed. Then he thought he could force the truth out of him and make him ask for forgiveness. But he couldn't. Michael persuaded Nitro to go with him to the lake. They fought there and Michael found a stone and smashed Arthur Crowder's head a few times before drowning him, dragging the body to the creek and pushing him in. The floodwaters brought the body down to the place where you and I found him."

"He had a rock in his hand the other night. I remember seeing it and then feeling it."

Reggie nodded grimly. "He must have learned to take precautions after Nitro put up a fight."

"Is Michael Duncan crazy?"

Reggie paused and collected his thoughts. "Let me put it this way. He's utterly convinced that God has told him to find sorry souls and wash away their sins and then give them back to God all clean and better. And by all clean and better I mean dead and drowned."

"How long has he felt this way?"

"We're not sure. Since coming to Boulder, at least."

"What about the girl in the lake?"

"Her name's Tess Jane Kipling. She's only seventeen. She comes from Galena, Illinois. She ran away from home. This is a truly sad story. She told it to Duncan at Lazarus. Apparently Tess went to a bar with her pals in town one night. She looks much older, uses a really good fake ID, has a few drinks and drives on home. She skids her car on a wet road and hits and kills a teenage boy on a bike on a dark night. She gets back home. Her Mom's been dead a few years. But she lives with her Dad who makes primitive pottery for tourists. She tells him what happened. He gives her a whisky. Then he gives her another. Later the cops show up. Dad tells the cops she hadn't been drinking that night but she was real upset after her accident so he gave her a few drinks to settle her nerves after the terrible fright she's just had. The cops can't prove she was drunk when she hit the kid on the bike and they can't prove it wasn't just an accident. Actually they can't even prove she had been drinking. The bouncer at the bar isn't even sure she was there. The bar was real busy that night. The guy behind the bar isn't too sure either. Her friends swear she wasn't at the bar with them that night. The kid on the bike tests positive for crystal meth and the road was real dark and he had no reflectors on the bike and he was wearing dark clothes in the rain. There's even a witness who says the kid on the bike was all over the road before he got hit. So the girl goes free and Dad figures she owes him, so he starts to sexually abuse her that very first night after the accident and for the rest of the next year. The sorry fucker keeps right on doing this to her and this gets to be old so Tess runs away and ends up in Boulder and it's cold one night so she goes to Lazarus House and she uses that fake ID of hers to stay there and she asks Michael for a blanket and he seems so nice and understanding and she tells him her sad story and he tells her that God will surely forgive her for killing that poor boy and for letting her piece-of-worthless-shit Dad fuck her, but she has to have her sins washed away and he can certainly help her out with that."

"Is she going to be alright?"

"Physically she'll be fine. She's still at the hospital, but that's because we don't know what to do with her. Sending her back home to Galena and her dad just seems stupid."

"Who did you have watching me?" I was suddenly curious.

Reggie shrugged. "Different cops."

"All the time?"

"Pretty much. One of our guys spotted you going under one of the underpasses."

"Did they ever wear red?" It was a long shot at best.

Reggie looked puzzled. "Seems unlikely. Why would they wear red?"

"I just wondered. Was Michael surprised to see me at the creek that night?"

"He said he was. He did recognize you from Lazarus."

So Michael Duncan wasn't my watcher on the creek. I

wondered who was.

Reggie looked sheepish for a second. "Was that really all you had?"

I nodded. It was my turn to look sheepish. "I had my hunch. I was only able to confirm that Andrew and Nitro both stayed at Lazarus last Sunday night when I had all the Lazarus records to look at. Michael was the person at Lazarus who spent the most time talking to the guests when I was there. The two reports for the nights that Nitro and Andrew were there both mentioned someone being upset. Andrew was mentioned by name. The tarot lady told me that Nitro was sad the night she was there. When I discovered that Michael Duncan was working there on both nights, I thought some more about him and the girl he was helping the night I was there. All the stuff about buses and cold weather wasn't that relevant although it was what kept me thinking about Lazarus. What was relevant was that Michael John Duncan found sinners and washed their lives away when the floods came. He did this twice. He would have kept on doing it if you hadn't stopped him."

"You helped a lot," Reggie said simply.

I laughed to hide my embarrassment. "I was mostly lucky."

Reggie laughed but he said nothing.

Then Reggie told me more stuff. Eileen had stepped forward and offered to have Tess come stay with her when she got out of the hospital, and no one in the police department could offer any real objection. Reggie's bullet had shattered all the bones in Duncan's shoulder and he would be in the hospital for a while longer. The Baptist Killer seemed neither happy nor sad to be shot and captured. He was now under twenty-four-hour guard at the hospital.

Reggie mentioned that the newspapers couldn't decide what to call Michael. John the Baptist. The Baptist. The Baptist Killer. The Boulder Baptist.

Reggie didn't much care what they called him.

Many years ago a very young girl with wealthy parents who dressed her up for beauty pageants had been murdered in Boulder. It was a famous and famously unsolved case and the Boulder police had taken a lot of flak in the long drawn-out aftermath. Reggie believed that whatever this new case would end up being called would be the case that would finally absolve his department.

As long as no one fucked it up.

I was worried about the publicity and Lazarus House. Reggie believed they might actually get more guests and way more volunteers. I wasn't so sure.

Reggie had another warm thought. "If my arm had still been in a sling you'd be deader than shit."

Then he came up with something else for me to ponder. "The first Sunday stuff is pretty weird."

"How do you mean?" I wondered.

He thought for a moment. "Duncan volunteered on the first Sundays. You volunteered on the first Sundays. The victims all stayed at Lazarus on first Sundays before they died."

"That many coincidences do seem like a lot," I offered lamely.

Then I reconsidered. "You're right. It is weird. But if Duncan had worked there on another day or worked at another shelter he still would have found a way to kill people. Different people maybe. But still people and still dead." I said this with complete conviction.

"Still pretty weird," was all Reggie could murmur to himself, as we both contemplated in silence, sipping at the last of our soups and our coffees, which were now both stone cold.

After Reggie left I looked at my iPhone. It had amazingly survived my ordeal zipped up snug and dead and useless inside my waterproof pocket.

I thought about the following things.

I didn't recall ever having let the battery go flat until that night. I did have a good excuse. I was no longer a young man and my newfound vulnerability was an unwelcome notion. Michael would have killed me in the creek without Reggie being there, watching out for me and saving my half-spent life. I wasn't sure how I felt about Eileen taking in Tess. I had been foolish and lucky. My head and my shoulder hurt.

It was definitely time for more turbocharged Tylenol.

SEVENTEEN

I woke up the next morning thinking about pornography. There had been two recent articles on the subject in the newspapers I read. In California, lawmakers were urging a condoms-only statute to be applied to the porn industry. This would allegedly halt the spread of sexually transmitted diseases in an industry where such safeguards were presumably deemed necessary.

But the *New York Times* piece I had read begged to differ. Porn stars generally arrived at a shoot and dropped their pants for medical reasons first. Seasoned filmmakers with trained eyes checked the stars' junk for oozing sores and the like. The performers also submitted to STD tests, often more than once a week, and databases were created and zealously updated. A positive test meant no legitimate movie work.

The results were interesting. The two stars interviewed, a young man and a woman with obviously bogus names, praised the preventative measures already in place. They both also insisted on condoms for their after-work recreational couplings. It was interesting to note the marked lack of enthusiasm they both displayed toward leisure time sex. But then the man who spends his days sampling wine probably goes home with little interest in sipping at a choice Burgundy with his dinner. They both further believed that dedicated porn watchers wanted their action barebacked, and condoms on screen would be detrimental to audience enjoyment and the long-term profitability of the business.

There was much more. A veteran female porn star and certified nurse testified to the dangers of severe chaffing with condoms being used for lengthy shoots. She also informed her captive readers that porn men are generally on the job for a good half hour, as opposed to the paltry ten minutes or so we common mortals can manage in the saddle.

The article succeeded in redrawing the image of the industry, heretofore either tawdry and exploitive or dangerous, as quite serious, oddly clinical, and unusually concerned with self-preservation.

It was an interesting article, which, after having now read twice was of no earthly use to me.

Next up was a short piece on porn and social networking in the Boulder free paper. Porn stars and their fans were rabid tweeters. Ashley Haze was as well known for her hardcore movies as for her informed blog on horticulture. She had a large wild garden in West LA and she regularly discussed the use of perennials versus annuals. She had legions of followers, including Neal the gay retired realtor and my volunteer yardman, who didn't know or much less care what she did with herself or with several well-hung men when she wasn't potting her plants and spreading her mulch.

Porn actresses had rabid fan bases and websites. They tended to earn much more than their male counterparts. Some grew older and less screen-worthy and became producers and directors. They all went to conventions and happily signed posters and body parts for the faithful.

The porn men usually worked more anonymously and for less pay. As a result, they tended to use the social networks feverishly to make a presence for themselves. One particularly vigorous tweeter was Jon Stone. He was reputed to have made literally thousands of films, but he needed a regimen of constant social networking to keep his career in the fast track and his fake name a household one.

So I tweeted Mr. Stone and told him that Nitro had died recently. I wondered if he had known him. And if he had, I wondered how I could find out more about him.

It was the longest of long shots.

I sat for all of three minutes without much hope.

Then Jon tweeted me right back.

Serious bummer. Nitro was the coolest guy. So sorry. Someone should tell StevieD@MILFrenzy.com.

I went old school and emailed StevieD. I told him Nitro was dead and Jon Stone had told me to tell him the news. I said I was sorry for his loss. Could he perhaps call me? I could tell him more, and he could tell me more. I gave him my cell phone number. I wished him well. I must have sounded more than a little desperate.

Not wanting to be idle, I fired up the laptop and made my way to MILFrenzy.com; purely for research purposes I hasten to add.

The site was hardcore. Women close to thirty pretended to be forty-plus and fucked guys close to thirty pretending to be under twenty on kitchen floors, teachers' desks, and office desks, against classroom walls and refrigerators, and sometimes in pool-boy uniforms by the side of a glittering pool in the warm California sun.

The featured women had names that were patently false but that at least appeared in the credits. Misty Daniels. Destiny Taylor. The one-sentence plotline merely gave the boys generically adolescent names like Timmy and Mickey. The lady sometimes opened the front door to her teenage son's classmate, the pool boy, or the young appliance repairman, who had come over to the house under the required slim pretext. Maybe her own kid and/or hubby had gone out somewhere, and she spent the next minute or two warming up the reluctant stud, who usually wore a baseball cap and grinned goofily. The mother was usually in classic housewife attire of platforms, tattoos, garter belt, and no body hair.

In a short time, mom was up against the fridge or on the kitchen floor, and Timmy or Mickey was going at it hard with a tadger big enough to throw over his shoulder when he finally finished up. He would presumably also get a big glass of milk and a still-warm cookie from the oven for his hard work.

There were several scant scenarios, but most worked pretty close to this fantasy. Some MILFs were hot teachers, some were the older hot babe next door, and some were the hot-bitch boss-lady tease at the office. The boys were chosen for their youthful looks and the size of their tackle, the women for flexibility, balance in high heels, staying power and determined displays of shockingly bad acting.

Each video had a free sample for three minutes or so, then the screen faded, and a credit card number was required to watch the whole epic.

I should mention that I'm no expert on porn for the following reasons. I don't watch it often enough to be jaded, so my resistance to its low-priced charm is lamentably low; I'm also a cheap date, and way too easily excited to have to pony up for more than the free three minutes as a result. I invariably tend to feel stupider than shit right afterwards, yet two months later I'll be sneaking back, eager and fresh-eyed with my middle-aged willy well rested.

As I speed watched, I looked for Nitro, and it occurred to me that I might inadvertently get a length on and have to hunt for a Kleenex. But I was wrong for several reasons; my head still hurt, I was sitting on my porch in the middle of the day, and, finally, there was the ultimate sadder-than-sad libido-destroying reality—I was primarily looking for a glimpse of a dead man, and decidedly not for a furtive wank.

After a while I began to doubt my ability to recognize Arthur Crowder if I saw him, and I suspected that I was giving my poor laptop enough viruses to choke it. My eyes were also hurting.

I took a respite from tramp stamps and studded clits and glanced up as a long shadow passed over me.

Nye was standing there on my porch and he was smiling. He had a Belvedere backpack I had never seen before over one shoulder. I didn't know we made backpacks. Where the hell was my backpack? He had a set of car keys in his hand and there, squatting like a garish gargoyle, was a lime green Kia Soul parked boldly outside my house. It could only be an economy rental.

This was certainly a surprise. Could he see the laptop screen from where he was standing? I prayed that he couldn't and tried to casually power the computer down.

His smile got a whole lot nastier. I was certain he could see the screen.

When Nye spoke it was with frosty disdain.

"I can come back when you're not so busy."

I told him I would have given him the bigger bedroom if he had given me any warning. He told me he was only staying for a few days. I asked him why he was here. He told me Jesse had emailed him.

While I got up and moved things around the porch randomly, Nye put his bag on one chair and sat down on another. He crossed his legs carefully and stared at me.

He got right to the point.

"I've heard rumors that you are getting yourself into all kinds of trouble."

"I don't know what you mean."

"Stop it."

"What did Jesse say?"

"Many things. He also wants to show me something, although he wasn't at all willing to tell me what it is. It was all very clandestine. Let's both go and see him."

We were soon walking along Pearl toward Cygnet in the late afternoon.

I tend to forget about the absolute blackness of Nye Prior. He's also quite tall and always manages to look much more regal than the people around him, like a Nubian prince in exile. Boulder is a place of both extreme liberality and pristine whiteness, so that Nye was drawing a handful of stares from the good folks, who would doubtless have been mortified to know that they were staring.

He never seems especially concerned by the attention.

"I do like your rental car," I ventured.

"It should prove relatively easy to locate in a parking lot."

"You could have gone for an upgrade."

He sniffed. "Who can afford luxuries like that when I have to support you?"

He did have a point.

Jesse and Rosie were waiting for us at the door of the cafe. Well, Jesse was waiting. Rose was lying down, sound asleep, seemingly all recovered from her surgery, and back to her regular vigorous regimen of sleeping and lying down and having her expensively restored eyes clamped firmly shut at all times. I was going to give her a good patting but fiend Nye got to her first.

"She's a savage killer," I warned him.

"Yes, I can see that," he replied as he rubbed the savage killer's stomach.

Nye stood up and shook Jesse's hand. Jesse looked slightly nervous. This was strange, but I had no time to evaluate the situation since it was my turn to pet the pooch.

Nye and Jesse were talking. They were both being, I felt, particularly mean, but I did my best to ignore them.

"I just caught Tom on the brink of pleasuring himself."

"That's not exactly unusual."

"Quite so. He claims it was research."

"He should have graduated with honors by now."

There was assorted smug chortling. At that point I entered the conversation with a choice bon mot of my own.

"Shut the fuck up, you assholes."

We sat down at a table near the back. The Handsome Family sang about Nikola Tesla. Jesse headed to the back, and Nye and I sat and waited in an amicable silence for a minute or so.

Jesse returned with a growler. There was something dark inside. He placed it on the table sheepishly. Nye raised one quizzical eyebrow but said nothing. There was a long pause as we all three stared at it. Jesse elected to break the silence.

"I made this," was all he announced in a slightly unsteady voice.

"You don't make beer," I countered sagely.

"Apparently he does," Nye said dryly. "Is this a stout?"

"It is a stout." Jesse sounded inches from an outright panic attack.

"Should we try it?" I asked.

"Obviously," Nye said haughtily.

Jesse produced three small glasses. He opened and poured and drank his first. I went second. After an eternity of sniffing and staring and swirling and sniffing, Nye finally sipped and then sipped again and then he looked at his glass thoughtfully. Jesse glanced at me and I smiled back. Then he stared at Nye, whose features were now molded into the very model of inscrutability. Then Nye took a third and final sip before he gently let a small smile slide across his features. And with that the spell was forever broken. He would make his pronouncement presently, but it would only confirm the evidence of the smile. I waited with interest, but Jesse waited as if his life depended on it.

Nye then spoke quietly, as if to himself. "We'll put this on nitro."

"Excuse me," I spluttered. "Don't I get a say?"

"Don't be silly." Nye turned to me. Then he turned to Jesse. "I assume you want Belvedere to make this?"

"I do."

"Good. It will be our singular pleasure. It's truly excellent. Do I detect molasses?"

"You do."

Nye nodded slowly and understandingly. Then he addressed Jesse again.

"Do you wish our self-abusing friend here to choose the name?" He gestured toward me.

"Do I have much choice?"

Nye shook his head unhurriedly. "Sadly not," his tone was mournful.

"What happens now?" Jesse asked Nye.

"In the days ahead we will good-naturedly haggle over a deal that we both want to make. You will make some money quickly. We might eventually make some money too. Belvedere Brewing will have an exemplary stout at long last. But before all that takes place, you and I will talk and finish this fine growler."

"What about me?" I whined piteously at that point.

"You're still recovering from your unfortunate injury," Nye said with the foulest grin he could muster.

While the selfish twosome proceeded to pour and plot, I checked messages. There were no calls, but Jon Stone had clearly alerted the porn world to Nitro's death, because I received several thoughtful and heartfelt missives asking for details and offering condolences. It was touching. Most of the people assumed I knew Art well. I replied with thanks and details and I sent on all the messages to Reggie. He would know how to contact Nitro's parents. I didn't know if they knew how their son had made a living. Perhaps they didn't and they would be upset to find out. Or perhaps they would be comforted to learn how many good friends he had left behind.

It occurred to me that I now had an extensive list of people who could tell me more about Nitro. Yet I hesitated. Jon Stone had offered up StevieD first, and perhaps that meant something. I decided I would give Mr. D a while longer to get back to me before inquiring elsewhere.

"Do you have a name?" Jesse asked me suddenly.

I must have looked quite blank for a moment.

"For the beer?" he persevered in the face of my unrelenting denseness.

I smirked conspiratorially at him. Actually I did. And it just might be my best yet.

Nye and Jesse began to ponderously plan drinking and dinner somewhere and sometime much later that night. Poor long-suffering Natalie was about to be dragged along to chauffeur and be bored shitless. I still felt less than chipper and hastily begged off.

The same Middle Brother song that had been playing on my last Cygnet visit came on as the two beer moguls continued to plot. Nye looked up in interest. I told him the name of the song and the artist.

"It's by Dawes," the stout master loftily proclaimed.

"It's by Middle Brother," I gently riposted.

"Dawes."

"You're an idiot." This was going nowhere.

I wandered back to my house slowly. My shoulder was starting to hurt. I got home just as Belle and Sebastian began to sing on my iPhone and a phone number with an area code I didn't recognize appeared on the screen. I managed to choke down a pain pill before answering.

The voice was ragged on the other end of the line.

"Tell me that the Nitro man isn't gone."

I couldn't.

Except for the stars on screen, MILFrenzy was pretty much a one-man porn-making operation, and Stevie Devine was that one man. I was able to provide him with a terse one-line synopsis: Nitro had been living in Boulder and he had drowned.

And that was about as far as I got in the dialogue.

Stevie D began to talk without any prompting. He told me that Nitro worked for him for a year or so in Los Angeles in the adult movies that Stevie singlehandedly made and marketed.

"He was the sweetest guy," Stevie recalled. "He usually worked for weed and cash. Mostly weed if he was flush. Mostly cash if he needed to help with the rent in whatever craphole place he was crashing. Most weeks he took a combo deal. I had sandwiches on the shoots, and Nitro ate like a horse after we finished up. There was usually some good beer in a cooler, so he was happier than shit. There was a no-brewski rule in place before the shoot for the Nitro man though. Booze and boners don't bring bank in porn, and the Nitro was a man good for wood at all times. Man was a rock-solid cocksman to the core. So how are you hung my man?" he asked me suddenly.

It was a question I was quite certain I had never been asked before.

"Like a cashew," I said.

Stevie burst out laughing. "Me too. Did you check out the honeymoon junk on the Nitro?"

"I surely did. Truly impressive."

Stevie chortled. "You got that damn right, my miniscule friend."

Mister Dee got right back on track. "Nitro was just much

loved, man. His face was super young looking, so he was great for MILF work. He looked like a little kid with a huge . . . what's that Scotch word you guys use for dick?"

And another unexpected question.

"Tadger?"

He laughed loudly. "Shit. Never heard that one. Must say I like it. "

"Willy?"

He laughed again loudly. "That's it. Nitro had himself a boss willy."

I asked Stevie how he made his money.

He came back with a question of his own. "You watch porn much?"

"Maybe once every few months," I confessed.

"Do you ever pay for it?"

I further confessed that I didn't.

He snorted. "Then you're a three-minute man and therefore fucking useless to me. I need guys who watch it all the time and get too used to it and need more than the freebie three to get off. These are the guys who pay for their porn and keep me in business."

I had another question. Why did Nitro stop working and leave Los Angeles?

Stevie went quiet for a moment. When he spoke again it was in a much softer voice.

"I make fantasy MILF movies. The older woman seduces the young guy. Nitro made a bunch for me and was pretty happy doing it. He worked a lot with Savannah Swift. She was a well-known porn actress. Worked most of the time for me. She also worked for a bunch of other companies. Always reliable. A couple of years older but looked great so it

kinda worked fine for the stuff that we made. Lived close by
in East LA. Really a fucking pretty girl in an industry full of
over-painted low to average lookers. Long legs that worked
like clamps. Big rock hard tits that weren't real and kinda
helped with the illusion of age-denying, if you know what I
mean. She had warm older-woman eyes. Savannah always
tested negative for our shoots. Limber as shit. She had no
tattoos, which I always liked. Like really, how many college
librarians are that inked up for Christ's sake, even if they
are falling tits-first out of hooker outfits? Nitro wasn't inked
either, so they looked kinda clean and right together."

"He had a tattoo on his ankle."

"No he didn't. Not in LA he didn't."

I figured Stevie D should know.

I changed the subject.

"So you admit your movies aren't exactly realistic."

"You think guys are looking for realism?"

"Do women watch porn?"

"Sure. A lot of 'em do."

"Why?"

Stevie hesitated before answering. "Some women just
want to find out what men like."

"Does porn influence people?"

There was another pause. "There's a lot more full-body
waxing going on, that's for sure." He hesitated. "But maybe
there's young guys getting a stupid notion about what love
should be all about when they watch it." Stevie was silent for
a moment. "Are you gonna get all fucking self-righteous on
me now?"

"I'm sorry. Tell me about Savannah Swift."

"Her and Nitro were like the ultimate soul mates/fuck

buddies combined. They were a hoot to work with because I always got the feeling that I was paying them to do something they would happily be doing for free. I paid Savannah pretty well, too. She made a lot of films with and without Nitro, but for my money she was best with him. They were bestest pals. They liked to hang out. They both dug prime weed. I know she lent him money when she was flush and he wasn't, which was pretty often. Nitro spent next to nothing on anything but he just never had a pot to piss in most of the time. Anyway there's a hangout bar called Ralphie's near where we shoot our stuff. It's a well-known industry hangout. Nitro really liked it. They had a bunch of good draft beers, and happy hour lasted most of the night. There was karaoke two nights a week. All the fans knew about the place and went there sometimes to meet their favorites but it was generally pretty mellow there. Nitro sung all these old Styx hits when he was plowed. It was just a good-time place."

"What happened?"

"Savannah got herself a stalker following her. His name was Terrence Jennings. He went to Ralphie's a few times and creeped everyone out, but the bouncers there got to know about him and they kept him out. So he waited outside for her one night. And Nitro goes in that same night. Jennings recognizes Nitro from his movies with Savannah. Fucking pay dirt, he thinks. So he waits and Nitro comes out later and Jennings follows him and fuck if Nitro doesn't walk straight to Savannah's house and knock on the door and she opens it and Jennings sees her and he waits some more and Nitro goes in and gives her some of the newest stash he just got probably with her money and they smoke some weed and then Nitro leaves and Jennings waits till he is gone and goes to the door and she opens it and he pushes his way in. He has a gun and he tells her that she's gonna be his girl from now on and no one else's and she needs to be true to him and not make porn films with other guys any more. And she laughs out loud in his face and tells him to go fuck himself and he shoots her in the stomach like it was nothing and she dies on the hall floor in a mess of her own blood then the cops come and he's sitting there stroking her hair and groaning and he hands over his gun all meek and mild and they take him away and lock him the fuck up."

Stevie doesn't speak for a while.

I wait. Then he continues.

"And poor Nitro is so far beyond being fucked up seriously by all of this. He stops showing up for work. He blames himself for leading the guy to Savannah's place. Then he gets a lot weirder. He gets into a bad fight at Ralphie's one night over nothing. Then he vanishes. And that's all she wrote. We don't ever see him again. Now you're telling me he's dead. And my pretty angel Savannah she's dead too. Shit, man. Their movies are still up on the website. People still like them. Have you seen any of them?"

I confessed that I hadn't.

"You should. Truly some of my best work there." He sounded suddenly cold and cynical.

I had a last question.

"What was Savannah's real name?"

"Her real name was Amy. Amy Secombe. Did I say that right? SEE CUM? Crazy-assed name for a porn star, right?"

I told him that there had once been a British singer and comedian with the same name. I thought it might have been

Welsh.

"Is that so?" He didn't sound particularly interested.

I told Stevie about the tattoo.

He didn't seem surprised. "She was the love of his life."

Then I told him about my beer plan. Stevie totally loved it.

After I finished speaking with Stevie I returned to MILFrenzy and looked some more. This time I was able to narrow my search for Savannah Swift movies. There were a lot and soon I was watching Nitro and Savannah. Stevie was right. They were shitloads better.

It was getting colder so I went inside and lay down on the couch.

I found their camping movie. Poor Savannah was lost in the woods in tight little shorts and hiking boots that improbably appeared to have high heels and a plaid shirt tied up high above the waist. Nitro soon showed up as Rick the young forest ranger who finds her safe and sound and clearly needs to be rewarded for his diligence. Right from the beginning the movie is different. They both laugh a lot. Amy leans up against a rock in the sun with her shorts gone and Rick the ranger is on his knees with his head between her legs. This takes a ridiculously large amount of screen time. It's hard to see anything, and the camera keeps cutting to Amy's face. As a piece of pure porn, even I can see it's hopeless. She's not even screaming and swearing over and over again. She's just smiling down at him, serenely happy.

Later Amy/Savannah hoists one long leg effortlessly up over Nitro/Rick's shoulder and the action gets to be more traditionally oriented.

Despite a sore head and shoulder and an amped Tylenol-induced semi-coma I'm aware of a fledgling stiffy firing up in the trouser department. I'm frankly a little surprised. These folks are both deceased, their lives violently cut short. Is a wank really the appropriate sign of respect for two professionals hard at their chosen craft, or is it an act of leering quasi-adolescent crudity?

It's certainly a pressing dilemma.

EIGHTEEN

Michael John Duncan drowned himself in a hospital bathtub two nights later.

The newspaper was tantalizingly vague on details.

Reggie was considerably more elaborate.

"We stupidly left him with just one guy. Late at night, Duncan craps the bed. He's beside himself. He begs the cop to be able to get himself cleaned up. He's actually sobbing. The cop walks him down to the showers. He's handcuffed. Duncan asks him if he can use the bathtub. He says he likes baths better. He's practically pleading with him. The cop finally says okay and even runs the water for him. It's a booth more than a room, with no door and no window. He isn't going anywhere. There's a wall fan and a light switch. The cop waits behind the wall. He can hear the bath water running all the time. The cop calls in a few times. Duncan says he's doing just fine. Getting himself all nice and clean, thank you so much, officer. The cop relaxes. He sticks his head out of the bathroom door to try and get a nurse to get the bed taken care of while Duncan finishes up. He swears it's just for a second. He gets a nurse on duty. He checks back on Duncan. The water is still running, only it's very slow now, almost to the very top of the bathtub and Duncan's lying there face up, stone fucking dead to the world."

"The last baptism."

Reggie isn't laughing. "Once again, we get to look like a bunch of small town assholes."

"He saved everyone a lot of trouble."

"Perhaps," Reggie acknowledged. "We had a good

confession. He'd maybe still have been let off for insanity once he lawyered up. But maybe this is better. All nice and clean."

"You don't sound convinced."

"I just wanted us to get everything right this time." Was he thinking of the little pageant girl's unsolved death fifteen years ago as he spoke?

"What will happen to the cop?"

"He's a veteran, close to retirement, with a good record and a reputation for being maybe too much of a nice guy. He'll face some level of internal investigative shit, but I suspect he'll walk away with a new asshole but his pension intact."

"Duncan was highly persuasive."

"That will be no doubt taken into account."

We were sitting at the creek near the library watching a family of ducks swim in the warm afternoon sun. I was waiting for Eileen to finish at work. In the morning, I'd been to the doctor. My head was much better. My arm was still a little stiff and the doctor had given me a sling to wear, more to stop me using the arm and let the shoulder get some rest. Reggie had smiled at the sling, but he resisted the urge to make an obvious remark. Instead he'd wriggled a green braided bracelet off his wrist and gently slid it onto mine.

"Are we dating now?" I asked glibly, although I was oddly touched by the gesture.

"I'm telling my girls that one fell off naturally. They do keep track. I figure as long as it stays intact during the switch we're still kosher and the mojo is still good. Let's hope it keeps you safer than you've been."

He changed the subject. "Tess is staying with Eileen now," he said. "I hear Eileen has some big plans."

I nodded. "She's got her working in the library stocking returned books and filing away stuff. She's also got Jesse working her part time at Cygnet, since he's now working as an indentured servant making beer for Nye. Tess was a good high school student so Eileen's looking at her going to college and the various residency issues for Colorado. That might all be a little further down the road. She's a very nice girl. They get on very well."

"You don't sound too confident."

"I just think Eileen's rushing it."

Reggie nodded. "You could be right. You should tell her."

"That's a wonderful idea."

There was a pause.

"You're not going to do jack shit are you?"

"You have that right, my friend."

The ducks were now swimming inches from my feet. One swam closer and chewed on my front of my shoe. It was gentle. Almost like a baby teething. I could barely feel the gentle pressure. Did the duck think it was food? Was it being friendly? Or was it warning me away?

Reggie was watching the whole performance with some interest.

He spoke after a while. "I didn't know they did that."

I smiled and shrugged. "Me neither."

I waited for a moment. The duck stopped chewing and swam away. I chose this as my moment to pitch my bold new idea to Reggie.

"So Jesse is busy making beer for Nye and me. It's a stout.

We don't have one. It needs a name and it needs a label. I've got a name and you're going to design the label."

Reggie didn't look as surprised as I thought he'd be. "You don't say," was all he said.

"It's called Art Nitro Stout."

"That's a cute name. Will you be paying me?"

"Of course we will."

Reggie thought for a moment.

"What does painting beer labels pay?" he asked.

"Next to nothing," I lied. Nye would be proud.

He snorted at that. "Nice try. What do you have in mind?"

"You're the artist," I answered.

Reggie thought some more.

"Okay. I imagine a person looking a lot like Nitro looked sitting at a place looking a lot like the creek on a warm day with a bottle of Art Nitro in his hand and a big joint in his other hand and a shit-eating grin on his face."

"What is he wearing?" I asked. "Can we see the Amy tattoo on his leg?"

"I hadn't even thought about that." Reggie paused. Then he continued. "He's dressed sloppy. He's wearing a T-shirt and jeans and bare feet, maybe a Belvedere T-shirt." Then he reconsidered. "The pant leg could be high up enough to show the tattoo," he continued to muse.

"That's funny," I said. "That's exactly what I was imagining. I also think it should look like your paintings—partly real and partly an obvious illusion, if you know what I mean?"

Reggie nodded. "I think I do. I'm going to have the grass along the side of the creek be a mixture of giant cannabis and hop plants. Or I will do when I figure out what the hell hops look like. Tell me, do you want him dead or alive? I ask because I generally do dead."

"I was actually thinking that he should look sort of stoned and drunk and happy but still alive."

"Isn't this all kinda strange for a beer label?" He asked.

I smiled. "You don't drink decent beer. There are some strange labels out there, and craft-beer drinkers aren't generally that sensitive." I hesitated for a moment. "So will you do it?"

"Absolutely," Reggie said.

"Should we tell Art's parents?" I asked innocently.

"You mean will I tell them?" Reggie laughed.

"Well, yes. If you could. Do you think they'll be okay with it?"

He laughed again. "We'll soon find out. But yeah, I think they'll be okay. They might even get to like the idea."

"You think so?"

"No."

"Oh."

"I'm joking. I went ahead and sent all the porn folks' emails on to them. They were really pleased that so many people had liked their son so much."

Eileen and Tess showed up then. Reggie left. I had walked along the creek path that day. My new secret undercover police bike would not be ready until the end of the week. The bike store had called and asked if I wanted all the same accessories as the old bike had. I said yes, as long as the cops were paying. I was looking forward to riding it. I figured no one would dare to steal it.

Eileen wanted to take Tess to the restaurant on Pearl

with the best beer in town. This didn't seem especially fair since Tess couldn't drink, but it meant Kind Ale and veggie chili for me and I had no serious objections to either.

NINETEEN

It was a warm day in May and I was waiting in the downtown Denver train station. The automaton voice had announced that the train from Sacramento was going to be delayed by almost an hour, and my already-tender nerves were immediately cranked one gear tighter. The sun's rays were segmented into rectangular sections of dust-infused light as they poured in through the glass-paneled station roof.

The large bedroom in my little house was tidied and prepared and ready for guests. A double room in the Lookout was also reserved as a backup if Lesley and Theresa didn't want to stay with me, or if things went tits up rapidly and we hated each other on sight, which I prayed wouldn't happen.

I had filled my fridge with goodies from Whole Foods and Sun Deli. I had reserved two Specialized bikes with helmets and locks. I had walked over to Cygnet to ask Jesse to try to be civil. There I had found Tess and Natalie hard at it, manning the fort, as Jesse was now spending lots of his time in Chicago, at Belvedere, with Nye, doubtless being driven insane by the overly demanding senior partner at that esteemed establishment, as Art Nitro Stout became a brewing reality.

Speaking of Art Nitro, the painting policemen had submitted his first draft of the label artwork. It was strange and it was unmistakably creepy but everyone loved it so far, including the demanding Lord Nye.

I planned to hike the Flatirons at Chautauqua with my houseguests. I had chosen an easy low-lying route, not because they were novices—they both liked to hike—but because the high altitude would be a new experience, and their Scottish lungs would have the traditional newcomer's reaction to what felt like a complete absence of available oxygen in the air.

Lesley and Teresa both thought the views of the Rocky Mountains from the train window were brilliant. I had just received an email telling me so. Teresa had brought a laptop. Neither of their mobiles were letting them call or send texts.

After some slight deliberation, I had decided to send the two women to the Admiral Fallow concert without me. The options were to buy another ticket and go with them or send them alone. When I had informed Eileen that the Fox Theater had the occasional all-ages show, that this was one such event, and that the under-twenty-ones were separated by a series of chest-high walls from the legitimate boozers in the venue, and that Tess would not therefore be standing beside us if we all went, she quickly begged off for the both of them.

I wasn't at all surprised. Eileen had made it clear that going to the show without Tess was not on the table. That was fine. What was also becoming abundantly obvious was that foster parenting for Tess was going to be Eileen's number-one priority for a while, and I could chose to be a good friend to the both of them or move on. Given the choice between having a date and having a daughter, Eileen was clearly more interested in the latter.

Tess was doing amazingly well. She was both resilient and lovely, and her dark recent past was quickly receding with the application of twin salves—a gentle period of personal stability and Eileen's patient care.

Eileen Arthur had wanted a child more than anything

in the world. I wasn't offended by that. Tess needed to be painstakingly remade as a whole new person. That one desire and that one need exceeded anything I could try to appropriate for myself.

Perhaps I would be a part of their future at a later date.

It wasn't by any means impossible.

I still had an hour to kill. I could walk back up the hill to the Falling Rock and choose a draft beer from their dismal selection. Or I could sit in the sun-infused atrium and stew some more. I chose the stewing option.

There was a copy of today's Denver newspaper on the bench beside me and I picked it up. A smiling face in a front-page picture caught my eye.

A gas station on Table Mesa had sold a winning lottery ticket last Friday. The Rocky Mountain Megapot had stood at a respectable if unspectacular $48 million. The station owner would pocket a few thousand for selling the winning ticket. He was well pleased, and I could understand his pleasure. More people would use his station. He would sell more gas and corn dogs and fountain soda and, despite no logical connection to the laws of probability, he would also sell more lottery tickets.

People were simply irrationally inclined to be superstitious.

But the story didn't end there.

The ticket buyer had come forward after the weekend. He had a credit card receipt for the gas he had bought that matched the exact time the winning ticket was purchased. The store owner even recognized him and remembered selling him the single ticket for cash at the same time. But the unlucky winner had lost his ticket the next day riding his bike along the creek with his daughter. He was a security worker at the university campus and lived in South Boulder with his wife. The lottery officials were unwilling to pay out without receipt of the winning ticket. According to a lottery spokesperson, their hands were tied in this matter, although they were naturally extremely sorry.

The media had breathlessly alerted the populace to the impending injustice, and on Tuesday a homeless man found the lost ticket close to the water and came forward. Our ticket-finding hero had insisted right from the start that he wasn't interested in the prize money for himself. He just wanted to make things right for the man who had bought the ticket and deserved the payout fair and square.

The ticket buyer was overjoyed and readily offered, with a microphone in front of his mouth and a TV camera turned on his beaming face, to split his winnings evenly with the man who had found the missing ticket. They had joyously met in a media-orchestrated event, shaken their two shaky hands, hired themselves a lawyer, and jointly presented themselves before the lottery officials who, after setting about a third of the prize money aside for the tax man, would now be more than willing to hand over two big cardboard checks with close to $16 million written on each one. More importantly, the lottery officials were also willing to cut two much-smaller paper ones, with the same numbers written, this time real-life promises that any reputable bank would be more than happy to honor.

I looked again at the picture and I smiled.

Devonte Williams was going to be a rich man.

ACKNOWLEDGEMENTS

Thanks to Barb Macikas, Jane Gibson, Shirley Murray, Julie Gaham, and Chris Watkins, who all took time to try to save this book from its blundering creator. You did your best, ladies. Any remaining errors are mine alone.

Peter Robertson
May 2013

ABOUT THE AUTHOR

Peter Robertson was born and raised in Edinburgh, Scotland. He lives in the Chicago area.

Made in the USA
Lexington, KY
17 May 2013